LIES THAT BIND US

LIES THAT BIND US

A NOVEL

ANDREW HART

LAKE UNION
PUBLISHING

Text copyright © 2018 by Andrew James Hartley
All rights reserved.

Published by Lake Union Publishing, Seattle

www.apub.com

Amazon, the Amazon logo, and Lake Union Publishing are trademarks of Amazon.com, Inc., or its affiliates.

ISBN-13: 9781503949379 (paperback)
ISBN-10: 1503949370 (paperback)
ISBN-13: 9781503953994 (hardcover)
ISBN-10: 1503953998 (hardcover)

Cover design by Shasti O'Leary Soudant

Printed in the United States of America

First edition

To my wife and son, in memory of a beach in Crete . . .

Part 1

Into the Labyrinth

. . . wandering in the labyrinth, and finding no possible means of getting out, they miserably ended their lives there: or were destroyed by the Minotaur which was (as Euripides hath it)

A mingled form where two strange shapes combined,

And different natures, bull and man, were joined.

—Plutarch

Chapter One

It's dark when I open my eyes. Utterly dark. I blink but it makes no difference, and for a moment I wonder if I have gone blind. I move my right hand up to my face and think the darkness thickens slightly, graying again as I take my hand away.

The back of my head throbs, and I feel for it, finding a lump at the base of my skull that sings out with tenderness when I touch it.

Where am I?

How did I get here?

What happened to me?

The questions crowd around me in the darkness like things I might reach out and touch. I cannot answer them. My memory is blank, the past a hole or a tunnel, deep and lightless, showing no more than the overturned car I am now in.

Except that it's not a car, and as soon as the idea comes, it goes again, and I have no idea where it came from. I'm not in a car. I'm somewhere else entirely.

A room.

The word flutters and alights in my head, then takes hold and becomes something firmer. I am not outside. The air feels still and close. I am lying *on my back on something soft—but not very—and when I shift it gives a little beneath me. My right hand strays beneath it, finds the plasticky fabric edge and then the hard, gritty surface of stone or concrete. I turn my head, and the darkness softens fractionally: a pale, thin mattress smelling of mildew and age. I sniff cautiously and catch something else, a scent I almost recognize but don't want to. Part of me noted it as I woke but pushed it away from my brain. It was stronger then. On impulse, I move my right hand back to my face and inhale.*

There it is. Sharp and edged with metal.

Rust, perhaps.

Or blood. Lots of it.

I snatch my hand away and make to sit up, only to be yanked back by something hard around my left wrist. I reach over with my right and feel the cold metal just below the heel of my left hand. I move it cautiously, testingly, bewilderment and curiosity drowning out all other feelings as I struggle to learn where I am and what is going on. I can move my left arm only a few inches before the resistance tightens. I roll onto my side and probe with the fingers of my right hand. The metal around my wrist is rough, its surface pocked and irregular but its core substantial, a good half inch thick. When it moves, it drags another weight, which I can hear: a heavy, purposeful chain. Sightless and fighting back the dull swell of alarm, I follow it with my fingers, a dozen or so coarse links that reach up, then loop through a heavy ring set into the wall beside the bed.

I don't know how I got here, but I know now where I am. I hear the flat echo of my breathing in the hard, confined space. I'm in a cell. Not the cell of a police station; the darkness and the manacle tell me that. I'm somewhere far worse. And now the panic spikes, my skin tightens all over my body, and I hear myself start to scream.

Chapter Two

One week ago

"Congratulations, Jan," said Camille, offering me her slim, dark hand and beaming. "Welcome to the land of the salaried."

I shook her hand, feeling the color rise in my face as a smile of joy, triumph, and relief broke out like a hot sun burning through clouds.

"Thank you," I said. "You won't regret it."

"I know," said Camille with an arch grin. "Else you wouldn't be getting it."

I laughed to show I knew she was joking, but it sounded too loud in my ears, so I bit the sound off quickly and reminded myself to let go of her hand. My own had started to sweat.

"Do you know how you are going to celebrate?" she asked.

"Actually," I said, "I do. I'm going on a trip."

"Good for you! Anywhere nice?"

"Greece," I said. "Well, Crete, actually."

"Wow," said Camille, looking more impressed by this than she had by my interview. "That's fantastic. Just don't forget us. Your first executive team–leader meeting is on the twenty-fifth."

"Got it," I said, grinning, and hoping she couldn't see the tears in my eyes.

The trip was an extravagance. Even on the roughly $70,000 a year I'd be making before bonuses—a significant step up from the hourly rate at which I'd been working for the last seven years—I would have thought twice about it if it hadn't been for Melissa and Simon, who had insisted on footing the bill for everything except airfare. They might have covered that too if the promotion hadn't gone through, but I was looking forward to telling them I wouldn't need their help on that front.

Simon and Melissa were loaded. I wasn't absolutely sure what he did—finance of some sort, the kind that got him apartments in London and New York—and she was an interior designer. I imagined she was good at it but figured she also moved in the right circles, where being glamorous and put together was worth as much as whatever actual talent she had.

Maybe that wasn't fair.

And I should say I didn't really know them that well, which made their generosity so remarkable, as if they were driven to share their good fortune. I had met them five years before, when I was still with Marcus and we were vacationing in Crete, and had seen them only twice since, both times when Simon was in Charlotte for work and Melissa was visiting her folks in Raleigh. Their connection to North Carolina had been part of our very first conversation, a welcome coincidence that bonded us over some terrible retsina and initiated the friendship that followed. I confess—and I know how dumb this sounds—that I had rarely been happier to be a Carolinian. The present trip was to be a sort of reunion, three couples getting together again to relive a glorious, boozy week from the finale of our twenties.

The other couple, Brad and Kristen, lived in Atlanta, though she was a Brit by birth and currently had a recurring role on a sci-fi show that was shot there. Brad was originally from some no-name town in Missouri. He was in real estate of some sort, but I didn't recall the details. Like Simon and Melissa, they had a shine about them, a glamour that made you want to be in their orbit, like a minor satellite, and I felt giddy at the prospect of being included in their presence again. It felt—to extend that orbit metaphor—like the Greek sun itself, warm and benevolent and invigorating. I just couldn't wait.

The timing was precise, if silly. The last night of this trip would mark the 1,999th day since we met. The idea had come to us near the end of that first week. We'd been mellowed by sun and drinking and by that special camaraderie that comes from feeling unbelievably lucky to have blundered into each other. Prince had been playing on the radio, and Kristen was talking about a friend of hers who had just had a baby and was obsessed with what she called "the first two thousand days," which was supposed to be crucially formative in a child's life. Somehow Melissa, who had never been much interested in children, latched onto the number and suddenly lit up.

"That's what we should do!" she said, the light of joyous revelation in her eyes. "To celebrate our friendship. New friendships are born, right? They have to be tended, nurtured."

"How much have you had?" asked Brad, checking her glass playfully.

"I'm serious!" she exclaimed. "We make a pact right now that wherever we are, whatever we are doing, we get together again, here, in two thousand days, just to do this all again."

"You're crazy," said Brad. "I like it."

"Wait!" said Simon. "Hear that?" He cocked his head toward the sound of the radio. "We're not babies. But I think we might party like it's 1999!"

Melissa's eyes and mouth widened with delight. "I knew there was a reason I loved you," she said, leaning over and kissing him loudly.

"Won't that be, like, October or November?" said Marcus, counting the months on his fingers.

"Fall break," said Simon, as if we were all still in college. "Perfect."

"Fall break!" sang Melissa. "We in?"

"I'm in," said Simon.

"Hell yeah," said Brad.

"1999," Kristen agreed.

Then Marcus. Then me. It was infectious—ridiculous, perhaps, but infectious just the same, because in that moment we were just so happy that anything, however random or goofy, that seemed like it would make it all happen again had to be grabbed with both hands.

"To us," said Melissa, raising her glass, "and to one thousand nine hundred and ninety-nine days till one hell of a party!"

I could see it all, feel the last warmth of the afternoon sun on my skin, the still greater warmth of being with them, of being *one* of them. The memory still made me smile.

It was going to be so very good to see them all again. That week when we had stumbled onto each other, clueless foreigners all, pointing our way through whatever the hotel bar had to offer because none of us spoke the language, had been, now that I thought about it, one of the highlights of my life. Perhaps *the* highlight. Till then, at least. Now I had other great things to look forward to, the vacation included.

Over dinner that night—takeout from Barrington's, which was fabulously expensive and deserved better than the mismatched china I served it on—Chad had taken a break from his pan-seared grouper to ask if I minded going alone and if I felt awkward about seeing Marcus again. I actually laughed.

"I honestly hadn't thought about it," I said, taking a sip of wine. "I mean, you know I still see him from time to time. We're still friends. But I don't miss him. Not in *that* way."

"Sounds very healthy," he said, returning to his fish. "Good."

"Chad Hoskins," I said teasingly, "are you jealous?" Then I kissed him so invitingly that he spilled his wine. "Goose," I said, laughing. "Now you're all wet. Whatever shall we do?"

⌁

I didn't fly much. The new job might change that, I supposed, and I rather liked the idea of jetting around with the sober business-suited bound for Tulsa, Newark, or Chicago on a Monday morning, gabbling instructions to my assistant in a no-nonsense way over my cell phone, asking for receipts with my steak dinner since I was "expensing" everything. Maybe that got dull eventually, but for now flying was still a little exotic, however much the airlines packed us in and gouged us for every inch of legroom and every bag of stale pretzels. The Aegean plane was nicer than the American Airlines one I'd crossed the Atlantic in: clean and sleek and new, with room to stretch out and everyone looking fresh faced and excited for the hop across the sparkling water.

I remembered the last time I had been to Greece, marveling at the blueness of the water that I had seen in books and brochures but assumed was a trick of filters or Photoshop, and my heart gave a little flutter of anticipation. I thought of Melissa and the others, and I realized I didn't know when everyone else would be arriving. I half thought Marcus might have been on the Charlotte plane and was a little disappointed when he wasn't. Just for company, of course. I had kept an eye open in the gate area at Douglas and made a couple of strolls down each aisle of the plane after they'd served dinner and dimmed the cabin lights, but there was no sign of him. One of the haughty, brittle flight attendants had pointedly asked me if everything was OK, like I might be planning some elaborate terrorist heist on my way to the bathroom, so I told her I'd lost an earring.

She hadn't believed me.

9

"I'll keep an eye out," she'd said brightly, daring me to push the issue further. She said *out* like there was a *W* in it. Canada, perhaps, or Wisconsin. I went back to my seat and stared fixedly at the little electronic map on the seatback screen, the tiny plane inching its way across the ocean and down. I think I may have slept for an hour or two at the most.

It was a long flight to Crete, with layovers in Rome and Athens. I saw the Colosseum from the air, which was exciting, and I had a plate of pasta at the airport in Rome, which wasn't. The connecting flight to Greece was delayed, and I had to run through the airport in Athens, dragging my carry-on like a wild-eyed bag lady, to make the Aegean Airlines flight to Heraklion. But the Crete flight was over almost as soon as we were in the air, and I found that the exhilaration at the prospect of seeing the others and rekindling our friendship from five years ago was turning into something hot and oppressive.

Calm down, I told myself. *You're as good as any of them. Executive team leader . . .*

I grinned privately to myself, but only for a second, and partly at the absurdity of my own pretense. Because no—my little promotion would hardly impress my ridiculously successful and beautiful friends, however much I told myself that I was somehow keeping pace with the jet set. But then that's how you get by sometimes, isn't it? By deploying those little half-truths that keep the world rosy enough to live in.

I came through baggage claim and out into the body of Heraklion Airport with a low-grade anxiety that everyone would have gone, that I'd be forgotten and would have no way to reach the house except on my own dime, which would probably cost more than I could afford. Then what? I ask Simon for reimbursement, show him my cab receipt, like I was filling out expense forms for work?

God, I thought. *That would be humiliating.*

And finding the place would be no picnic. Melissa had refused to tell me anything about where we were staying except to say that it wasn't a hotel. I had an address but had not bothered to look at a map to gauge how long a journey it would be. Having already traveled for a dozen hours on practically no sleep, I hoped it wasn't far, but Melissa's dangled promise of an "exclusive luxury villa away from the resort set" didn't bode well. My nervous exhaustion spiked again, and I felt my pulse quicken.

Get it together, Jan, I told myself before taking three long, steadying breaths—one of Chad's tricks designed to soothe my ragged nerves.

Thinking of Chad calmed me as much as the breathing exercise. This would all have been easier if he were with me. I had told him so, and he had smiled that gentle, thoughtful smile of his and said, "You can tell me all about it when you get back. Take lots of pictures."

I would. I did the breathing thing again and felt better.

The arrivals area—*lounge*, which I thought implied chairs, was the wrong word—was a wall of watchful faces: men in close-fitting dark suits and no ties held signs—some were dry-erase boards, some computer printed, most just blocked out in Sharpie—all blaring names of passengers. I scanned them hurriedly: Blunt, Kastides, Ferguson, Alexandros, Merrimack, and more.

No Fletcher.

I stopped in my tracks, craning to see some of the signs casually held up from the back row, and a woman with a pair of pink roll-on cases jostled me out of the way, shooting me an irritated look.

"Sorry," I said, but she was already walking away, welcomed by a lean, angular man in his fifties, who gave her a perfunctory nod and took one of the cases. As they moved away a space opened in the throng, and there, like Apollo himself, was Simon, handsome and tanned, flashing me that toothpaste-commercial smile of his, blue eyes glinting.

"Jan," he said, striding over. "So glad you could make it!"

I half extended my hand, but he closed in for the hug and pecked me once on the cheek. I burbled into his neck, flustered, scanning the space behind him for signs of the others.

"Just me?" I asked, trying to sound like it didn't matter one way or the other.

"Marcus and Gretchen are already here. And Melissa, of course. Kristen and Brad get in later. I figure we'll get you settled; then maybe we'll head down to the beach at the Minos for the afternoon. For old times' sake. It's a bit of a trek, but I'll be able to collect Kristen and Brad around five before we go home for the evening."

The Minos was the hotel where we all met five years ago. Well, not quite "all." One name stood out and made me stare at him like a startled bird.

Who the hell was Gretchen?

And not just Gretchen. *Marcus and Gretchen.* As if they were together. My stomach squirmed and knotted, but I said nothing.

"This everything?" asked Simon, eying my luggage approvingly.

"Yes. It's only a week, after all."

"Travel light, travel fast," said Simon. He was wearing short sleeves, and his arms were bunched and veined with the fruits of his hours in the gym. Slim jeans—designer, I suspected, but not showy or broadcasting the brand—and brown leather loafers without socks. You'd never mistake someone so fair for a local, but he looked in his element, absolutely comfortable. But then, he always did. As I said, I had no idea what he did beyond the fact that it involved moving around millions of dollars of other people's money—and earning millions for himself in the process—but I imagined he looked just as at ease and in control on trading floors, in board rooms, on golf courses, and in high-end cocktail bars, dressed in each case appropriately, fashionably, and with that apparent carelessness that made it all look so effortless. Marcus used to have a word for that last part, an old Italian term I couldn't remember. It meant something like the ability to pass off as natural and spontaneous what was actually studied and deliberate. I'd have to ask him when I saw him.

If you can tear him away from Gretchen.

The name annoyed me. It sounded vaguely Nordic or German, and the image that popped into my head was the St. Pauli beer girl, with braided flaxen hair and cleavage you could lose a rabbit in.

Simon was talking, and I turned my attention back to him as he led me through the airport toward the doors that opened onto the hot, bright parking lot. Looking at him from behind, I wondered if some of that sartorial effortlessness was actually Melissa's handiwork, though I found it hard to imagine her picking out his ties and brushing lint from his jacket like some fifties housewife.

"I said, 'Did you see much of Rome?'" Simon repeated.

"Oh," I replied. "No, it was just a layover. But I saw the Colosseum from the air."

"Really?" he said, pulling a face. "Did the plane have to circle or something?"

I hesitated.

"I don't think so. Why?" I said.

"The airport is close to the coast," he remarked. "You'd have to go pretty far inland to get a look at the city, and then I'd imagine you'd be too high to really . . ."

"Must have been mistaken," I said quickly. "I slept a lot on the way in. Maybe I dreamed it."

He gave a little laugh, but I saw nothing else in his face as he pushed through the outer doors, so I decided to leave it alone.

It was pleasantly, surprisingly warm in Heraklion. I remembered the June heat of my last visit as a physical shock, a blistering, searing sunshine that stood breathless and unmoving in the shadeless parking lot. Charlotte was hot and I was used to it, but the air in Crete had felt thinner somehow, and while that meant it didn't have the mugginess of home, the sun seemed more intense and relentless: a desert heat. On the plane I had remembered how much I had burned on that beach five years ago, and another stupid pulse of panic coursed through me then even as I reminded myself that it was November. But now the weather was glorious. Midseventies, the sky clear, a slight breeze full of promise and comfort, and Simon had already said we were going to the beach after all. Like the old children's game, if Simon said it, you had to go along.

Simon made for the biggest, sleekest, shiniest car in the lot and made it beep with a fob in his pocket. It was a huge boatlike Mercedes van, black and new and screaming money. It had tinted windows and looked like it should come with champagne on ice and celebrities fleeing paparazzi.

"Nice," I said.

"Only the best for our friends," said Simon.

My heart sank a little, but I rallied. I was newly promoted. A salaried executive team leader. Moving up in the world.

"Gonna be a great week," he remarked, pushing a pair of Ray-Ban aviators on and turning the engine over. "Lots to catch up on. Old haunts to revisit. Remember that guy who used to sell peaches from a stand outside the Minos? The one with the mangy dog who peed on Brad's foot? I drove by today, and I swear he was still there. Same guy. Same dog!"

He laughed delightedly.

I looked out of the heavily tinted windows as we pulled onto the road, and I tried to laugh along, but it was cold in the car with its blasting AC, and all I could think of was *old haunts*.

I shouldn't have come.

Chapter Three

The screaming doesn't last. The sheer volume in my little prison shocks it out of me long before it can shred my throat, the sound of my own terror jarring me into numbness. Still, the exertion of all that crying leaves me light-headed, and that's scary too.

I sit up as best I can, my left arm resting unnaturally far from my body because of the manacle, and I try to decide if the darkness has lessened. I don't think it has because I can make out no light source, so the softening of the blackness, the vague sense that there are shapes only a few feet from the concrete platform where I am chained, must be my eyes adjusting. I remember dimly from one of my biology classes that the sensitivity of the human eye increases massively in the first few minutes of being exposed to the dark, but I am pretty sure it's a short-lived phenomenon. It's not like the longer I sit here, the better my night vision will be. I've been awake several minutes now and am sure this is as good as it's going to get.

Thinking about such things has slowed my heart. I can feel it easing in my chest, as if I were over-revving an engine but have now taken my foot off the gas, though my breath is still thin and gasping. It's noisy, more sobbing than breathing, and the air feels strangely thin. The room smells of damp and earth and the very slightly chemical staleness of old concrete, and on top of it is the vibrant, rusty tang of blood.

What the hell is going on?

I force myself to be quiet, to sit and listen for any sound that isn't made by me, like I'm reaching out with my ears into the darkness. Then I take a breath, swallow, and say "Hello?"

There is no reply, but I say it again, louder this time, listening to the fractional and instantaneous echo. I try it again, speaking like a sound engineer at a concert Marcus and I went to years ago.

"One, two. One two," I say, spitting the T *sound as the roadie had done. "One, two. Two. Two. Two."*

It had amused me at the time, his earnestness as he made the nonsense noises before giving his thumbs-up to some invisible colleague in the sound booth at the back of the hall. I hadn't really processed what he was doing, but I understood it instinctively now. He was listening to the shape of the sound as it went from microphone to speakers, the pop of air on the consonants, and I realize I am doing the same. I am doing what bats or dolphins do, bouncing sound to get a sense of where things are. I can't read the results like animals, but I feel in my bones the way the sound brings the walls of my cell in. I can't see them, but I instinctively know that the room is very small. Maybe only ten feet square. And while three walls are hard and flat—stone or concrete, probably the latter—the fourth is somehow different. Not softer, exactly, but more absorbent. A door. Large and wooden. Sensing that it is there, I think now that I can almost see it, a deeper blackness in the gloom.

I frown, marveling at my little discovery, trying not to admit how little that gave me to work with. There is also an irregularity in the wall directly across from the bed, the way I am facing and almost level with my steady, if largely useless, gaze. A panel? Or a cupboard mounted on the wall? I can just make it out as a dark rectangle. I reach for it, stretching as far as I can, but get nothing but air. I swing my feet down to the floor and get the uneven shock of finding I have one bare foot and one still wearing what feels like a sandal.

My *sandal.*

Thin leather straps and a little thong over the top of my foot gathering around the ankle and looping around the big toe.

My sandal. *I can see it in my head, and with it comes the sense of things remembered but hidden in shadow just out of arm's reach.*

Crete. I came to Crete. To see old friends.

I remember packing, laying out colorful clothes on the bed at home, taking the plane, but after that . . . I frown and regroup. I am Jan Fletcher. I live in Charlotte and work at the Great Deal store on Tryon in the University area. I drive a white Camry, bought secondhand from the Town and Country dealership on South Boulevard. I can see my apartment in my head: the fading, hand-stenciled vines on the bathroom wall, the smell of the neighbor's ratty terrier that poops under the gardenia bush by the front door. I am on vacation . . .

The word sounds bleakly funny, but I brush past the urge to laugh because I know it will turn into a sob, and I try to remember more. What happened after I arrived? Was I in a car accident?

I squeeze my eyes shut, trying to make sense of why I think of that first, but can recall nothing relevant, nothing connecting me to a car or a wreck. I came to see Simon and Melissa, Brad, Kristen, and Marcus. That, I'm sure of.

Marcus . . .

Did I see them? I feel sure I did but the details don't come. I reach for them, and the effort to push through the haze to the truth of what happened next is almost physical, like straining against a heavy door in my mind.

It doesn't open.

I set both feet and rise unsteadily. I can stand straight without straining my left arm unduly. I turn onto my side on the concrete bed with its thin mattress and take a long step with my right foot, feeling all the slack leave the chain around my left wrist as I lean away from the ring in the wall. I stretch out with my right hand, straining, reaching . . .

Nothing.

I am covering about six feet of the cell, and the cabinet on the wall—if that is what it is—will be at least a foot deep, maybe more, but if my echo-location guesstimate about the size of the cell is right, that leaves me still two feet short of reaching it. It may as well be a mile. I pull at the manacle, twisting my wrist back and forth, but the bracelet lodges at the base of my thumb and won't move. I lean away from the wall till the pain becomes intolerable, then give up.

I sag back onto the bed, feeling far more weary than the action merits. I still can't remember how I have wound up here and, coupled with my thin, ragged breathing, I wonder suddenly if I have been drugged.

Or assaulted.

There is still the smell of the blood, on my right hand particularly, though when I rub my fingers together, they feel dry and grainy, not slick. I smell them again, recoil at the scent, and begin feeling for injuries. The back of my head is throbbing and tender, but there's no wetness:

a bump, not a cut.

My fingers go to my face. Then my arms. Then my legs and, with a little sob that forces its way out, up my thighs. I am wearing a dress, knee length, lowish at the neck and short sleeved. It is light and simple—cotton, I think. It feels familiar.

Mine. I know it. I can almost remember putting it on. In Crete. In a hotel? No. A house or . . . a place we had rented. A place Simon *had rented.*

I have a bra on underneath, also soft and comfortable, and panties, all of which feel intact. I feel no bruising, no tenderness anywhere except on the back of my head and a little ways above my right eye. A fall? Or a blow? Maybe both.

But no cuts and no sign of sexual violence.

The words come to me from a TV crime show. Sexual violence. *It is one of those phrases whose bald factualness dodges a million horrors.*

I have not been raped, or at least not in ways I can detect, though that is an uncomfortable proviso and points at the hole where my memory should be. I shy away from it again, the dark pit of unguessable depth, and cling instead to what I can deduce. Someone has put me here. I do not know why. If they wanted me dead, I would be. But I am not.

Which means they will come back.

I shift uneasily. My left arm already feels tired from the awkward angle I am holding it, and the wrist is chafed from the metal of the manacle. I tug at it till my hand protests but feel no give in the chain or the ring in the wall. Someone is coming back, and I am stuck here. Powerless.

And then there's the blood, *I remind myself.*

Yes. I have blood on my hands, and my dress around the waist feels stiff with it too. I can't be sure, not without light, but in my heart it makes sense, as if there is something I will eventually remember that will make sense of the gore on my hands and clothes. The dried clumps of it I feel in my hair.

I can't remember how it got there.

I feel my body over again, rolling and adjusting to probe every inch of flesh. My head has been battered, and I must have a nasty black eye, but it is no ragged wound, no slash or puncture that would have bled like that.

Which can mean only one thing.

The blood I am caked in belongs to someone else.

The thought stops my breath for a moment. I was thinking that I have been . . . what? Trapped by a psychopath? Something like that.

But what if it isn't that at all?

What if I have been walled up in here because of something else? Something I have done?

Chapter Four

It was a long drive. Over an hour to Rethymno, where we stayed last time, along the coast road that was sometimes labeled E75 and sometimes just 90, and then as much again as we cut in from the shore and up into the mountains, where the previously straight road became narrow and circuitous.

"Where are we going?" I asked, trying not to sound exhausted and apprehensive. It was good of Simon to have picked me up on top of covering the costs of the lodging. I had asked if I could give him anything for gas, but he waved the offer away with a smile, as if we were talking about sums so small, he could cover them with what he found in between his couch cushions. Maybe he could.

"You're gonna love it," said Simon. "It's fantastic. Kind of in the middle of nowhere, but yeah. Fantastic. Perfect for us."

I shifted in my leather seat.

"Us?" I said.

"All of us," he qualified, giving me a look I couldn't read because of the sunglasses. "The reunion."

"Right," I said. "Great."

I was sitting with my carry-on in my lap, which felt ridiculous and uncomfortable. The car was huge, and I could have easily tossed it into the back seat or the trunk, but now I was belted in and had been there for so long that turning around and trying to get rid of it felt stupid for reasons I couldn't explain. So I sat with the bag in my lap and my arms around it, like it was one of those under-seat float cushions the flight attendants had told us about "in case of a water landing." The phrase had amused me in a bleak kind of way, like it was something the pilot might choose.

You know, copilot Bob, I think we'll skip the runway and just put down in the ocean today, whaddya say?

Or maybe the bag in my lap was a shield.

Of course there was no reason to protect myself—even psychologically—from Simon. He was great. Gorgeous, friendly, generous. Flattering, even.

Apollo, god of the sun, the golden charioteer with his bow . . .

I took another of Chad's long, steadying breaths and stared out the window at the craggy slopes with their clusters of dust-colored olive trees, ramshackle farm buildings, and bleached, crumbling churches. It was beautiful. I needed to get over my stupid, halting inadequacies and enjoy what I'd come here for.

"You heading straight back to Charlotte after our little get-together?" asked Simon, idly watching as an ancient man in worn and faded clothes, which might once have looked quite formal and must have been insanely hot, shooed his goats to the side of the road.

"I think so," I said. "I had wondered about going to Turkey, but I have to fly again for work soon, so we'll see."

I wasn't sure why I said it. It just came out. His suave composure, the luxurious car . . . I couldn't help myself.

"Where to?"

"What?" I asked, already back pedaling.

"Where will you be flying for work?"

"Vegas," I said. "One of our head offices is there. Not really my kind of place but . . ."

"You have got to be able to have fun in Vegas!" Simon exclaimed. "Something for everyone there, right?"

"Right," I said. "Gets kind of old after a while, though."

"I guess it could," he said. "Where do you usually stay?"

"Oh, various places," I said airily. "Work takes care of the arrangements."

"Close to one of the casinos?"

"Always," I said with a theatrical eye roll, as if nothing could be more tiresome.

"Which one?"

"What? Oh, what's it called . . . the one with the pyramid."

"Luxor," said Simon.

"Right. Of course. Forget my head if it wasn't attached."

"The sky beam is something, isn't it?"

"Yes," I said, anxious now. "Really is."

"They say you can see it hundreds of miles away."

"I bet that's true," I said. "So tell me about the place we're staying here. You made it sound quite mysterious."

He turned and gave me a look, as if he knew I was changing the subject, but I couldn't read his face to be sure, so the half smile that hinted at something private might have been about what we were just discussing or what he knew was coming.

"Oh, I don't want to steal Melissa's thunder," he said. "Wait and see." For a long, taut moment we rode in silence, and then he started fumbling with the radio controls, scrolling through station after station of tinny Europop and sighing. Last time we were here, there had been a beachside DJ at the hotel, a buff local guy in shades and a do-rag who spent his breaks windsurfing and looking cool for the girls. He had thought Melissa was the greatest thing since . . . well, whatever the Greek equivalent of sliced bread was. It was as if she were an icon, a walking, talking model of everything his American surf-suave pose was supposed to be. She was the thing itself. Simon had rolled with it all, used to his wife getting this kind of attention, befriending the guy with a nod and a knowing grin that showed he didn't feel threatened. From that point on the DJ had been sure to play whatever she asked for, even hunting down the tracks he didn't have just so he could blare them for her. She had been on an alternative eighties kick, so my memories of Crete had a soundtrack by Depeche Mode, Tears for Fears, and the B-52s.

"No 'Rock Lobster'?" I asked, grinning.

"What?"

"The B-52s song," I said. "'Rock Lobster.' Melissa was always singing it, and . . ."

He was still smiling, but his face looked blank. Then his brow furrowed and the smile widened.

"Right!" he exclaimed. "'Rock Lobster.' Yeah. I'd totally forgotten that."

I grinned, pleased by his remembering, feeling once again that shared glow, and wondering how anyone could forget the way she had been. The way we had been.

Well, I thought. *We would rebuild it all, down to the last bass riff and ridiculous vocal trill . . .*

And as if to complete the memory for me, Simon finished fiddling with the iPhone he had plugged in and gave me an expectant look as he pushed the car system's volume up. A moment later the familiar anthemic keyboard chords crashed in, the drums filled the gap, and the bass started, Prince's "1999" rocking.

"Yes!" I said. It was happening. I had made it to Crete, and we would slide not forward in time like the song suggested, but back to that glorious week and all the promise it held. Simon read my look and nodded emphatically along to the music.

"1999!" he yelled.

Pleased, I looked out the window, seeing the increasingly rugged hills and ravines we had not so much as glimpsed on my previous trip. That had been a beach holiday, pure and simple. Days in and by the water, nights in the bar, occasional dancing, constant drinking. We had seen nothing of the surrounding countryside or the ancient Minoan sites for which the long, sprawling island was uniquely famous. In fact we barely left the resort except to eat and return to the airport. Except for the last day.

The cave.

I frowned to myself. The cave had been the exception, an excursion that we hadn't enjoyed and that made me feel like we should never have left the beach, should never have looked up from our drinks, our toes in the sand at the water's edge . . .

Five years later that vacation seemed both naive and kind of glorious, a last drunken farewell to our twenties, our youth. What we would do now, up here, bumbling through our thirties and as far from the ocean as Crete physically permitted, I had no idea. I shot Simon a sideways glance, looking for signs of age: crow's feet by the eyes or a hint of silver at the temples, but I couldn't see them. Maybe it was just me who felt older.

And as fun as it would be reliving our last visit through drinks on the beach, I had to admit that I was ready for something different this time. Whatever my job had been and would be, working at Great Deal didn't exactly fulfill all my intellectual needs, and I found myself thinking wistfully about all the things we'd missed last time, and what it would be like to stroll the island's ancient ruins with Marcus, talking history, mythology. Though I had been a biology major, I had also been an English minor and had considered flipping them at one point. I wasn't especially interested in the politics that seemed to inform—or infect—everything in the classroom, but I loved story, the shape of it, the inventive audacity of stringing together characters, places, and events to make up something that felt absolutely real but existed only in the head of the writer or their readers. If I'd had any talent or willpower in the matter, I once thought, I would have been a writer: a novelist rather than a poet, though a playwright might be good too. I liked the way stories lined up behind each other like mirrors, reflecting little bits back, sometimes direct and straight on, sometimes distorted and crazy, Joyce growing out of Shakespeare, who grew out of Ovid and all those ancient tales of gods and goddesses, some of them cobbled roughly together a stone's throw from this very spot.

Jason, Medea, and the Golden Fleece . . . stories of magic and madness, passion, and divine intervention. Most of it I'd half forgotten till a couple of days ago, when I dug out one of the textbooks that had been sitting untouched on my shelves for at least a year and found the ancient tales waiting, fresh and familiar, ancient but edged with something sharp and urgent. I reread them with a similar urgency, a hunger I could not completely explain.

This was a land of legend, of ancient myth, of story. It was the land of King Minos and the mazelike complex of tunnels beneath his palace known as the labyrinth. Inside the maze lived a terrible monster, half man, half bull—the Minotaur—to whom victims were sacrificed annually, trapped down there in the darkness of the passages where the monster hunted . . . It was great stuff, reeking of danger and heroism and strangeness. For a second I forgot Simon, humming tunelessly next to me, forgot the inevitable partying the reunion would center around, the willful, gloriously frivolous stuff we would laugh about over the next few days, and I felt those ancient stories in the air like incense, sweet and fragrant.

I have left behind my job, I thought, *my ordinary, humdrum life in an American city, and I have become Medea, a woman of magic and mystery . . .*

Grinning to myself again, I watched the road signs to neighboring villages as we drove. "Georgioupoli," "Fones," "Alikampos," "Kryonerida." None of them meant anything to me, and as the roads got smaller and the gaps between habitation larger, the settlements themselves shrank till they were mere clusters of ancient houses and an occasional tiny monastery. I wondered what I had gotten myself into. The last village we saw was Empresneros, and then nothing, just a slow and winding climb into the pale mountains as I tried to check my e-mail on my phone.

"Are there hotels round here? Stores? Restaurants?" I asked, hating the timidity in my voice.

"Nope," said Simon, shooting me a wolfish grin. "Isn't it awesome? Out in the wilds. We figured we'd done the hotel scene and were ready for something a bit more authentic, you know? This is real Greece. You may as well put your phone away. You won't get a signal up here."

"Right," I said lamely. "Wow. Great."

There were no cars on the road. No gas stations, just these endless, rubble-strewn switchbacks, the land climbing on the one side as it fell away to the ever-present sea on the other.

"Good thing it's fall," said Simon. "In the winter this whole area is buried in snow, and the roads all get closed. It's why so few people live up here. The mountain range is . . . I don't know. Forgot the Greek name, but it means white mountains, or something like that. It's the limestone, I think."

We had been driving through the ubiquitous olive groves, but there were fewer and fewer signs of cultivation here, and the land was heavily wooded. I think Simon picked something up in my watchful silence because, out of the blue, he remarked, "When I got the keys for the place, I asked if there were bears or wild boar we should watch out for, but apparently they don't live here. There's a rare Cretan wildcat and some kind of ibex, but that's about it. Nothing to worry about."

"Good," I said. I'd never been outdoorsy. I doubted Simon was either, and I was as sure as I could be that Melissa was a confirmed urbanite. We might be out in the wilds, but the house—or whatever it was—would have all modern conveniences, and if Melissa came down to breakfast not dressed to the nines and made up as if she were featuring on the cover of *Cosmo*, I'd throw myself to the rare Cretan wildcat. Hell, I'd *eat* the rare Cretan wildcat.

"What?" said Simon, who had half turned and caught my grin.

"Nothing," I said. "Just, you know . . . looking forward to seeing everyone and hanging out."

It sounded so pathetic when put like that, deliberately so. I didn't want him to know just how excited I really was, how delighted that I had managed to hold on to my slender connection to them. I felt the way people may once have felt in the presence of royalty, except this was better because they were my friends. I knew that was lamer still, and I privately mocked myself for being so much the devoted hanger-on. It was tiredness, I told myself, the kind of exhaustion that makes you weak and emotional. I should have slept on the plane.

Chapter Five

I lie against the wall on the bed, my knees drawn up to my chest, my back to the room. It's a defensive posture, an animal curling, as if I'm presenting an array of spines to the world. It has the added advantage of taking the strain off my wrist since I'm now close enough to the iron ring in the wall that I can smell the rust. Unless that's more blood. For all I know the room could be caked with the stuff.

It is still mine dark. The kind of pitch blackness I can't recall ever experiencing before, as if my head is in a velvet bag. It is numbing. I cannot tell how long I have been awake or if I have been continuously so. In spite of my alarm, the strange amnesia weighs on me so that I feel only half-there, and I wonder if I am drifting in and out of slumber without realizing it. In the dark, when you can't move, there is little difference between sleeping and waking. It is nightmarish either way.

You have been in darkness like this before, *I think vaguely.* You woke up on your side in the black, smelling of blood . . .

I run from the memory. It's like I'm on a railroad track with the train bearing down on me. I leap aside and suddenly the train was never there, even the memory of it boiling away to nothing, so that I can't understand why I was so spooked. What could I have forgotten that was worse than where I was now?

I have taken off my one sandal because wearing it left me feeling unbalanced, but being barefoot makes me feel naked, vulnerable.

You're in Crete, *I remind myself, hoping that will jog more from my memory. I can picture the sea, the sky. A house, strange in its mixture of old and new . . .*

The memory, if it is indeed that, makes me shudder, a deep, cooling flicker that runs uneasily through my body like an earthquake and leaves my skin puckered, each hair rising. There's something about that house that I don't like . . .

The blood on my hands . . .

. . . something about the house that a part of me needs to forget.

So I have. I push at the memory, trying to draw it out of the shadows, but it slithers away, not wanting to be found. I am almost relieved, though I don't understand why my memory feels so fuzzy. The bump on my head feels superficial, and I don't believe I was concussed.

The amnesia—if that's not too grand a word for it—also feels selective, only blacking out the last few days. Older stuff is still there, and as if to make the point, my brain dredges up something I would have happily forgotten: a book Marcus bought me, paintings and poems drawing on the Greek mythology he knew I was so attached to. And though I had loved the book, the pictures had been a little too good, some of them so dark and creepily atmospheric that I skipped over them to get to lighter, happier material. One of them was the picture of the Minotaur brooding in the shadows of the labyrinth. It brimmed with strangeness and menace so that you could almost smell the musk of the creature. I had hurried past it, jumping to the end of the tale so I wouldn't have to look at it or—ridiculously—feel it looking at me. The isolated Cretan house in my memory is like that, a vague and unsettling dread waiting for me when I turn the page.

At last I roll onto my right side and open my eyes, though that makes no difference either until, very gradually, I see, or feel that I see, the thin variance between the wall and door, the dark patch across the room that might be a cabinet.

And something else.

There is another darkness, one that I am almost sure was not there before. It nestles in the corner by the door, a squat dense shadow, like a rough, tall pile. I stare at the spot, feeling the nameless horror of it and trying to remember. It is like reaching across the cell, straining with my mind the same way my body tugged at the chain fastened to the ring in the wall, and as with that physical stretching, I find nothing but my own tiredness. But I am almost sure.

The pile, or whatever it is, was not there before. And that can mean only one thing. As I slept, overwhelmed by whatever drug-induced exhaustion led to my imprisonment, someone has been in.

Chapter Six

"Ta-da!"

Simon sang it out as we pulled up a long, narrow driveway and the house was suddenly visible through the trees, as if he were pulling the dustcover off an antique or a gift. I hunkered lower in my seat to get a better view and managed an awed "wow."

It was huge, three stories tall in parts, a rambling and imposing oddity of jumbled styles and periods. Parts of the outlying structure looked ancient, built out of weathered gold and amber stone blocks, part palace, part fortress. They included what looked like a bell tower on the west side of the house and a wing with large and regular arched windows flanked by relief-work pillars. The central block, by contrast, was an angular mass of glass and steel, built into the older stonework and roofed with pinkish tile. Still other parts of the house—the word felt inadequate for something that was more like a small modernized castle—looked rustic and unpolished, especially sections of the ground floor that had been patched together with rough stone and concrete blocks. All told, it managed to be whimsical as well as impressive, and under the blue Cretan sky, I found my doubts and anxieties melting away in a kind of surprised joy.

"Only a rental," said Simon, "but should do us for the week." He said it as only he could, in a tone that sounded both proud and dismissive, what my coworkers would call a humblebrag. "Parts of it are Venetian, so that's, what? Sixteenth century? Seventeenth?"

"I don't know," I confessed.

"Pretty cool anyhow," he said, shrugging as he guided the Mercedes into the corner of a spacious forecourt, gravel roaring under the tires. "The original design was obsessively symmetrical—everything doubled and balanced for proportion, I guess—but the upper stories have been heavily remodeled, and at some point they got rid of the eastern tower. I think it looks better this way. Let's get you inside and see if Melissa's got the fog cutters going."

"Fog cutters?" I echoed.

"I know," he said, rolling his eyes. "Kind of last year, but we got this kick-ass recipe from a bartender at Satan's Whiskers in Bethnal Green."

"In London?" I said. I was trying to process information that otherwise meant nothing to me, like a school kid preparing for a test in a class she had never attended. Being with Simon and Melissa often felt like that, like you were working to show that you deserved to be with them. Pretending, really.

Simon gave me a quizzical smile.

"Yes, Jan," he said. "In London."

I laughed self-consciously and opened the car door to hide my face. Before I came I had thought about switching my prescription glasses for those with the lenses that adjust to the light, but it had seemed like an extravagance and maybe like I was trying too hard to look cool. Now I wished I had them, even if they wouldn't fully hide my blushes. But then Simon was talking again as he walked down the drive to close the wrought iron gates, saying how I really should go over and visit their "flat" there, as if that was a normal thing for someone like me to do, and I felt better again.

I was moving to the trunk to get my suitcase as the front door—a heavy, varnished thing with a massive bronze knocker in the shape of a lion's head—banged open, and there was Melissa, arms spread wide as her smile, dressed in something white and flowy that made her look like a goddess.

"Jan!" she squealed, moving down the steps toward me, her arms still open, as if she were trying to catch the whole world to her. The welcoming hug felt like it took place in slow motion, like I was surrounded by love and warmth so acute, so wanted, that it brought tears to my eyes. She squeezed me to her Chanel-scented breasts, burbling about how happy she was to see me, how delighted that I had made the trek. Then, still holding me, she leaned back to look at me, drinking me in. I adjusted the glasses her overenthusiastic embrace had dislodged and smiled back shyly before she pulled me to her again.

"It's been years!" she exclaimed. "You look wonderful!"

"One year," I said, "near enough. When you and Simon came to Charlotte to see your parents." I didn't bother contradicting the other observation. That would only lead to more disingenuous compliments on her part and poorly hidden inadequacy on mine. Melissa looked like Aphrodite, as imagined by the Hollywood of the 1960s: alabaster skin, flowing chestnut hair, and eyes of cornflower blue. I looked like . . . like I'd just gotten off a plane. Like I lived alone and spent my days—beginning at three in the morning—in a yellow polo shirt with my name on a brass badge . . .

Not when you get back, I reminded myself. *Executive team leader.*

I forced an unsteady smile and told my inner voice to shut up for once.

"It's good to see you," I said, meaning it.

Simon had taken my luggage.

"I can manage," I protested, but he waved me off.

"I've got it," he said. "Come on. I'll show you your room."

"Don't be long," said Melissa, more to him than me. "I'm adding the ice to the drinks. Gretchen and Marcus are parched!"

I opened my mouth to say something but couldn't find the words. As she bustled off, turning that beatific smile of hers on me like a lighthouse scanning the horizon for whoever needed it most, I lowered my gaze to the tiled floor and followed Simon.

The foyer was cool and dim, with a hanging tapestry and a little central table, upon which sat an ancient black rotary telephone with a braided, cloth-wrapped cord.

"Our one link to civilization," said Simon, grinning.

This was one of the older parts of the house, I assumed, and the stairway in the tower—a tight stone spiral—seemed to come from the same era. It felt cool and massive. When I saw stonework on Charlotte houses, it was always obviously a shell tacked up around the house for old-timey decoration. This, by contrast, was structural and genuinely, unpretentiously ancient. On the next floor up, however, everything changed, opening up, most of the house's antiquity vanishing, the angles getting crisper, more precise, the space airier and glowing with large modern windows. The next flight of stairs was polished pine in a black-steel frame that rang with each step.

"Just one more floor," said Simon, wheezing slightly. "What do you have in here, the kitchen sink?"

"Sorry," I said. "Never been a very good packer."

"It's fine," he said, turning down a hallway with a lush blue carpet runner down the center. "Melissa and I are in the east wing. Master suite. Here you go. All yours."

He unlatched the door with the heavy, old-fashioned key that had been left in the lock and pushed the door open, stepping aside so I got the full effect as I strode in.

It was a beautiful, simple room. There was a sink with a mirror in an alcove and a great rustic bed heaped with a cloudlike white duvet, a single wardrobe, and a bedside cabinet of polished close-grained wood, warm to the touch. Otherwise, it was just white plaster walls save for the one opposite the door, which was the raw amber stone I had seen outside, and a great arched window that dominated the chamber and white linen drapes. It looked out over the grounds, over treetops, and down the coast to the bright sea and the open sky.

"Wow," I said.

I really had to stop saying that. It made me sound like a teenager.

"Right?" said Simon. "Thought you'd like it. Bathroom's down the hall. That door there. You need to rest or something, or can we expect you downstairs for fog cutters?"

He gave me an imploring smile and looked, for a moment, so genuinely happy to see me that I forgot all my previous anxiety.

"Give me ten minutes to change," I said.

Actually it was going to be more like fifteen. I checked my phone, even though Simon had said I wouldn't get a signal, and saw he was right. But I had told Chad that I would text him when we arrived, so I sat on the end of the bed and tapped my way through the phone's settings menu and hunted for a Wi-Fi signal, but there was nothing.

Will have to wait till you're back in civilization, I told myself. *No biggie.*

As much as I loved the simplicity of the room, built as it was around its ancient view, I found myself a little disappointed that I was sharing a bathroom, something I had been hoping to get a break from. I barely saw Becky, my roommate in Charlotte, because we kept such different hours, but it was a mark of my relative poverty that I had to deal with someone else's smear of toothpaste on the sink and her pubes on the toilet seat, like I was trapped in an endless adolescence that I couldn't afford to escape. A trip overseas, I had thought, meant a hotel room to myself. Total privacy. And a bathroom I could call my own.

Some people like to imagine the other guests who have been in the hotel room they are staying in before—their histories, the things that brought them there, and what they were up to before checking out.

Not me. I liked to pretend a hotel room has just been built, that I was the first person ever to sleep in its crisp linens and shower in its spotless bathroom. I don't like sharing my space, even with people I know. Especially, in fact. So when I checked on the bathroom and found it clean and dry, as if it hadn't been used for weeks, I took the opportunity to grab a much-needed shower and was able to sustain the illusion that no one else had used it yet.

It had to be quick, and not just because I had drinks waiting. The water, which began so piping hot that I was instantly pink across my breasts and shoulders, cooled fast. I got out before it was stone cold, but I couldn't help wondering how we were going to manage with seven of us using the same supply.

Maybe there are separate cisterns, I hoped, *or some sort of heater that hasn't been switched on yet.*

I remembered Simon's throwaway remark about the lack of cell phone service and wondered what other comforts I might have to do without.

But if I was honest, the shower had been a stalling tactic. Marcus was downstairs. So was "Gretchen," probably slopping fog cutters from a fistful of beer steins while singing selections from *Cabaret*. I needed a moment to prepare myself.

Marcus and I dated for a little over three years and had known each other for eight. We'd both been at college in Chapel Hill, where I was edging cautiously through a biology premed with a side order of English while he was doing history and secondary education. We'd met at a party, introduced by a theater major who knew us both a little and could have been sexually interested in either one of us. I think it was the weirdness of that encounter that drove us together. Marcus had been wearing a bizarre orange sweater and a pair of heavy-rimmed glasses, both of which I had teased him for, and he had responded by mocking my taste in music (I was going through a hair-metal phase, which I don't talk about anymore). Marcus said he had an off-campus girlfriend at the time, and I was semi-interested in a guitarist who played in a jazz band, so we weren't looking for anything other than someone to share the pretty miserable experience of a house party where the only people we knew either hadn't showed up or were more interested in their other friends.

I should say that I'd also never been involved with a black guy before, and while I wasn't against the idea, I'm sure it made me cautious. Him too, probably. Race used to make me wary, careful about the signals I sent out and the ones I thought I was getting, terrified of making assumptions or saying the wrong thing based on . . . God, I don't know: Movies? Social media? Dumb stuff. Anyway, we spent half the night talking and both had way too many tequila shots, so much so, in fact, that if there had been a moment we might have gone home together, we had drunk right past it and wound up staggering off separately. In hindsight this had seemed like a godsend. We saw each other from time to time, but nothing happened between us till half a decade later, when we were, we decided, older, wiser, and free. If we'd gotten together that first night, we said sagely, things would have gotten messed up, and we would never have had a real relationship.

But then we'd messed that up too. It had just taken longer.

The breakup had come six months after our trip to Crete when we had fallen in with Melissa and Simon, Kristen and Brad. I sometimes wondered if the cracks had already been there then but we had chosen to ignore them. How else do you explain a young couple on a romantic vacation on a Greek island spending all their time with complete strangers? The trip was certainly a factor, even if I couldn't put my finger on how.

And now they were all downstairs, fog cutters at the ready, waiting for me, along with a mysterious spare called Gretchen. For a second I looked at myself in the steamed-up bathroom window and wondered again why I had come.

But I had, and now that I was here, I was not just going to endure it—I was going to enjoy myself. I turned from the bathroom mirror, put my glasses on, wrapped a towel around myself, and tripped barefoot back to my room, confident that the view through the great arched window would lift my spirits.

I didn't get that far. I was unlocking my bedroom door when I heard footsteps on the stairs behind me and turned to find Marcus looking at me, frozen with indecision. He was wearing khakis and a white open-necked shirt, the sleeves rolled up, showing slim brown forearms. I'd always liked his arms. His hair was cut short, trimmed at the edges to a razor-sharp line. He had new slightly odd-looking glasses with ironically purple frames, and his feet were bare so that he looked quite unlike himself, or the version of him I had seen last. A bit hipper, maybe. The cool teacher. He had been waiting for me to go inside, hoping I wouldn't see him. I felt it in his stillness, and the impression was confirmed as he tried to blunder his way out of it.

"Hey, stranger!" he said, a thoroughly un-Marcus thing to say. "I was just going to . . . is the bathroom free?"

"Hi, Marcus," I said, clutching at my towel, terrified that it might shift. "Yes. It's right there."

"Right," he said. "Cool. OK, then. What a great place, huh?"

"Yes," I said, wishing I was somewhere—anywhere—else.

"Gonna be fun. Us all together again."

"Yes."

There was a fractional beat, just a breath longer than was comfortable.

"OK," said Marcus. "Well, we'll do the reunion thing when you're dressed, yeah? Hugs and such."

"Sure."

"OK, then. I'll see you in a few . . ."

I opened my door and slipped inside without looking back, closing it behind me and leaning against the wood, my heart racing.

The reunion thing.

Jesus. I didn't know which of us had been more mortified. It was the suddenness of the thing. And the towel. Jesus, yes, the towel.

I mean, Marcus had seen me naked in the past, but . . .

And he might be remembering that now . . .

God. It was a mess. And what if he thought I had deliberately bumped into him like that, like it was supposed to be seductive?

I sat heavily onto the bed. It was soft, layered with the thick, fluffy duvet, and suddenly I wanted to slip out of the towel, burrow under the covers, and not come out till morning.

What a fool you are, I said to myself. *You came back for him, and in thirty seconds it's already clear that he's embarrassed to see you, that he secretly hoped you wouldn't show, and now he sees you're here and trolling the hallways in a fucking towel for Christ's sake, trying to lure him into your bed like some desperate divorcée who stakes out college bars . . .*

Shut up.

Why? You know it's true.

It wasn't like that. None of it. I didn't come here for him. I wasn't trying to lure him anywhere. I was just taking a fucking shower . . .

He won't believe that. That's the one thing you know for sure. He doesn't believe a word you say.

I got under the duvet and pulled it over my head.

Chapter Seven

I stare into the darkness, focusing my gaze on the shape between the cupboard and the door, but I am not even sure it is there or, if it is, that it was not there before. I feel like a child in bed, fixating on the shadow of a shirt on a hanger, trying to decide if it's a monster.

"Hello?" I say. It takes me two attempts. The inside of my mouth is dry and my tongue sticks. I swallow, suddenly realizing how thirsty I am, and say it again, clearly this time. "Is there anyone there?"

It should be funny, I think, that movie cliché, but I don't laugh. I listen hard, but there is no response. I think I can see the shape still, but it's a mere craggy blackness against the fractional pallor of the wall. If it is a wall. What I think is a cupboard may not be. The door may not be a door. I can't tell. It's just too dark. The only thing I know for sure is that I'm chained to a ring in the wall beside a bed that is really just a mattress on a concrete block.

But I feel it. Something, nestled, squatting there like the nightmare demon in a painting, though this is not squatting. It is sitting in a chair, slumped forward. Unmoving. I'm almost sure.

And I'm also almost sure it wasn't there before. My skin creeps, my heart races, and my eyes strain wide, afraid to blink and miss . . . what? The thing rising? Looming over me?

The sob breaks from me and I fight to stifle it.

"What do you want?" I gasp to the thing that might not be there.

Still no response, but now I'm sure I did not feel like this before. I was scared before. Confused and frightened by the chain and the darkness. But something has changed. I must have slept, and now things are different. Now I feel . . .

Watched.

I can't see them, but there are eyes in the darkness. Perhaps. I can't be sure, and the uncertainty is killing me. I want to get up and lean across, to touch, just to be sure. Because knowing would be better than this dreadful uncertainty. I can't, of course, and not only because the chain won't let me reach that far. I can't move. My muscles have shut down, paralyzed by fear.

I have to know, *I think again. Whatever is there is less frightening than not knowing.*

And as the idea of this takes hold, I hear something that proves me wrong.

A breath. In and out. Almost a sigh. Coming from the corner by the door.

I stop breathing. I feel my heart tighten in my chest, as if, for a second, every cell in my body just ceases whatever it usually does. I am lifeless. Iron, like the ring in the wall against which my wrist chafes, or ice.

I am fear, and no other thought, feeling, or sensation registers.

I had thought that not being sure was the worst thing I could feel here in the dark, but someone is there, and knowing that is far, far worse.

Chapter Eight

"Oh my God! Did you fall asleep?" said Melissa.

"Sorry," I said. I had slept for an hour and a half and now felt sluggish and stupid. I had dressed reluctantly and tiptoed down, half hoping everyone would be gone and I could let my humiliation leech out of my system slowly and alone.

"You missed the drinkies," said Melissa.

At the foot of the stairs I had ducked away from the sound of raucous talking and laughter in what I took to be the living room and found her in a rustic but well-appointed kitchen next door, loading glassware into the dishwasher.

"Not to worry," she said, giving me a sympathetic look. "There'll be plenty more. Poor lamb, you must be exhausted."

"I am, kind of," I said.

"Tell you what," said Melissa, taking charge. "Get your bikini on and we'll spend the afternoon at the beach. Nice and easy. Then drinks and dinner, and you can get an early night."

"Oh, I don't know, Mel," I said. "I'm pretty beat."

"Nonsense. You've come all this way, and if you go back to bed now, you'll never get your body on schedule. Gotta tough it out till sundown, and then you'll be set for the rest of the week. Only way. Oh!" she exclaimed suddenly. "You haven't met Gretchen! You're gonna love her. Right this way, missy."

She took my hand and led me in the direction of the voices. For a split second I considered pulling back, just tensing the muscles of my arm enough to send the message and stop her in her tracks so she'd know I didn't want to go in. But then again I didn't really want her to know. To tell you the truth, it was almost impossible not to want to please Melissa. She was the sun.

So I walked, and we went in and there they were, Simon in his short sleeves as before, a half-empty cocktail glass in his hand; Marcus smiling faintly from him to me, his eyes evasive, both hands clasped around a beer glass as if afraid he might drop it; and a girl. A woman, I should say, but she looked young, waifish, if pretty, a less confident version of Melissa. She was wearing a summer dress and chunky jewelry that made her look like a college student, and her face was tanned, as if she had been out in the sun for several days already. I glanced at Marcus again but couldn't read his attitude toward her.

"Gretchen, this is Jan," said Melissa. "She used to be with Marcus, ages back, when we first met them. Now they're just friends."

I gaped at Melissa, who gave me a blank look as Gretchen awkwardly got to her feet and offered me a slender white hand.

"Hi," she said. "I'm a friend of Mel and Simon."

"Hi," I said. Marcus was looking at Melissa with the same disbelief I was sure was painted all over my face.

"What?" asked Melissa, apparently genuinely confused.

"Nothing," I said hurriedly, trying to move past it.

"There is," said Melissa, taking in Marcus's expression. "Oh, I'm sorry, was that a secret? Did I . . . ?"

"No," Marcus and I said at once.

"Of course not," Marcus added.

"I thought it was, you know," said Melissa, "common knowledge or whatever."

"It is!" I said, beaming manically.

"And you are still friends, right?" Melissa persisted.

"Absolutely!" said Marcus. "Great friends."

"Always," I agreed.

"We just don't . . . ," Marcus began, then looked panicky. "Not anymore. We're just . . ."

"Friends," I said, staring at him, horrified, wishing the floor would open and the earth would swallow us up. Gretchen gaped at us, eyes wide, smile fixed tight.

"OK," said Melissa, shrugging the moment off as if it hadn't happened and going right back to where she had been before. "So, beach, yeah? A little dip before dinner."

"Won't it be cold?" asked Gretchen, glad of the chance to change the subject.

"Apparently not," said Simon, brandishing a guidebook and reading from it theatrically. "*'While the air cools in the fall, the sea retains most of its summer heat into November.'* Apparently we should expect the water to still be in the midseventies."

He let the book slip from his fingers and fall into the lap of a startled Marcus, its apparent owner, like he was dropping the mic. Everyone laughed with just a bit more verve than the moment deserved.

"I'd better change," I said, still avoiding Marcus's eyes.

"That's right, missy," said Melissa. "Time to get some sun on that pasty skin!"

I turned to the stairs and she slapped my ass—not hard but somehow managing to get a resounding thwack that echoed round the room.

"Yes!" said Melissa. "Beach! I can't wait."

I fled, jogging upstairs and barely breathing till I had the bedroom door closed behind me. It was going to take an act of will to get me to open it again.

But I did. I changed into my swimsuit, slipped a cheery orange sundress over the top (purchased at employee discount but not, I thought, obviously so), and considered Gretchen. She was, I thought, like me in her diffidence, her slightly awkward, hesitant way of carrying herself, even if she did look more like Melissa's brand of bombshell. It was an odd combination and I wondered how it evolved, how someone with such obvious good looks grew up so mousy.

I still didn't know who she was or why she was there, nor did I have any idea about whether she was involved with Marcus, or if Melissa had brought her there to become so. It seemed an odd thing to do with me here. I mean, we were just friends, me and Marcus, but Melissa couldn't know that romance was absolutely off the table for us, not unless Marcus confided way more to Simon than he let on. I felt mildly affronted, then reminded myself that I had no right to be.

And what if Gretchen did get involved with Marcus? What was that to me? He wasn't why I was here.

I considered myself in the mirror over the sink, staring myself down for a long minute, then snatched up my purse and went downstairs, where the others were waiting.

We piled into the huge Mercedes with our beach bags, chattering happily and smelling of suntan lotion and, in the case of everyone but me, rum. The car was warm, the sky blue, and Melissa's enthusiasm for the excursion infectious.

"Oh my God, this is so great!" she said. "This place! The weather! All of us together again. And with Kristen and Brad on their way!"

"I can't wait to meet her," said Gretchen, starry-eyed. "I love her show."

"We are going to have the best time *ever!*" said Melissa, barely listening.

Gretchen gave a shrill whoop and shouted "Yeah!" so unselfconsciously that I was quite impressed, though it also struck me as strange since she didn't actually know the *all of us* who were getting back together. Then Melissa was turning up the radio and we were rocking out to the Black Eyed Peas, which, anywhere else, at any other time, would have been absurd but here was perfect, so even Marcus sang along. I felt ten years younger and forgot my annoyance with Gretchen. Melissa was right. This was going to be great after all.

That feeling flagged a little after an hour and a half but perked up again as we pulled into the Minos. We were still singing, bobbing in our seats like kids.

"We are so white!" Gretchen exclaimed to Marcus. "Aren't we just so white?"

Marcus's eyes widened slightly and he smiled that puzzled, disbelieving smile I knew so well.

"Pretty white," he agreed, indulgently.

"Right?" said Gretchen. She shrieked with laughter at her own outrageousness.

"You are so random," said Simon consideringly. He was smiling, but it wasn't quite a compliment.

"I know, right?" said Gretchen, delighted. "Seriously random."

Melissa had booked lounge chairs on the beach behind the hotel in the exact spot where we had sat five years ago, and we took our places without thinking. The sand was warm underfoot, rather than the searing heat we had so bitched about last time, a heat that had actually burned your feet if you didn't get to the water fast enough. The beach was quieter too. In my memory it had been crowded with Germans and Russians, the latter mainly bullish men and sculpted, hard-eyed women who might have been TV news anchors or models. The relative quiet calmed me, and for a moment I just sat in my beach chair, staring happily at the water, the years falling away like curls of old skin. When I turned to see that Marcus had, on some old instinct, taken the chair next to mine, we smiled at each other unselfconsciously, amazed at how easy it all was.

I looked at Gretchen, slathering oil onto her trim belly, apparently unaware of her status as interloper. I had not seen so much as a glance or gesture between her and Marcus suggesting they were a couple, but I couldn't think of a way to find out for sure. She caught my eyes on her and said, apparently unsarcastically, "Makes a change from Great Deal, I bet."

"It does," I said.

"Do you still have that pink top that you got on employee discount?" she asked. "The one with the seashell pattern around the neck?"

I blinked. I knew exactly which top she meant, but I'd spilled wine on it at Christmas and had had to throw it out.

"How did you know about that top?" I asked.

"You were wearing it in a picture, right, Mel?"

"Oh my God!" said Melissa, wriggling out of her top to reveal a stunning black bikini that made her look like a Bond girl. "Do you remember when we went to that cheesy disco and had to get a cab back, and we told the driver the hotel was Midas instead of Minos, and he drove us, like, halfway across the island?"

"When *you* told him it was Midas," said Simon, smirking.

"And then he wouldn't bring us back when we realized the mistake!" Marcus chimed in.

"You say Midas!" Melissa mimicked, hunching her shoulders and flapping with her hands. *"Now you not want Midas. What is wrong with you?"*

"And then he wanted double the money!" Simon added. Gretchen, I noticed, was laughing with the rest of us as if she'd been there, the Great Deal pink top forgotten.

"I took down his name and cab number," said Melissa, delighted, "and when I spoke to the concierge at our hotel—finally, after driving around for hours—the guy just shrugged and threw it away! I was like, *excuse me?* And he was like, *meh*. You know, *whatever*. I was furious. And I still hadn't realized we'd been saying the name of the wrong hotel, and the concierge was like, 'If you want to get back to *this* hotel'"—she said, making her voice slow and serious—"'you might try saying the right name.' I felt so stupid that I told him they should rename the hotel Midas because that was someone everyone had heard of."

She laughed at herself.

"I'm sure he was like, *yeah, lady, we'll get right on that,*" she added. "What an idiot. I still get it wrong. It's Minos, right?"

"As in minotaur," said Marcus. "Mythical king of Knossos down the road. Heart of the Minoan civilization."

"Thank you, professor," said Melissa, sticking her tongue out at him, then grinning. "God, look at this place. Is this awesome or what?"

We considered the beach stretching around a rocky headland toward the town of Rethymno in one direction and the long golden stretch back to Heraklion in the other, the view of the blue Aegean so vast and unbroken that you could see the curvature of the earth itself.

"Pretty awesome," said Simon.

"Totally awesome," said Gretchen. She shaded her eyes to look at Marcus, who, feeling everyone's gaze on him, chuckled, shrugged, and played along.

"Awesome," he said. "Jan?"

"Awesome," I agreed.

There was a reverential silence while we considered the general awesomeness, and then something occurred to me.

"Why was the minotaur named after the king?" I asked.

"What?" said Simon.

"Minos. Minotaur," I said. "What's the connection?"

"Minos. Taurus," said Melissa. "Well, Taurus means bull, right? Like the star sign."

"Right," I said. "So why Minos?"

"The monster was actually the offspring of King Minos's wife," said Marcus. "That's why it wasn't killed at birth. It lived in the complex of passages under the palace."

"How do you know all this stuff?" said Melissa. "You are so smart. Isn't he smart, Gretchen?"

"Super smart," said Gretchen. "I mean, I know you made the dean's list every year, but still."

"It's a weird monster, don't you think?" I said, cutting across Marcus's baffled surprise. "I mean, yes, it's sort of creepy, and I guess the horns would be dangerous, but it's a male cow! Cows are cute, kind of. If you were trying to tell a story about a monster who lived in a complex of underground passages to scare the living crap out of people, half man, half bull seems like an odd choice. You'd think the head of a lion or something would be more frightening."

"The minotaur was carnivorous," said Marcus. "Being an unnatural creature, it had no suitable food and could only eat people. Tributes to King Minos were sent by surrounding countries every year from the neighboring regions."

"People," I said.

"Right," Marcus replied.

"To be fed to the monster."

"That was the only way they could control it once it had reached full maturity."

"OK, that's less cute," I conceded.

"Hold on," said Melissa. "You said the monster was the child of King Midas or Minos's wife?"

"Yep," said Marcus.

"And . . . how'd that work exactly?"

"Well, I guess Jan isn't the only one who thinks cows are cute," said Marcus.

"Hey!" I protested.

"Minos's queen, Pasiphaë, fell in love with the sacred bull of Poseidon and had a famous craftsman, Daedalus, build a life-size wooden cow that she could climb into . . ."

"No!" said Gretchen.

"Yep," said Marcus again. "It was also Daedalus who built the labyrinth where the monster lived."

"But wait," said Melissa, grinning, "so the queen climbs into the wooden cow, and the sacred bull or whatever just . . ."

"Exactly."

"OK, professor," said Simon, his eyes down on the *Sports Illustrated* he had brought with him. "I think that's enough of that."

"It's interesting!" I said.

"It's gross," said Gretchen.

"It's not real," said Simon. "Bunch of old made-up crap. I don't know why you waste your time with it."

I frowned at him but didn't get the chance to argue, and I wasn't sure what I would have said anyway. Melissa had turned her lighthouse smile on us again.

"OK," she said. "So swim, then drink; or drink, then swim?"

"Swim," said Simon, leaping to his feet.

"Swim," agreed Melissa, continuing the game.

Gretchen predictably followed suit, and Marcus gave me a look.

"Swim?" he said.

I didn't want to. I doubted the water would be as warm as Simon claimed, and I felt uncomfortable stripping down to my one-piece in front of all these near-perfect bodies, but it was impossible to say no.

"Swim," I said.

~

I wore my glasses in the sea, partly because I wanted to be able to see what was going on, and partly for the same reason I had kept my hand luggage in my lap as we drove in from the airport. They made me feel a little less naked, which, after the towel incident with Marcus, felt important. It was choppy but the water was indeed warmer than I had believed possible, especially a few inches under the surface, so I waded out till I was chest deep and then half squatted, half floated between the waves, my chin just under the surface, my feet touching down on the rippled sandy bottom to push myself up and over each new surge.

I had an OK body. Paler than I would like, a little heavier and less toned than I had been, but I wasn't neurotic about it. I ate reasonably well unless money was very tight, and I did enough walking at work that I didn't feel bad about letting the gym membership slide. I had some cute dumbbells and a Pilates ball that I dragged out from time to time, but I didn't obsess about my body—though I'd be lying if I claimed not to have noticed the very slight spread and sag around my boobs and butt. When I was working reasonable hours and pulling down a healthier salary, I'd take them on, I told myself, and the occasional pizza wasn't going to kill me, was it?

That's what I had thought a few days ago as I modeled my bathing suit in front of the mirror in my apartment.

Not bad, I had thought. Not as bad as I had feared, anyway.

But that was then, and now I was here with Melissa and Gretchen, who had basically the same body as each other, lithe and toned, everything still tight and perky like nymphs, goddesses. It was impossible not to stare. I stayed under the water, even as the waves swelled in the wake of a passing speedboat, watching Melissa and Simon swimming like Olympians and play wrestling, kissing each other wetly, and doing God knew what with their hands under the water. I turned away quickly and found Marcus looking at me.

"Water feels good," he observed.

"Yeah," I replied. "I'm sorry about before, when we bumped into each other. When I was coming out of the shower—"

"No, that was my fault," he cut in. "I guess we weren't expecting each other."

"Not in that moment, no," I agreed, smiling. He wasn't wearing his glasses, a rarity that made his face strangely open and young. It reminded me of waking up next to him.

"And then there was the *Introduction to Gretchen* debacle," added Marcus, still pained.

"Yeah," I said.

"Sorry," he said. "I just didn't know how to . . ."

"And Melissa said . . ."

"Right," he agreed before I could say any more, not needing me to. We nodded at each other, smiling, finding an odd kind of familiar ease in discussing our previous awkwardness.

"You doing OK, Jan?" he said. "You look good."

"Yeah," I said. "You too."

"I mean, outside e-mail and Facebook we haven't spoken for . . ."

"It's been a while," I agreed, still smiling, glad we were having the conversation and that Gretchen had taken herself after Melissa and Simon, splashing less expertly in a ponderous crawl.

"Oh, and how about that promotion?" he asked, his eyes wide and encouraging. "The executive team leader thing."

I should have been ready for the question, but I had been thinking about other things, other times, so home—*work*—was the last thing on my mind. I looked down. Just that. A momentary, reflexive gesture that would have meant nothing to anyone else. But it was Marcus, and I just couldn't get my face to do what it needed to do fast enough.

"Oh, I wouldn't have been right for it," I said in a low voice, my eyes flashing to Melissa, who was screaming with delight as she straddled Simon's broad shoulders.

"What? Jan! I thought you were really excited about it."

"The salary wasn't that much of a step up, and there was a lot more responsibility," I said breezily. "I'm better off on the hourly plan. The benefits are still good and—"

"Jan?"

"What?" I said, my smile fixed.

He was giving me that look, the one that made my heart race and my skin break into pink blotches. He lowered his head slightly, and when he spoke his voice was little more than a whisper.

"I'm sorry," he said. He looked sad and embarrassed.

"Why?" I said with manic brightness. "It's fine."

But Marcus always knew when it wasn't fine. When I was fibbing. In my head I saw it all as it had happened two days before I got on the plane for Greece.

"I'm sorry, Jan," Camille had said, offering me her slim dark hand and smiling apologetically. "We just didn't feel you were ready for this much responsibility."

I shook her hand, blinking, feeling the color rise in my face.

"It's fine," I said. "I understand."

I reminded myself to let go of her hand. My own had started to sweat.

"Maybe you should take a few days off," she suggested. "Just till you feel ready to . . ."

"Actually," I said, "I plan to. I'm going on a trip."

"Good for you! Anywhere nice?"

"Greece," I said. "Well, Crete, actually."

"Wow," said Camille, looking more impressed by this than she had by my interview. "That's fantastic. Just don't forget us. I hope you have a great time."

"I will," I said, grinning and hoping she couldn't see the tears in my eyes.

⌒

OK, yes. That's how it actually happened. I prefer the first version, and I'd worry less about my bank account had it been true, but yes, I made that up. I do that sometimes. My application to move into the executive team for one of Charlotte's best-known megastores had been unsuccessful. Again. Which meant that I would still be going into work at three in the morning, making sure the backroom kept the store stocked and that the previous day's sales were steadily, constantly replaced, a new item slotted into the shelves as its counterpart left the building in Great Deal's ubiquitous and horrible yellow shopping carts. That was my life. Another cog in the great yellow machine, working my eight or nine hours till I crawled back to my apartment at lunchtime, to the roommate I needed to share my rent but never saw because I was in bed by six every night. That was my life. Nine dollars an hour with a degree in biology and a minor in English, subjects almost comically irrelevant to what I did for a living, a job I had taken on as a way of building up cash while I was a student with the vague idea that it would help me prepare for med school. But I hadn't gone to med school. Hadn't even applied, though sometimes I pretended I had.

Once last week, I told a new employee in hardlines—cute in his way, but far too young for me—that I had been accepted at Chapel Hill and would start next fall. It was a stupid and unnecessary lie, and I knew it would bite me in the ass even as I was saying it, though even I was surprised at how quickly he started avoiding me. No biggie. I am used to being alone.

While I'm making my confession, I should also say that Chad Hoskins wasn't my boyfriend and we hadn't had dinner together the night before I left Charlotte. He was my occasional therapist, the closest thing to a psychiatrist my health insurance would cover, and though I fantasized about him occasionally, we had no relationship outside of his dingy office.

And there you have it. Me. Jan the liar.

Voted—in a dazzling bit of mean-spirited group creativity—most likely of her graduating high school class to have flammable pants.

So yes, I'm used to not being believed. I'm used to feeling stupid and humiliated, caught in the web of my own fantasies, mocked, passed over, and rejected, usually for reasons entirely in my own control.

Except that—painfully, inexplicably—they're not.

I lie. I can't help it. I don't mean to. Not usually. I just prefer the version of my life that I make up, but then I say it, not out of malice or the desire to trick or mislead others, but to get that nicer, happier version of the world out there where I can see it, where I can believe in it . . . but then that's not true either, is it? Of course I mean to mislead others. Or myself.

It's pathetic. And it's why Marcus left me.

Chapter Nine

He sits there in the dark. He? I have no idea, but I'm chained up, impris-
oned, and someone is there, someone I assume is responsible for my situation,
so yes, decades of books and movies and damsel-in-distress crime TV says he.

Unless . . .

"Are you stuck here too?" I say to the darkness, somehow steadying the
quaver in my voice till I can barely hear it. "Are you tied up? Manacled?
Can you hear me?"

Nothing.

I strain to see, leaning closer so that the chain around my wrist clanks
and I feel its weight shift, but the movement doesn't make my eyes any better,
and I can't make out anything in the darkness beyond that lumpen shape.
Maybe he is asleep, drugged like I was, dragged in and left to wake in his
own time. The sigh could have been a snore.

But he hasn't moved, and what little I can see suggests he is sitting.
People sleep sitting up.

But the breath . . . if it was a snore, surely there would have been more
than one? I stare harder into the blackness, not wanting it to be true, wish-
ing I were anywhere other than here. I want to roll onto my side with my
face to the wall, to pretend none of it is real, but I daren't turn away. I can

see almost nothing, but I can't take my eyes off the shape, a huddled, oversize crow perched there in the corner.

"Can you hear me?" I try again. "Can you? Speak to me. I just want . . . I need to know what is happening to me. What is . . . going on. What . . ."

And suddenly something inside breaks, and my voice, which had been low and raspy, is a ragged, full-throated scream that bounces off the walls like gunfire.

"What do you want?" I shout. "What have I done to you, you sick bastard? What do you want?"

And then there are almost no words. Just my screaming, crying despair, raw as the howl of a wounded dog. It gets me off the bed and a step toward the corner, to the full limit of the chain around my wrist, and my fury yanks at it, though I barely feel the pain, a squall of bellowing and cursing that takes the air from my lungs. It rings in the silence as I collapse back onto the mattress, trembling all over, unable to stand, sprawled on my side, my left arm keening from the edge of the manacle, my anger and fear folding around me. I have never done anything so clearly futile in my life. I'm weak from the exertion, cowed by my own powerlessness and terror.

For several minutes, everything is quiet. Then . . .

I barely notice at first, but it comes again—the faintest creak—and I see that the shape in the corner is different, taller, as if he has sat up straight. There's a long, empty silence, and then a prick of light comes on at what I take to be waist height. It's red, but it turns green almost immediately, and now the breathing sound is louder and different, sibilant somehow, like wind in dry grass or breakers coursing over shingle.

I go very still, not daring to swallow or breathe, too terrified to speak or move a single muscle. I am tense with the strangeness of what is happening, eyes and ears straining for something, anything that will make sense of the sound, the tiny green light. A moment passes, and then a strange inhuman voice uncurls from the corner of the room. It's slow and deep, distorted so that it drags and rolls like a steel barrel on a hard floor. It is neither male nor female, and it says only one thing:

"Jan."

Chapter Ten

Lying is creation ex nihilo. It's parthenogenesis, the goddess Athena born fully armed from the head—the *mind*—of her father, Zeus. Lying is making things up out of thin air. Except that the air is toxic, corrupting everyone who hears the lie, and the liar most of all.

I want to believe that it's harmless, a coping mechanism that makes a pretty shitty reality seem bearable, but it always catches up with me, a black cloud that engulfs me with a sense of failure, of stupidity and worthlessness. In college I lied about why I hadn't done assignments as a way of buying myself time and sympathy—a grandmother's funeral here, a self-harming roommate there—and initially it had been fine. I even made the dean's list in my first year, and I never pushed beyond simple lying into other moral or criminal areas, like plagiarism, which—though related—felt like theft. But getting away with a lie brings its own particular euphoria, a secret pleasure like an adrenaline high, and if you're not careful it can become an end in itself. I said that my excuses, the assorted variations on *the dog ate my homework*, bought me time, but midway through my second year, it became clear I wasn't actually using that time to finish the work I had dodged. I was using it to build more lies, more escape hatches. In my third year I took two incompletes that I never finished; and in my fourth, I ran headlong into Dr. James Bancroft and his developmental biology course. The class wasn't especially hard, but I didn't like it, didn't like his pedantic, robotic teaching, and I resolved to find a way to skate through it with the minimum amount of actual work.

From time to time I ran into people who saw through me. Not completely, and usually not right away, but they were hardwired to sniff out bullshit and—and this was worse—to call you on it. Most people are too polite to see a lie for what it is. They sense something is off, but you seem so nice—or so upset, whatever—and they just assume they've miscalculated somehow. *After all,* they say, *why would she lie?*

Why indeed?

Anyway, Bancroft was one of the few who were just primed for untruth. I'm not sure why, though I suspected afterward that he knew me like an alcoholic recognizes other alcoholics, picking up the little tells in the way your eyes go to the bottle just before you sit as far away from it as possible. Or maybe he had seen the behavior in someone close to him and was just alert to it. In any case, my little elaborations, what I used to call my *fibbing,* didn't wash with him. I tried to avoid a paper on morphogenesis not once, not twice, but three times, spending more labor on inventing reasons why I couldn't do it than I would have done on the actual paper. The first time Bancroft shut me down so completely that I should have known I was on a losing tear, but some stupid part of me treated it as a challenge. The second time I was actually affronted by how unmoved he was by my tales of hardship, as if my inventiveness had actually deserved the pass.

I failed the class, a shock so unsettling that I lost control of my grades in every other course that semester, failing to show up for finals in two of them, including one in my beloved mythology class. By the time I graduated, the 4.0 I had maintained through my first year had dropped to a 2.7, and my future was in burnout. I applied for lab positions and internships, never lying in my applications but always in interviews, upping the ante as jobs came and went, and I was still getting up at three in the morning to oversee the stocking of shelves at Great Deal. The more desperate I became, the more reckless was the lying, so that I was soon telling stories of my past employment that were in direct contradiction to my own résumé. I got used to the ripple of confusion on the faces of my interviewers, the way their gaze would go back to the papers in front of them while I backpedaled and unraveled.

I told myself it was fine. I was moving on up. It would all be fine. *I was fine.* And I continued to do that, right up to this day at the beach in Crete.

They were all still in the sea, but I had splashed a little distance away to be alone with my humiliation. The lie I had told Marcus about the promotion not being right for me was nothing like as great as the one I had been telling myself: that I'd gotten it, been welcomed to the upper echelon of the company with open arms, that I could afford a solo apartment or, for that matter, this vacation. That was the greater lie, the one that said life was good. That I didn't mind my spreading body, the increasing gap between me and the friends I had made on this beach five years ago, the longing for the rum I had missed while taking the nap I had pretended was from tiredness rather than retreat, rather than panic, dread, and rushing inadequacy. They were all paddling back to their deck chairs now, and there would be more rum, or whatever newfangled cocktails Melissa had discovered in the trendy London bars I would never visit. I wanted one of those drinks more than anything. No, I wanted six. But I couldn't face the way Marcus would avoid my gaze, as you might avoid looking directly at a beggar.

I was an embarrassment.

So I swam farther out as the others went in.

I swim like I do everything else—badly, with neither grace nor power—but I felt my feet leave the bottom and labored on out to sea. The horizon sparkled through my speckled glasses and I fixed my eyes on it, pushing through my clumsy and inefficient breaststroke, glad I couldn't see the others settling happily on the beach talking about . . .

what? Old times? Recent triumphs? A new kitchen, even a new house? I doubted Simon could afford a private jet, but a boat was surely within his means. Maybe he already had one. Maybe Marcus was telling them all about the excavations at the palace of King Minos. Or Midas, who turned everything to gold just by touching it. Or maybe he was telling them about Jan and her lies, her dire financial straits and professional failures, Queen Jan whose touch turned everything to shit.

I kept swimming. Someone went buzzing round the headland on a Jet Ski. We'd used a Jet Ski or two when we were here last. I remember seeing Simon on a big blue one, looking like a latter-day Poseidon shooting across the waves, his face dark with focus, his chest and arms braced. He had been—as always—confident, impressive, even when he ran it aground on the pebbly shore on our last day and had to pay for the damage.

"Why you drive so fast, man?" the rental guy had yelled. "Why you not just shut it off? And why you come from over there? I told you, you only go round the rocks *that* way!"

It should have been funny, but I guess we were tired and stressed about leaving.

The jet skier wasn't Simon this time, though. *Not one of my group,* I thought, marveling at the ironic inaccuracy of that *my*. I had thought Gretchen was the interloper, the hanger-on, but suddenly it seemed more likely that that was how they saw me. Jan the Pathetic, the charity case who had to have her way paid for her.

A horrible thought struck me, and my stroke faltered. What if I was the only one who wasn't chipping in for the cost of the villa? What if the others had gotten together to help out poor Jan and they were all covering my expenses? What if Gretchen was auditioning to be the group's *new* Jan, a better prospect for Marcus: cuter, less of a downer, someone who could be counted on not to lie about what fucking day it was . . .

The Jet Ski whipped past, a good twenty yards in front of me, but the wave from his wake caught me by surprise. It slapped me hard in the face before I could float over it. I came up sputtering and realized immediately that what had been crisp and clear was blurry, a smudge of light and color.

My glasses.

I had lost my glasses. I flailed in the water wildly, but I was out of my depth and couldn't fix my position as the sea moved round me. I thrust my splayed fingers through the water, hoping to catch the drifting frames, staring down, my face almost under the surface, but I touched nothing, saw nothing.

"No," I said aloud, hands raking the water desperately. *"No!"*

It was futile. And stupid. I had lost them. My only pair—of course they were—and I had lost them. I was more than angry. I was humiliated, ashamed even, because this was just *so me.*

I continued to tread water a little longer where I was, sobbing quietly, my piggy snuffling loud in my ears as the infuriating fucking jet skier zoomed away so that I had the Aegean to myself. At last I began my pathetic splashing back to the shore.

I remembered coming out of the optician's shop when I was twelve in my first pair of glasses, astonished by the clarity of the bricks in the wall across the street.

People can see like this? I had wondered, amazed to the point of disbelief. It had always seemed to me quite logical that things got harder to see the farther away they were, and I had breezed through the first decade of my life sure in my own mind that there was nothing wrong with my eyes. No one else had figured it out either because I developed ways of hiding the truth, even from myself. I sat at the front of class; I kept clear of sport, professing that I would rather read books; and when other people pointed things out that I couldn't see, I pretended I could.

More coping strategies. More lies.

But my eyes were terrible. So bad, in fact, that it was only because the beach was largely deserted that I was able to find the others as I splashed my way out of the water. If it had been crowded, my humiliation would have been increased by having to wander from group to group, peering . . .

But I found my chair without a word and braced myself for the questions about what I had done with my specs. But the questions didn't come. No one noticed. Not even Marcus, and while it was a relief not to have to explain my idiocy aloud, this too felt like a kind of defeat.

I lay in my recliner, eyes shut, angry at myself and at the others for not realizing I was upset. I stayed like that for ten whole minutes, so locked in my own head that it took me a while to note the edge in Simon's voice.

"I thought the whole point was that we would come to the beach on our way to get them from the airport?"

"But we're hot and sweaty and covered in salt and lotion," Melissa wheedled. "It's over an hour in each direction to the airport, and we'll just take up space in the car."

"Kristen and Brad are expecting to see you there," said Simon. "I'm not the fucking chauffeur, Mel."

"Come on, Si," said Melissa. "It's such a waste of the afternoon . . ."

"For you," Simon shot back. They were keeping their voices low but everyone could hear. "I have to drive there and back regardless."

"And I appreciate it," said Melissa.

"So you say," Simon snapped. "But you'd rather lie in the sun."

"Of course I would! Who wouldn't? Right, Gretchen?"

"Well, sure," said Gretchen, guardedly.

I kept my eyes shut, determined not to be drawn in.

"Maybe we could call a cab to get them," Simon mused. "Bring them here, then we all go up to the villa . . ."

"They're expecting you," said Melissa.

"They're expecting *us*," Simon returned.

"Come on, sweetie," said Melissa. "Don't make us all go."

"Fine," said Simon, standing abruptly and snatching up his towel so fast that I felt a faint shower of sand on my legs.

"Simon!" Melissa exclaimed. "Careful!"

"Oh, I'm sorry!" Simon replied with mock politeness. "Did I disrupt your busy day of sitting?"

"Don't start, Simon," said Melissa. "I've done as much as you to make everything nice."

"I'm the one ferrying everyone back and forth from the airport! By myself."

"I'll go with you."

It was Marcus. I turned in surprise and opened my eyes, dismayed to find how indistinct everyone looked.

My glasses.

But I didn't need perfect vision to see that Simon was glaring at Melissa.

"That's OK, Marcus," he said. "This isn't your fight."

"It's OK," Marcus answered, sitting up. "I could use a break from the sun, anyway."

Simon turned to look at him, and everything about him softened a little, the tension draining from his face and shoulders.

"Yeah?" he said.

"Sure," said Marcus. "Gives us the chance to do some manly bonding. You know . . . talk football. Boobs."

"Deal," said Simon. "I have things to say on both."

"As do I, brother man, as do I. See you all later."

I nearly offered to join them, but I couldn't, and not just because it would feel disloyal to Melissa. Simon walked away without another word.

"Big baby," said Melissa, pushing her sunglasses back into place and sitting back in her lounger. "I'm ready for another drink."

I had seen Brad and Kristen less than the others, only once, in fact, since our first visit to Crete, and even then they had been more peripheral to the group, though I suppose that was true of everyone but Melissa. She was the sun at the heart of our little solar system, the gravity that drew us in and held us together. Simon was next, of course, a giant planet like Jupiter or Saturn, though with the looks of Apollo, as I've suggested, and the personality of Mars. I said this once to Marcus and he had agreed, though he'd suggested that since we were in Greece, we'd be better off thinking of Simon as Ares rather than Mars. He had said it half to himself, as if he was making a point, but when I asked him why he had corrected me when he knew it had just been a mental slip on my part, he replied, "Oh, you know me. Always the teacher." He had said it miserably, with a kind of low-grade contempt for himself that bothered me.

But a certain amount of self-loathing was inevitable around our newfound friends. They all had a glow about them, the halo of beauty and prosperity. If Melissa and Simon were the heart of our solar system, Brad was its Mercury—sorry, Marcus, *Hermes*—shimmering and changeable but fascinating and, in its way, beautiful. My first thought was that Kristen was our Venus—Aphrodite—but with hindsight, she was more a comet: mystifying, spectacular, and rare.

"And what are we?" Marcus had said, indulging me. This was after the only other time we had seen them, at a holiday party in Brad and Kristen's colossal Buckhead home.

"Minor moons," I said.

"Or Pluto," he added, cracking himself up. We were both pretty drunk.

"Discredited," I agreed.

"Invisible to the naked eye," he said.

"And named after a cartoon dog," I added.

"Well, not exactly *named after* . . . ," he began, catching himself and rolling his eyes. "God, I'm boring."

"No, you aren't," I said. We were still together then. Just.

"Well, we can't *both* be Pluto," he pronounced. "I called it. You have to be something else. What do you think? Which of the Greek gods was the biggest underachiever?"

He grinned as he said it. He'd had at least three beers and a couple of large shots of whiskey. He didn't even see my reaction, an involuntary wince like a muscle spasm. But I played along.

"Maybe I'm not a planet at all," I said. "I think I'm more . . . a black hole."

"Ooh," he said, nodding. "That's good. Sucking everything around you into your own darkness. That's perfect."

"Yeah," I said. "Perfect."

Anyway, Ares and the comet—they sounded like a band, or the hosts of a New Age radio talk show—arrived on schedule and met Simon and Marcus at the airport. I could picture exactly what that moment was like, Brad and Kristen drawing every eye, movie stars in their shades and casual couture. And I guess they were, one of them at least. Kristen had joined the cast of *End Times*, the Atlanta-based sci-fi show, in its second season but had quickly moved from being an occasional guest star to being a core character. She played an alien who had survived the apocalyptic war with humanity that had left the world in ruins. I didn't know why the alien had a British accent, but people loved her. They were on season four now, and she had become the face of the show, so while I'd seen her only once since we met on Crete, she now eyed me from billboards and the sides of buses almost constantly. It was a bit unnerving. The accent was real. She was born and raised in and around London to a white mother and an Asian father and had done some theater and TV there as a child before maturing into the bombshell she was today—light-tan skin and black hair complemented uncannily by ice-blue eyes and the kind of elegant calm that made her ethereal, angelic. Not angelic in the sense of prim or sexless—her TV roles had often been pretty spicy, so watching her as someone I knew, albeit slightly, made me feel like a voyeur—but with that chill, otherworldly strength you sometimes see in medieval paintings. Michael. Gabriel. Angels with flaming swords and eyes to match. She was perfectly cast in *End Times*: beautiful, sexy in ways that felt deliberately manipulative, and ultimately unreadable. It was no surprise that Hollywood had come calling.

Brad, as I think I said, was in commercial real estate. He found and brokered land for powerhouse companies to open new branches and franchises. That was about all I knew of it. It was very lucrative and meant that he traveled a lot, but it had none of the glamour of his wife's profession. They had met in London while he was negotiating a deal for an Atlanta-based company, and she had looked him up when she first went to the States. He was, apparently, the only person she knew in the city who wasn't working on the show. They had only just become a couple when we met them, and her first *End Times* episode hadn't yet aired. They married a year later, just as her star—her comet, I should say—was really taking off.

"Good timing," Marcus had remarked cryptically.

"What do you mean?" I asked.

"Nothing," he said. "But I mean, he's a regular guy, right? Smart, good-looking, and rich, but still a regular guy. He buys and sells land for Wendy's and Wal-Mart."

"So?"

"So she's a star, and she mixes with stars. Gets a lot of attention."

"You think that he married her because he wouldn't be able to compete with the Hollywood A-listers who were starting to pay attention to her? That's pretty cynical."

"Just honest," said Marcus, who always was. "I mean, if I were with someone like that, I'd be worried, what with all the fame, the glamour, the celebrities, and fancy parties, you know. That I couldn't keep her."

As I said, we were only just still together. I opened my mouth to say something, but I wasn't sure what it was that I wanted to know or whether I really wanted to know it, so I left it at that.

Simon's earlier irritability had utterly vanished as the four of them met us at the Minos, and he made a point of tacitly going straight to Melissa and kissing her on the cheek. They muttered privately to each other and hugged, their differences forgotten, and I felt a twinge of envy. Brad hugged me warmly, like he was genuinely pleased to see me, and his smile was wide as a child's, a happiness at seeing us all that seemed so deep and genuine that I was momentarily thrown. Brad was the driest of the group, the most implacable, and his wit had a fine, cutting edge. Kristen hugged me too, but she said "hiya" first, a word that sounded so comically, stereotypically English and unselfconscious, that for a moment I couldn't connect her to the ice queen I saw on television. I wondered briefly if I'd had it wrong all this time and this wasn't actually the same woman at all. Her manner was—I have to say it—nice. Ordinary. Less the comet of my imagined recollection and more a person I had once met. She was still exotically beautiful, still English, as her husband was still rich and handsome, but they were also just people, less glamorous in some ways than Melissa and Simon, younger and less polished. That all made Kristen a better actress than I had thought her, and that slightly mean-spirited compliment made me like her more and myself less.

So, nothing new there . . .

Brad looked older than he had. His auburn hair was cropped very close at the sides, and his forehead was higher than I remembered, but he looked more buff than he had been too, his arms long and muscular. He had blue eyes so bright, I had always assumed he wore colored contacts, though he claimed not to, and they flashed when he cracked wise, which was most of the time. There was something slightly skeletal about his face, like the skin had been pulled tight at the back of his head, so that when he smiled he got a manic look, eyes wide, teeth exposed like little chisels. Kristen's hair was also short—amazingly so—cut to within a couple of inches all over. It should have made her boyish, but it only showed off those knife-sharp cheekbones, so she looked like the magical princess from some strange Japanese anime. She didn't pulse like Melissa did, didn't glow, and you might not notice it at first, but she really was exquisite.

"Oh my God!" said Melissa. "Your hair!"

"I know, right?" she said, ruffling it self-consciously. "Too butch?"

"No!" said Melissa. "It's fantastic. Very chic."

"Makes it easier to deal with wigs. And I get recognized less off set."

"That must get to be a drag," I said, not really believing it.

"It's mostly OK," said Kristen. "But it's nice not to feel like public property all the time."

We had left the beach when Simon phoned from the road and waited for them in the hotel's airy lobby. Our reconnections done, Brad made a pit stop to the men's room, and we then climbed back into the Mercedes: Melissa in the front; me, Marcus, and Gretchen in the back; Brad and Kristen in the middle. It was tight, but the AC was cranked up and as soon as we were pulling away, Simon had "1999" blaring away on the stereo again, and everyone was whooping and singing, reveling in being there again.

"Can't believe he died," said Kristen, as the song finished. "I was sad about Bowie, but Prince? I couldn't believe it."

Marcus nodded. "A piece of my past," he said. "I remember my mom dancing around to 'Little Red Corvette,' and I used to crank *Sign o' the Times* all through college, remember?"

"Yeah," I said, suddenly wistful.

The mood in the car had inverted in seconds, as if Prince's death had cost us something we hadn't noticed before.

"We need a new anthem," said Melissa, scanning the iPhone's playlist with determined focus. "You guys know any other good millennium songs?"

No one did.

I kept my eyes on the passing scenery to stave off motion sickness. Not that I could see much beyond the blur of color and shape.

"So, Jan," said Brad, turning right on cue. "Contact lenses, huh? Looking eagle eyed. Nice."

I colored. Beside me, Marcus frowned with bewilderment. He knew how bad my eyes were, but he also knew that I had an aversion to anyone—myself included—touching my eyes. I had tried contact lenses one time, and it had taken me twenty hellish minutes to get one of them in. I never got the other in and fled from the optician's, weeping, the moment I had managed to get the first one out. Neither Marcus nor any of the others had noted my missing glasses.

"Just trying something new," I said.

A stupid, unsustainable lie, but sitting there with them all, the Pluto, the black hole of the group, I just couldn't say "No, I lost my glasses in the sea because I'm a pathetic, clueless, moron." Marcus's eyes narrowed doubtfully, but it was too late. I just couldn't bear the idea that I'd tell them the truth and they'd laugh at me. Or that they'd stifle that honest impulse out of pity. That would almost be worse.

"Good for you!" Brad said.

"Thanks!" I replied.

The trees sped past: blobs of dull green and pale, sandy ground, illegible road signs like teasing question marks all pointing at me, Lying Jan . . .

How was I going to get through a week like this? I couldn't see shit beyond about three feet. There was no way I would be able to sustain the pretense that I could function normally. I was used to covering my ass like that, keeping track of my various exaggerations, elaborations, and flat-out untruths so that I didn't catch myself out, and generally I got away with it. And usually I was also careful about the initial lie, floating it only in situations where I knew nobody or was about to leave so that the chance of being exposed was minimal. This was different. A week in close quarters with people I knew pretending I could see? I could barely tell them apart!

I bit my lip hard, punishing myself till I felt the blood run.

Idiot. Pathetic, lying, idiot.

Chapter Eleven

My name. The voice in the dark—strange, sexless, sepulchral—says it and I clench every muscle. I can hear the tremble of my limbs in the miniscule shaking of the chain around my wrist, drawing myself together like some shell-less turtle.

"Jan."

"Who are you?" I manage. "What do you want?"

The silence that follows lasts an age. All I can hear is the thin hiss from the corner that sounds dimly like radio static, and the stuttering quaver of my own breathing. The pinprick of green light doesn't reveal anything more in the blackness, but then, I remember with a start, that might not just be the lightlessness of the room.

I lost my glasses.

In the sea. I lost my glasses in the sea. I remember now. My mind tries to hold on to that thought, to anchor the person I am now, chained in the blackness with this . . . this thing that is talking to me, as if having a past will somehow explain the present, make it manageable. But I can't remember anything else; the attempt is drowned out by the dread of whatever is sharing the cell with me. It speaks.

"Tell me about before."

I stare blindly into the dark, my eyes fixing pointlessly on the green-glowworm brightness.

"W-what?" I stammer. "Before what?"

Another long silence like a chasm, and I feel like I'm on the lip of a pit peering down, terrified of the black depth, and even more terrified of what might come out of it.

"Last time," says the voice.

"What?" I say again, confusion and panic making me stupid. What does he want me to say? What will he do if I get it wrong? "I don't understand. Last time when?"

"You came to Crete five years ago," the rolling, droning voice intones, each syllable dragging like snagged audiotape.

"Yes," I say.

"Tell me about it."

The panic rises again, kicking mulishly inside my head. I don't understand and I'm going to get it wrong. I'll die because he—or she or whatever the fuck it is—has me confused with someone else and I don't know what he wants to know, and he'll reach out with a blade I won't see coming and I'll bleed out here in the dark . . .

"Five years ago," says the voice. "When you were here. Tell me what you did."

Chapter Twelve

"So, Brad," said Simon, "how's life in commercial real estate?"

"Awesome," said Brad. "Just reeled in a deal for sixteen new Value Auto Parts stores across the southeast. A little economic downturn, and suddenly everyone wants to work on their own cars!"

"Gotta love that," said Simon, laughing.

"No kids to put through college, so I guess we'll get that boat!" Brad cooed, reaching for the high five. Simon responded on cue, as if the whole thing had been carefully choreographed, and their two palms rang out crisply. It looked like a scene from a movie, the two of them, with their easy *GQ* elegance and professional good looks, like brothers, in sync, comfortable and on top of the world. "Or a zeppelin," he added musingly. "Always wanted one."

He gave me his trademark skull grin, and his blue eyes flashed.

We were sitting in the villa's glorious glassed-in lounge, its rustic stone floor and great fireplace flanked by immense windows looking down over the patio to the rugged coast and the sea. The golden light of the late afternoon had reddened into sunset as vast purple clouds rolled in, crisp-edged and solid as heaped boulders. It was extraordinary.

"I'm looking at getting into a little real estate dealing in London," said Simon. "Might want your input. Residential rather than commercial, but still. Man, the appreciation there is through the roof. It takes a little capital down, but if you have it, there's serious money to be made. If you're in the right spot, you can charge what you like. Fifty million dollars for an apartment. More. I shit you not."

"Yeah?" said Brad. "Some people have a lot more cash than brain cells."

"Ain't that the truth. Some of these Saudi businessmen, man. You wouldn't believe what they walk around with in their pockets. But if it's a swank London apartment they want, overlooking Hyde Park or whatever, and they can afford it . . ."

"Oh hell yeah, I'll sell it to them," Brad said with a laugh. "Their ill-gotten oil money will do a lot more good in my wallet. Sure, send me what you have and we'll talk."

"You should come over soon. These post-Brexit prices won't last forever. I'll walk you through some options. Might be something you want to get into. I gotta show you the new Panamera. The Turbo S, baby, it's a sight to see!"

"Absolutely," said Brad, nodding. "And we can talk about that wine dealership idea too."

"Yeah," said Simon, making a face. "Not so sure about that. Looks to me like most guys who get into that do it so they can score some deals on a few crates. I doubt they're making much more than pocket change. I mean, could be a tax write-off, but it's more of a hobby than a real business enterprise."

"Maybe," said Brad, "but if you can get your foot in the door with the big distributors . . . Total Wine, the supermarket chains . . . you put enough investment in . . ."

I caught Marcus's eye, and a private smile rippled the corner of his mouth. It had been like this last time, the two business guys trading tales of profit and loss, stock market tips and portfolio recommendations in a language where every fifth word sounded coined by some MBA textbook, and me and Marcus looking at each other, feeling both out of it and on the edge of giggling. Of course, the first time, we had then taken solace in each other, celebrating our difference from them with little looks and grins that would, later, become whispers, kisses, other things . . .

Now, with the weight of my professional failure hanging around me like a wet coat—the heavy woolen kind that holds rain like a camel's hump—the humor of being so obviously excluded was harder to find. Even Marcus's wry amusement looked weary, as if he had dug out some old TV comedy that had once seemed so hilarious and found it dulled by repetition and familiarity. We were sitting across the room from each other. Gretchen was one seat over from him on the couch, but she was too entranced by Melissa's iPad pictures of the house she was redesigning for some newspaper magnate, and when Marcus's eyes wandered toward her she didn't react, so he got up and went to the bar by himself. I considered going after him but didn't know what I would say and, without my glasses, couldn't read his face well enough at this distance to see if I was welcome.

Brad was still pitching his wine-supplier idea.

"I don't know," said Simon. "Risky commodity. Too fragile, too niche . . ."

"But with the right capital outlay and people on the inside who really know the product . . . ," Brad persisted.

"Yeah, but the hardcore enthusiasts aren't your market, are they?" Simon quipped. "Or if they are, your market is too small and you'll never earn out. And if they're not your market, if your target consumers are people more like . . . well, *us*, who frankly don't know that much about wine . . ."

"Hey," said Melissa. "I know wine."

"You know what you like, honey," said Simon, indulgently.

"Same thing," said Melissa, kissing the top of his head and taking his empty glass to refill it.

"See?" said Simon to Brad. "Expert opinions don't matter to most consumers."

"But people want the best!" said Brad. He was leaning forward, his shoulders locked, spine straight, and it struck me that he hadn't made a smart-ass remark for a while. Usually, every other sentence had a barb or a punch line.

"But when you're talking about wine, that's just opinion, isn't it?" said Simon, lounging.

"No!" Brad replied. His grin was a little fixed and his voice a tad louder than it had been. We had all been drinking since we got back to the house. "It's measurable! There are experts whose judgment—"

"Nobody cares!" Simon laughed. "They like it, they drink it, and then it's gone. The only people who are going to pay top dollar for what they think is the best are collectors, not consumers, and that's too small and volatile a market."

"But that's not a concern for investors, is it?" said Brad. I was weary of the conversation and wished they'd shut up, but Brad wouldn't let it go. "So long as they see their money growing, who cares whether it's coming from a casual drinker who buys a few cases a year, a store that buys thousands, or a collector who buys one bottle of Châteaux Margaux 1875 but spends a quarter of a million dollars on it?"

"But that's the thing, isn't it?" said Simon, less playful now. "I don't see investors making their money back on this."

"Simon . . . ," Brad began, earnest to the point of frustration.

"Leave it, Brad," said Kristen, reaching over and patting his hand. He looked at her and she smiled. "Let's have another drink, shall we? You can talk about this later."

Brad hesitated for a second, then the tension in his face eased a little and he smiled.

"Sure," he said. "Later. How about we open that Peter Michael Oakville Au Paradis? Gonna blow your mind."

"I want something with vodka," said Melissa.

"Yeah," said Gretchen. "Get that voddy out." She gave me a quick look and hesitated. "Voddy's OK, right, Jan? It's brandy you don't drink."

I was momentarily taken aback, wondering when I had let that slip, then nodded.

"Voddy is fine," I said.

"Ah," said Simon getting up. "But vodka and what? I spotted some elderflower tonic, and I had a case of basil spritzers flown over yesterday."

For a moment, as Melissa and Gretchen *oohed* and *aahed* from the adjoining kitchen, Brad kept looking at the chair Simon had just vacated, his fists balled, and then he sat back and turned away. His gaze fell on me, and for a moment he looked—what? Caught out. Embarrassed and angry. Something hard and dark went through his eyes, and then he shrugged it off and turned to the rest of the group, getting to his feet and turning his back on me.

"Vodka it is," he said, suddenly cheery. "Where's my glass?"

"Are those words?"

It was Kristen. She was standing at the French doors that opened onto a brick patio with ornamental shrubs in terra-cotta pots between faded wicker furniture and a large grill, her head tilted on one side. I moved to join her.

"There," she said, pointing at what seemed to be just dead leaves on the ground. They looked like they had been left over from someone sweeping up, the edges of former piles straggling into each other. But as I looked, squinting to wring a little focus from my terrible vision, I saw that she was right. The crisped fall leaves trailing together in little heaps of dust, sticks, and other debris formed what might be capital letters. An *A* stood out. And a spiky *S*. The rest were less clear.

"*Hanos?*" she murmured. "*Nanos?*"

"*Nanos*," I said, still squinting. "But that's not a word."

"Just fell like that, I guess. Random."

"Or someone swept up with a dust pan. I get those little lines on my floor where I can't get the dirt up no matter how many times I sweep," I said. I wasn't sure why I wanted it to be nothing, a chance event.

Something about it bothered me, partly the way it seemed arranged to be read through the window. If it was an accident, it was a strange one.

She laughed and nodded but turned from the window, still puzzled and thoughtful.

"Come on," I said. "Let's get a drink."

An hour or so later we all went out into the garden for a few minutes, and I went back to the spot by the French doors to see if I could still read it, but the word, if it had been one, had been blown away, though there was no wind to speak of.

"OK," said Melissa, standing up, "you guys have to promise not to get all miserable if we play the Prince song, yeah? Coz we're gonna party."

"Deal," said Kristen.

"Wait," said Brad. His previous mood, whatever it had been, was utterly gone, and he was genial and funny again. "By my calculations, we're at day one thousand nine hundred and ninety-six. We don't get our millennium-even party till the end of the week."

"I can't wait that long," said Melissa. "Plus, who says we only get to party once, am I right?"

"You're right," said Simon.

"OK, then," said Melissa, satisfied. "So I figured we would start at the very beginning. Marcus, you're up."

I gave him a quizzical look as he rose and began hooking his iPad up to the flat screen on the wall, muttering about compatibility issues.

"Right," he said, turning and smiling at the rest of us. "Melissa asked me to cobble together a little presentation—sorry, Gretchen, this might be boring for you—to remind us all of why we're here." He tapped the iPad and the TV on the wall came to life, displaying a truly glorious photograph of the original six of us, sitting in our swimwear in deck chairs, toasting the camera with multicolored drinks. We were joy personified. Across the top, in large, festive letters, it said, "1999 days of friendship!"

Marcus made another click, and the inevitable keyboards, drums, and bass kicked in. As Prince crooned away in the background, everyone cheered and the slide show began. Every swim, every meal, every dance was catalogued, the images full of life, energy, and flashing smiles. Here was Brad with a towel on his head and an eye patch made from a napkin, waving a bottle of rum and pulling an *argggh!* face.

"Pirate Brad!" shouted Melissa. "I'd forgotten Pirate Brad."

"Well, he hasn't forgotten you, me hearty," said Brad in his best Captain Jack Sparrow voice, leering at her.

"Check us out!" said Kristen as a picture of just the women came up, all modeling the same Charlie's Angels pose in our bikinis. "We are *svelte*!"

The next image added the boys to the picture, all mimicking our look and holding halves of oranges and melons up for breasts. Gretchen about wet herself at that one. Then we were splashing each other in the sea, unwrapping grape leaves at our favorite taverna, and posing with the staff.

"Waiter boy!" Kristen exclaimed. "I'd forgotten him. He *loved* you," she said to Melissa, teasing.

Melissa always seemed to be the center, the focus of attention, but she wore it so well that no one minded. There was one where you could see Brad looking at her with a kind of mute adoration that was both touching and hilarious.

"Hey, mister!" said Kristen, reaching over and slapping him lightly on the back of the head. "Save those looks for me."

Brad winced.

"Honest to God, Officer," he said to Simon in a bizarre hick voice, "she beats me something rotten, so she does! Domesticated abusing, it be!"

"Not to worry, my lad," said Simon seriously. "We'll put the mad witch behind bars; just you see if we don't!"

"You've got your own little show going here, huh?" said Kristen, grinning.

"You just don't recognize good art if there are no aliens in it," said Brad, earning another slap upside the head.

Next up in the slide show was a gallery of each couple gazing lovingly at each other. I blushed when the one of Marcus and me came up, surprised that he had included it, but could not look at him, even as Kristen made *awww* noises beside me. Then there was more dancing and toasting, Melissa looking sour on a donkey, some gloomy cave formations, another meal, another round of drinks, and our notably tanned faces gazing back at the camera, smiling still, if a little weary.

"Boy, we look exhausted," said Simon.

"Partied pretty hard," said Melissa.

"Still going strong!" said Gretchen, as if she had been part of it all. I wanted to feel sorry for her at the way she was being excluded, but she either didn't notice or didn't seem to care.

The final slide was a view of the coastline from above, onto which had been Photoshopped the words: *Here's to the next 1999 days!*

Marcus received his applause with a modest bow, and I found myself gazing at the blank screen in the hope of seeing more, of falling back into those pictures, that time. I don't think I was the only one. After a moment I refilled my drink and caught Marcus's eyes on me.

※

It rained that night. I didn't notice at first because it was so dark outside and I was so tired, but then I noticed the streaking down the great windows and saw, when I shaded my eyes and pressed my face to the glass, the way the cedars on the cliffside were bending in the wind.

The lights flickered, and Kristen gasped an uneasy "Uh-oh."

"No worries," said Simon. "The landlord said they lose power here all the time. AC burnout in the summer, snow on power lines in the winter, storms in the fall. Flooding, downed trees. You know the drill."

"Maybe we should have come in the spring," said Kristen, who sounded spooked.

"It's fine," said Simon. "There's a generator and lots of gas. Eight hours of power in one tank, if we need it. Sound good?"

Kristen leaned into him and smiled vaguely. She looked unsteady, and I wondered how much she had drunk. The look she gave him was more than flirty. It was secretive.

"Sounds good," she said and drifted away, her private smile still in place.

Simon watched her, his eyes dropping unconsciously to her ass as she walked away, then turned back to the window and stared fixedly into the rain-swept night.

"Did someone go out?" he asked, still looking out the window.

"Huh?" said Melissa, who had been drowsing absently on the couch, her long legs stretched out in front of her.

"The gate's open," said Simon. "I closed it when we came in. Has someone been out? Come on, people, let's try to be a little careful."

"You're afraid we'll fall prey to Zorba the Ripper?" asked Melissa.

Gretchen laughed, a high, unsteady laugh, too loud and long, until Melissa gave her an arch look and said, "No more voddy for you, little Gretchen."

"I'm fine!" she sang back. "Totally down, right Marcus?"

"I'm sorry?" said Marcus.

"I'm down. You know. *Down.*"

"I don't know what you . . ."

"You know," she said, her eyes unfocused. "It's a street thing, dog. *I'm down with OPP, yeah, you know me . . . ,*" she sang, flashing ludicrous gang signs.

"Oh boy," said Marcus. "You need to go to bed."

"Just tryin' to keep it real, homes."

"OK," said Marcus.

I moved quickly, getting up and sliding in between them and taking hold of her hands. I couldn't see Marcus's face, but I didn't need to. I could hear the tightening in his voice.

"Come on, Gretchen," I said. "Bedtime."

"Okeydoke," she said, beaming sweetly, her eyes vague, head lolling. I hauled her to her feet, but she shook me off and made a show of taking a few steps unassisted. I threw Marcus a glance. He was watching Gretchen leave, scowling. When he caught me looking, he rolled his eyes.

"That's my girl," said Melissa absently, though I wasn't sure which of us she was commending. Her attention was on Simon, who was still scowling into the darkness outside.

"I'm sure it's fine," she said.

"Not worried about us," said Simon, terse and frowning, oblivious to the almost-drama with Gretchen. "Worried about the house. We paid a significant deposit to cover any damages. I'd rather not lose it because we invited the local hooligans onto the property."

"I don't think there are any hooligans round here," said Melissa. "Goats, maybe."

Again, Gretchen's manic laugh.

"Jeez," said Melissa to her, "Marcus is right. You need to go to bed."

"Not a bad idea," said Marcus. "I'm beat."

"Yeah," I said. "Me too."

I couldn't see Marcus's face properly, but I thought he flinched or blinked or . . . something.

God, I thought. *What if he thinks I'm fishing for an invitation, a drunken quickie for old times' sake?*

I nearly made a show of changing my mind and pouring myself one last drink, but I already felt wobbly and a little nauseous and wanted nothing more than to get into bed. It was only midnight, but I had been traveling all day and suddenly realized that the time difference made it seven in the morning. No wonder I felt like an extra on *The Walking Dead*. I turned to say my good nights, but Brad and Kristen were already asleep—or pretending to be—on the loveseat, and Simon was still staring out the window down to where the open gate was swaying back and forth in the wind. When I looked back to where Marcus had been, he was gone. I took my time, washing my glass out and wiping the sticky counter down so that I wouldn't bump into him on the landing.

Unless he wanted me to and was deliberately hovering outside the bathroom . . .

I pushed the thought away decisively.

I was right to. I saw no sign of him upstairs and moved quietly to my room, unlocking the door and closing it behind me with something like relief. I couldn't afford to confuse my life further by getting entangled with Marcus again, even if he wanted to, which seemed unlikely. And besides, I was here all week. Plenty of time for that kind of bad decision.

I stepped out of my clothes and left them where they fell, suddenly so tired I couldn't think. The bed was soft, softer than I generally preferred, but tonight that didn't matter. I was, for the first time in years, asleep in under a minute.

⌐

I woke with a start. It was still dark, and I had no idea what time it was or, for a moment, where I was. It took me a second to orient myself: the bed, the window, the door.

The door.

My blurry eyes latched onto it as my brain connected the dots, trying to recall what had woken me. A knock? Footsteps in the hallway as someone blundered to the bathroom? Or the door handle?

I had locked it when I came in. I was almost sure.

I lay where I was, huddled in the duvet like a child hiding, and then I got up, flinging the covers aside and stalking across the room with a muttered curse of decision. I tried the handle.

Locked.

I went back to bed and lay very still for a long time.

Eventually I fell asleep again and heard nothing more till I woke and found the room full of soft light. It was muted by the drapes, but it was clearly morning. Or afternoon. I had no idea. The room felt muggy, the air stale. I peered through the drapes, squinting at the brightness of the sun outside, to see if there was a window I could open. They all had little locks, the kind that required a screwdriver-like tool to unfasten before you could unlatch them. There was no sign of it.

I flung myself back into bed and fished blindly for my watch on the nightstand. I had to hold it right up to my face, and I sighed, recalling the whole swimming-with-glasses fiasco.

Idiot.

I had reset my watch on the plane as soon as we touched down. Now I stared at it, trying to make sense of how long I had been asleep.

Jesus.

Almost eleven hours! I stared at the ceiling and gauged how tired I was, how hungover, and found that however long I had slept, I still felt woolly headed and exhausted. I listened to the house, trying to detect the sound of movement, water running through pipes, distant laughter.

They might have all gone to the beach or into the town.

I felt a pang of disappointment. However intimidating I sometimes found them—well, most of them—I didn't want to be left out. Perhaps if I went down now, without showering, I could catch them.

And meet Melissa the Radiant with her British TV star sidekick, oozing perfection over spinach and egg white omelets? I don't think so.

The bath was wet, and there were half-empty mini bottles of shampoo and body wash, one of which had its prime ingredients—ginseng and extract of pomegranate—laid out in faux French. Well, maybe it was actual French, but you know what I mean: the kind of French chosen to feel chic (!) without actually being a barrier to anyone who didn't speak French. Basically, just English words with a few accents and a couple of letters rearranged, like in some restaurants that offer salads with "bleu" cheese dressing, which they then pronounce *blue*. Anyway, I took some, and my irritation at the Frenchified marketing made me feel less bad about using it without asking. It smelled nice—not synthetic, like you might expect—and I gave it a closer look, upending the bottle to read the embossed stamp in the base: FABRIQUÉ À PARIS.

So . . . not your Great Deal knockoff after all. Awesome.

I dried myself off, donned a towel, and made the sprint back to my room, whose stale air was even more obvious now that I had been out of it. I needed to find one of those window keys. As I had crossed the landing, I'd heard desultory conversation from below. *Brad,* I thought. So at least some of them were still there.

I put on another sundress and tried to recall if anyone had floated a plan for the day. I couldn't remember. The whole evening was foggy and vague. Either I had been *really* tired, or I'd drunk more than I thought. Probably both.

I drifted down slowly, cautiously, keen to see who was there before they noticed me, though I wasn't sure why. Brad and Kristen were sitting at the kitchen table, and Melissa was going through a cupboard on the far side by the stove.

"Morning," I said.

Brad and Kristen looked up and smiled.

"Hey," said Melissa. Except that it wasn't Melissa. It was Gretchen.

Damn my worthless, shortsighted eyes and damn my moronic impulse to wear my glasses in the sea straight to hell.

"Was it you creeping around upstairs last night?" she asked. "About gave me a heart attack."

"No," I said. Gretchen's room, like Brad and Kristen's, was on the floor below mine. "I thought I heard something but figured it was just my imagination. You know, unfamiliar place . . ."

"No," said Gretchen, very sure of herself. "I heard someone. It wasn't Brad or Kristen."

"Maybe it was Marcus," I said.

"I don't think so," said Gretchen.

What the hell did that mean? Like she'd know where he'd spent every second of the night? I didn't believe it.

"And the master bedroom is on the other side of the house," said Gretchen, conspiratorially. "With its own bathroom."

"So you think what?" I pushed. She was annoying me.

"Someone is obviously telling porkies," said Gretchen.

"Porkies?" said Kristen.

"Pork pies," said Gretchen. "Lies. You know. Rhyming slang."

"Oh," said Kristen vaguely. "Right."

"Are you saying I'm lying about not sneaking around the house last night?" I demanded, my spine stiffening.

Gretchen turned to me. Her face was both baffled and shocked.

"Of course not," she said. "I was kidding."

I stared at her, feeling the color rise in my face.

"Oh," I said. "I'm sorry. I . . . God, I'm still really tired. I don't know what I . . . sorry."

Her uncomplicated smile flicked on and the confusion was gone.

"Know the feeling," she said. "Coffee?"

"Oh God, yes."

"Just a heads up," said Brad. "Greek coffee is terrible. It's either instant Nescafé, which tastes like gray Kool-Aid, or it's the Turkish stuff that should be spread on roads."

"She has been here before, dear," said Kristen, not looking up.

"Just pour me a cup," I said.

He grinned and shrugged.

85

"Your funeral," he said.

"Morning darlings!" called Melissa from the foyer. She was leading Simon in by the hand. They both looked slightly tousled but wide awake and brimming with health. "Lots of fun things packed in for today!"

"Good God," I said, "can't you be like regular people for once?"

"It's a glorious day," said Simon, grinning from ear to ear.

"And we've been up hours," Melissa stage whispered. "You should see him when he wakes up. Like a bear in January."

"Is Marcus not up?" I asked.

"Went for a walk," said Brad. "Wanted to see the sights. Trees, presumably. And stones. There are lots of stones. It's awesome."

"OK, Mr. Grumpy," said Kristen. "Time to shake it off."

"Well, I hope you can get a taste for stones," cooed Melissa, "because we're gonna see lots of them today."

"Uh-oh," said Brad. "I don't like the sound of this."

"It's gonna be great," said Melissa.

"What is it?" asked Brad, still dour.

"Finish up your breakfast and we'll head out," said Melissa. "Bring your bathing suits."

"Seriously, Mel," said Brad. "What is it?"

"Just get your things together—" Melissa began.

"What if we don't want to go?" said Brad, an edge to his smile. "I mean, we were flying for about a week yesterday. I thought we'd have a lazy day."

"We can do that tomorrow," said Melissa. "Last time we were here we barely left the hotel bar. This time . . ."

"Oh God," said Brad. "If I'd wanted a tour I'd have booked one of those geriatric educational cruises."

"Mel's laid on some great stuff," said Simon loyally. "Gonna be fun."

"I'd just like to be able to provide a little input—" said Brad.

"It's a mystery tour!" said Melissa. "Trust me. Gonna be a blast. And there'll be plenty of time for lounging and drinking later."

"Too bad there's no pool," said Brad, gazing out onto the patio. "Bit of a swim, no salt sticking to you for the rest of the day. That would hit the spot."

Melissa turned to Simon, and her face, which had been so full of light, looked fractured, as if she was barely holding in a sob. It was so surprising I didn't know what to say, but Kristen saw it too, and turned abruptly to Brad.

"Let's get ready, Brad," she said. "I think you've had enough coffee."

There was something in her voice that I hadn't heard before. Her soft British vowels and tight consonants were almost gone and she sounded like an American, all the Mary Poppins falling away. It made her sound sharp, forceful. Brad said nothing but got to his feet. I focused on stirring my coffee, as if I had stumbled onto something embarrassing.

"What crawled up his ass?" Simon muttered once they were out of earshot.

"Simon!" Melissa scolded.

"He's being a prick," said Simon. "Was he always a prick? I don't remember."

I wanted to say yes, he always kind of was, but we liked him anyway because he was usually funny with it and was mostly a prick to other people. He was the one with the snide remarks about the fat German on the beach, the one who teased the cab drivers for the age of their cars and mocked the waitresses for their patchy English, using words he knew they wouldn't understand, then translating with even harder words. He did it gently, playfully, always with a smile so no one could take offense, but yes, he'd always been sort of a prick. The only thing that was new was his directing it at us. I wondered why.

"I'm gonna go get ready," said Melissa. "Don't take all day."

"Absolutely, your highness," said Simon. Melissa tapped his cheek lightly as she walked by, and he grinned after her just as her voice came back from the foyer.

"See any birds?" she called as she made for the stairs.

"A few."

It was Marcus's voice. Gretchen winced, suddenly small and chastened, and I turned to see that he had just walked in, looking braced and happy.

"What a day!" he said.

"Good walk?" I asked.

"Yes," he said. "Not much to see in the way of civilization, but yes. Amazing views. There's some sort of old gun casement in the cliffside below the house. World War II, I guess. I looked for a way up but couldn't see one, then walked all the way round the other side. There's a little church or monastery or something with a tower over on the far side of the valley. Beautiful. But nothing in walking distance. No houses. No shops. No gas stations. I hadn't realized just how isolated we were. It's kind of wonderful. I mean, I'm sure you could get to a village if you kept going in the right direction, but, yeah, we're pretty much alone up here."

He said it musingly, smiling at me, and I remembered why I had liked him. Loved him.

"Dude," Simon remarked. "You make it sound so lame. This is just a base. We're gonna do some great shit."

"Morning, Marcus," said Gretchen, putting a show of cheeriness on.

"Morning," he said, smiling after the briefest hesitation, like he'd decided to just ease right past last night's awkwardness.

"Listen," she said, glancing around the room as if deciding whether to ask the rest of us to leave. She clasped and unclasped her hands. "I don't really remember last night, Marcus, but I think I might have said . . ."

"It's fine," said Marcus. "It was nothing."

"It's just that . . . ," she continued, as if he hadn't spoken. "I don't know. I didn't mean anything bad. The opposite really. I just don't generally . . ."

"You don't have any black friends," said Marcus. He was being patient, but there was a stillness about him that said he hadn't made up his mind which way this was going to go. It would probably depend on her. Simon and I watched, tense and not sure how to help. "It's OK. It's pretty common."

"Thanks. I mean, I don't know how . . . I just want to . . . understand. Your people."

"My people?" said Marcus, stiffening again.

"I don't mean . . . oh, I don't know. I don't understand why this is so hard . . ."

"Look, Gretchen," said Marcus. "I know you mean well, but I don't want to play cultural translator for you right now, OK? I'm on vacation. Can I just be a person for a while?"

She gaped a little, then nodded.

"Thanks," said Marcus, his smile warming.

"But you know what I mean, right?" said Gretchen.

"Let's let it go, OK?" said Marcus.

She looked at him, and he held her eyes, still smiling but with a note of caution in his face. She nodded quickly.

"Sure," she said. "Absolutely."

He took a step toward her and put an arm around her shoulder and gave her a little squeeze. Gretchen's face lit up. She didn't understand what had just happened, but she felt forgiven, and that was all that mattered.

"Aaaaanyway," said Simon.

I started laughing and Gretchen joined in, hesitantly at first, sensing she'd done something silly and endearing but not entirely sure what.

"So," said Marcus, turning to the room as a whole. "You were about to tell us all this great shit we were going to do."

"Right," said Simon. "We have the car. Big plans."

"Like what?" asked Marcus.

"Well, don't tell her I gave it away," said Simon, double-checking that Melissa had not returned. "But we've got scuba diving this afternoon, then an hour in Knossos right before it closes."

"The site?" said Marcus, perking up like a dog who has been promised a treat. "I thought no one was interested in that stuff."

"Well, we're not, to be honest," said Simon. "Consider it a gift, professor. But hey, we're in Crete. Gotta do some Minoan shit, right?"

"Right," said Marcus, clearly delighted.

"But first," said Simon, rather more enthused, "scuba! Better check the equipment."

"We don't rent it at the beach?" I asked. I wasn't crazy about the prospect of diving. "Isn't there some kind of mandatory training or something . . ."

"It's fine," said Simon. "I'm a certified instructor, and we hired the gear for the week. I'll talk you through it."

Right, I thought dismally as he headed out, whistling. He was certified. Of course he was.

Marcus caught my look.

"If you're not comfortable doing it . . . ," he began.

"It's fine," I said. Another lie. "Thanks. And then we get to do some Minoan shit."

"For a whole hour," said Marcus with a wan smile. "Yeah."

"Think we'll be able to fill the time?"

"In one of the most important archaeological sites in the world?" said Marcus, deadpan. "I don't know. Maybe we can pick up some sudoku books on the way."

"Maybe there's an extensive gift shop," I said. "Case after case of plaster Minotaurs."

"We can but hope," Marcus agreed, grinning.

"Better get my swimsuit," I said. "See you in a few."

"We're kind of the odd ones out, aren't we?" he said.

The remark stopped me. He was chewing his lower lip and gazing at the empty living room and its sprawling rented opulence. For a second we said nothing, then he made a tight little smile and a decision.

"Swimsuits," he said.

"Yep."

Chapter Thirteen

I have not moved except to take some of the tension out of the chain that binds my arm to the wall.

"I don't understand," I say at last. "Five years ago we were here. Not here in this place," I say, though I'm still not sure where exactly I am, "but Crete. The hotel Minos."

There is another loaded, expectant silence, and then the voice winds out of the dark once more.

"And what happened, Jan? What did you do?"

I am scared and flustered again, not knowing what to say but desperate not to get it wrong.

"I'm sorry," I say. "I don't understand. I didn't do anything. I don't know what you mean."

"I think you do," said the voice, quicker this time, and I felt the irritation. The more I heard it, the more I was sure the voice was being electronically modified, distorted. That was what the green light meant. Some kind of device. Perhaps the idea that the questioner was just a person using some kind of gadget to disguise their voice should have made me feel better, but it didn't.

"I don't," I say. "What do you think I did? Perhaps if you explain . . ."

"What did you do? What did you see?"

"I don't know what you are talking about! How can I answer you if I don't understand what—"

The light goes red and then goes out. I hear movement, and my eyes detect the vaguest shift in the shadows. He's standing now.

"I'm sorry," I gasp. "I'll tell you anything. I just don't know what you mean—"

There's a metallic snap, loud as a gunshot in the dark, then a juddering creak, and I can see a graying of the darkness. He has opened the door.

Oh thank God, I think. He's going to let me go.

I sit very still and then I feel a hand on my bare ankle. I bite down the shriek of horror and surprise, pulling my foot away, but the grip tightens, and then I feel something cold and flat against the flesh of my calf.

Metal. I can't feel the shape of it properly, but I think it is a blade.

Again I try to pull away, kicking with the other leg, but then the knife—if that is what it is—pivots, and I feel not the flat, but the edge, sharp and biting, inching up the back of my leg.

It presses but does not slice, and I take it as a warning rather than the beginning of something more *awful that may or may not follow, so I go still. In the same instant, I get a sense of his*

His?

presence, his body close to mine, and I realize with a start that something is wrong.

The head is too large. I can barely see anything, so it's as much an impression as it is anything certain, but I am suddenly sure of it. The head is too large and the breathing is strange, animal. Drunk with fear, some primitive, reptilian part of my brain says, Minotaur. The body of a man, the head of a great bull . . .

I don't believe it, but I freeze. I want to say that I'm sorry, that I will try to remember whatever he wants to know, but the words won't come. All my senses close in around the few square inches of thigh above the back of my knee, where his knife has come to rest. I think of the muscle and tendon there, the femoral artery. If he cuts that, I bleed to death.

I do not move. I wait, locked in powerless terror.

And then the pressure on my leg is gone. The cold of the blade, the grip around my ankle, the sense of him looming there, deciding what to do, are all gone. Almost immediately the door closes again, thudding shut. I don't hear footsteps, but I am sure he

It

is gone, and I am alone again. I should feel better, but I don't because I know he's coming back. He'll ask again, and again, and then, when I cannot answer, when I can't begin to give him whatever it is he wants, he'll kill me.

I know that as I know the concrete beneath me is hard and cold. It's a certainty. I don't understand why I am here or what he wants, but I understand that, and for the first time I know something else with the same hard surety.

I have to get out. Somehow, before he comes back, and regardless of what labyrinth I am trapped inside, I have to get out.

Chapter Fourteen

I rather liked swimming, even if I wasn't much good at it, but scuba diving was a different thing entirely and it frightened me a little. Once—spring break in Cancun, if you can believe the cliché—I had gone snorkeling with some friends, none of whom I was still in touch with. It had been a disaster. I hated the taste of the mouthpiece, the way I had to bite down on it to keep the water out even as it kept my airway open. It felt weird, and the first time a wave lapped over the top and flooded my throat with salt water, I was done. I faked it, splashing around, even diving beneath the surface holding my breath, and managed to see some fish. That's the one upside of being a habitual, even pathological, liar: you get good at pretending all kinds of things. An old boyfriend once told me I was the most fun in bed he'd ever had because I made him feel good about himself. There is, after all, more than one kind of performance.

But I wasn't going to be able to fake scuba diving. Swimming on the surface and pretending you'd just come up when everyone else surfaced was fine when you were all just floating about with snorkels, but twenty, thirty meters down? Not so much.

"You're gonna love this," said Simon at the quayside as we boarded the boat at the dive center in Agia Pelagia. We had been driving for over two hours, and I had been getting increasingly restless and apprehensive along the way. We could have just donned our stuff and then waddled out from some beach, puttered around for a few minutes in the shallows, and come in, but Simon was in charge, so naturally there was a boat and state-of-the-art equipment, all hired at considerable expense for a serious expedition. "For those of you who are comfortable underwater and are used to the usual half mask and octopus, there's these." He indicated a set of gear, including air tanks, carefully lined up in the well of the boat, a substantial motorized thing maybe twenty feet long, with a little cabin, a wheel, and a burly local captain who kept leaning over the side to spit. "For the others, you get something a bit special."

He held up the other masks proudly. They were larger, designed to come all the way down over the chin, sealing around the neck, and had an airflow unit built into the faceplate. They looked like the kind of apparatus firefighters wear.

"No mouthpieces to bite down on," he said, as if reading my thoughts. "And you can talk. There's a radio link to earpieces we can all wear and to Archimedes here on the boat." The captain gave a mock salute and a little grin. "It's all perfectly safe. The water is not super deep, so you don't need to worry about pressure, and you can toggle between your tank and the ambient air when you surface, so you don't need to take the mask off at all once you have a good seal. We'll all stay together. If anyone feels light-headed or disoriented, or you otherwise think you aren't getting enough air, you tell Archimedes and he'll give you this." He indicated another, smaller tank. "Three liters pure O2. Emergency use only. OK? Let's do this."

The boat's engine rumbled, blew out a puff of brown smoke, and came to life. Archimedes cast off and we began chugging out of the harbor. I caught Marcus watching me and gave him a brave smile over Simon's shoulder as he walked me through my equipment and helped fasten the air tank to my back. It felt clumsy, doubly so with the ridiculous fins on my feet, and I felt both absurd and scared. Melissa and Brad were, predictably, as much in their element as Simon, trading stories of wreck dives and shark sightings in Mexico and Costa Rica. Kristen looked wary but game, and Marcus, apart from his concern for me, seemed happy to at least try. The only person who looked as uncomfortable as I felt was Gretchen, and I found myself warming to her a little.

"You OK?" I asked.

"Not much of a swimmer," she said under her breath, thumbing absently through a homemade picture book of the creatures we might see that Archimedes had given her. "Or sailor," she added.

"Oh," I said, making a sympathetic face. We had barely left the dock, and she already looked a little green and was sitting very still, as if refusing to move at all would compensate for the bouncing of the boat's nose on the water.

"I'll stay close," I said.

She managed a smile.

"Thanks," she said. "Do you do this a lot?"

"First time," I said, resisting the impulse to lie and then, as her smile stalled, wishing I hadn't.

"You think it's safe?" she said. "I'm not sure I should really be trying this in the ocean. Shouldn't we have training first? In a pool?"

"Simon knows what he's doing," I said.

She nodded, watching him, but murmured, half to herself, like it was a mantra, "I'm really not a strong swimmer."

"It's just kicking," I said. "You don't have to work to keep yourself afloat. The gear gives you a kind of neutral buoyancy, so you just pick the direction and go."

"I thought you didn't know anything about this stuff?" she said. Her nervousness gave the remark a sharpness and her eyes were faintly accusatory, as if I had misled her on purpose.

"My sister does it," I said. "Loves it. She's always trying to talk me into joining her."

"Family Thanksgiving under the sea," said Gretchen mirthlessly.

"Oh, I won't be seeing her this year," I said. "She lives in Portland. We don't connect much."

"Had a falling out?" said Gretchen, pleased by the idea of something else to talk about. Or by someone else's unhappiness.

"You could say that."

"Over what?"

I looked away.

"Go on," said Gretchen with a pleading smile. "Take my mind off being about to drown."

I smirked at her, then shrugged.

"Nothing exciting," I said. "What sisters always fight over, I expect. Our parents. Who loves whom most. Who's doing the other person's share of the work, the care, the worry. The usual."

"What line of work is she in?"

"Software development for movies," I said. "CGI and such."

"Ooh, fun," said Gretchen, managing a real smile for the first time since the boat hit open water.

"You'd think," I said. "She spends most of her time talking about how companies are constantly shopping for cheaper labor. The people who actually do the work don't get to stamp the finished product with their name and face like actors do, so it's hard for them to demand what they're worth when less-skilled companies elsewhere are prepared to do the job for less. And then the studios are constantly adding work to the contract— more scenes, more edits—and expect not to have to pay extra. CGI takes time so the work starts early, but then the script changes or the director goes in a different direction, and all the digital work that was already done is useless and has to be scrapped, but the contracts are structured so that the studios don't have to pay for anything but finished product. It's a mess."

"Sounds like you know a lot about it," said Gretchen, impressed.

"About as much as I do about scuba diving," I said. "I can tell you what Gabby—my sister—bitches about, but ask me to add a troll to a battle scene, and I'd be drawing on the film with a Magic Marker. Let's hope my diving is better."

"Stay close to me," said Gretchen. "We'll drown together."

"Terrific."

—

Archimedes doubled as gear tech as well as captain, and we spent twenty minutes or more being poked and scrutinized once the boat came to a halt. He was a big guy, a decade older than the rest of us, broad shouldered, strong, and tanned to the color of tea. His black hair was silvering at the temples and he was developing a gut. He smelled, not unpleasantly, of sea and sweat and oil. As he tightened the straps around my tank, he managed to be careful not to brush against my body while still giving me a mischievous look that reminded me of the awkwardness of being so close to a strange man while wearing very few clothes.

"Now this," he said, giving me the mask Simon had already shown me. He guided it over my face and inspected the seal. "Breathe OK?" he asked.

I tried, feeling hot and claustrophobic, my peripheral vision lost, and nodded.

"Talk," he said, pointing at his mouth. "You can talk."

"Oh," I said. "Yes. I can breathe."

Talking and breathing at the same time was hard, and I had to pause, feeling my heart racing, to steady my nerves. I took longer, slower breaths and felt better. Archimedes took my hand and guided it to the airflow regulator in front of my mouth.

"This air," he said, gesturing vaguely at the sky, then turning the switch. "This tank. OK?"

I nodded.

"Talk," he said.

"OK," I said. "Yes."

I wished I could see. The scuba gear was handicap enough without me being close to blind to begin with.

"If you like this," said Simon, "we could come back. There's a World War II German fighter farther out. A Messerschmitt. That would be pretty cool, right?"

"A 109?" asked Marcus, clearly excited.

"How the hell should I know?" Simon quipped. "What do I look like, a historian?"

"Could be a 110, I guess," Marcus mused. "Or a Focke-Wulf. A 109 would be neat, though."

"Whatever, professor," said Simon. "It's an old plane. Who cares what kind?"

I looked at him through the diving mask, and it was like I wasn't really there or was watching the scene on television, so I could do or say anything I wanted and they wouldn't know. The effect gave me an oddly critical distance. Simon was joking, boisterous and grinning in a matey way, but the remark had that casual unkindness he and Brad so easily slipped into. It wasn't malicious exactly, just dismissive, as if there were a line between what was cool and what was dorky that they instinctively recognized. People like Marcus were always straying over it. For his part, Marcus shrugged the moment off, laughing at himself, and I couldn't tell if he felt stung.

We hadn't actually gone far from the boathouse—a half mile, perhaps, maybe less—and I found myself both relieved and disappointed. Not that I could see the shore, but Gretchen kept checking. Everything was a blurry vagueness to me, and I suddenly wondered if that would also be a safety hazard on top of making the whole expedition a bit pointless. I considered Archimedes, and as soon as he was finished with Melissa—clad today in a vivid yellow bikini worthy of *Sports Illustrated*—I got his attention.

"I'm sorry," I said, still speaking through the mask to his earpiece, "but do you have any lenses? I left my glasses at home and . . ."

"Lenses?" he said, frowning at the word.

"My eyes are . . . not good, and . . ."

"Ah," he said, holding up one hand and beckoning me over to the stern of the boat, where a series of plastic baskets were heaped with snorkels and life jackets. He pushed things around, grunting to himself, and came up with a box of single-piece goggle inserts. He pushed it over to me and pulled my mask back.

"Sorry," I said. "Should have done this before. Sorry."

There were only four options to choose from, and he pressed each in turn into the faceplate of my mask. They were a little fogged and scratched, but one of them improved my vision significantly, and I thanked him, delighted. He grinned back, pleased by the improvement in my mood, then resealed the mask in place.

"I thought you were wearing contacts," said Brad shrewdly.

"Not while I swim," I said. "Too easy to lose them."

Almost as easy as glasses . . .

He nodded and looked away, and I grinned to myself, glad of the way the mask hid my face. I could see. For the first time in twenty-four hours, I could see. I would happily stay here all day, scuba diving or no fucking scuba diving.

Archimedes called the dive spot Daedalus, and he asked if we knew the story of the man who had designed the labyrinth for King Minos and then built wings for himself and his son to escape the island.

"Like bird," he said, flapping vaguely with his arms and smiling.

"Icarus, right?" said Marcus. "His son was Icarus."

"That's right," said Archimedes. "He fell. Drowned."

"Let's hope that's not an omen," said Gretchen, gray-faced, worried eyes fixed on the water, as if something might emerge that would save her from going in. A submarine, maybe. I felt for her, and not just out of pity. The water looked deep, and I was suddenly sure that making a fool of myself was the least of my worries.

"Icarus," sneered Brad, catching Marcus's eye and shaking his head. "Jesus, professor. You teach this stuff?"

"Not my field," he said.

"So why do you know it?"

"Just think it's kind of cool," he said, looking abashed. "Icarus is . . . I don't know: aspiration and daring but also arrogance and hubris. It's a cool story, the boy who flew too close to the sun so that the wax holding the feathers in his wings melted, but it's also a great tragic metaphor for overreach, not knowing your limitations."

Brad just shook his head again and made a face.

"The things you choose to care about," he said. "Yo, Simon! We there yet? Let's get to it!"

Marcus seemed to hesitate, as if waiting for Brad to speak to him again, and then, when he didn't, just turned away. I was going to say something, but I didn't want to draw attention to the moment or let him know I'd seen it, so I studied my gear and went back to wishing it would all soon be over.

But the dive was more than fun. Against all the odds, even Gretchen didn't drown. We braved water that was about twenty-five meters deep, navigating a reef with sizeable rocks that formed a kind of underwater cliff face that was home to all manner of plants, fish, and other creatures. Kristen and Brad saw an octopus, and I saw some kind of pink, squiddy-cuttlefish thing with big baby eyes and little flouncing tentacles jetting over the reef, which was, I had to admit, pretty damn cool. Simon guided us all to a hole from which a speckled bluish moray eel watched us, all beady eyes and nail-like teeth that gave me the willies. We moved around with flashlights, scanning the pocks and hollows in the rock for crabs and little lobsterlike crustaceans and anemones, but I was at least as transfixed by the luminous blue of the water around us, the sensation of looking up through cascading bubbles and schools of flashing silver fish toward the surface. It was electrifying.

And I was graceful. I'm used to feeling bumbling, clumsy, and the gear—especially the flopping fins on my feet—had made me feel worse in the boat, but in the water I became a mermaid, moving effortlessly with little kicks, rolling and turning in a kind of disbelieving rapture. I had been so glad when I found I would be able to talk with my mask on, to stay connected to the others, but once in the water, exploring the darker depths and glimpsing the first gleaming shoals of colorful fish, I didn't want to say anything. I wanted to keep it to myself, the thrill, the surprise, the simple pleasure of it.

And amazingly, everyone felt the same way. Not the quiet secrecy part—the joy. In fact, the less experience we had, the more we reveled in it, so that those of us who had been most apprehensive—me, Gretchen, Kristen, and Marcus—had the best time. Simon and Melissa exulted in our pleasure, vindicated, and only Brad showed any sign of sourness, the dive not "challenging" him as much as he wanted, not showing him marvels greater than he had seen before. Everyone, Kristen included, ignored him, and eventually he came round, joining in the general exuberance even as we bundled into the Mercedes, crooning, à la Dean Martin, "When the bite on your heel's from a massive great eel, that's a moray!" The fact that it was him made it funnier, and the moment became rare and precious because you know in your lying heart that nothing this good can last; you want to preserve it in crystal forever, a few perfect minutes in time that you can hold and step back into whenever you want.

We had an early dinner—*linner*, Simon called it, after *Seinfeld*—at a harborside restaurant in a town whose name I didn't even catch, and it too was perfect, higgledy-piggledy houses, all painted bright, cheerful colors long ago and then left to age in the sun. They might have been there centuries, repurposed from time to time, added to, renovated, but essentially the same. I suspected that some of them, like the villa we were staying in, had Venetian or Ottoman roots, and I found myself thinking amazedly of how houses got knocked down at home, scooped off the landscape to make way for something bigger and shinier in ways that left not so much as a scrap for the archaeologists of the future to see what might once have sprouted from the Carolina clay. I thought of Mrs. Robson—Flo—who had moved into assisted living at the age of eighty-five, leaving the house she and her husband had built half a century ago across the street from my Plaza Midwood apartment. The house was demolished two months later, a pair of tracked diggers breaking it down to the foundation and a bulldozer scraping the remains away while Flo stood by, watching for as long as she could stand it. The shiny new condo that had taken its place was half-finished now. I doubted I'd ever see Flo again, and the only trace of her presence would be in aging town records.

Here there was continuity, the past reaching back centuries, always lived in, always handed on to the next generation. No doubt I was romanticizing something fundamentally un-American, something that would lose its appeal if I had to actually live in it for any length of time, moldering and small as it was, no doubt I would soon be crying out for the neat, pristine newness and flexibility of life in the United States, but right now, through my out-of-focus tourist eyes, it looked pretty great.

Even the food was unreasonably good. Though we had chosen the place at random, we couldn't have hoped for better: mussels cooked in white wine and crispy fried sardines with olive tapenade and crusty bread brought to the table beside the marina by the elderly lady who ran the place and her bashful daughter. Simple food, made from fresh local, staple ingredients according to family recipes and prepared exquisitely. More tradition and continuity.

"You know what you'd pay for this in New York?" Melissa remarked, pouring more wine.

"Or London?" Simon agreed. "Forget about it."

"Not sure you could even get this in Charlotte," said Marcus.

"Well, no," said Simon with that knowing smirk that pulled the side of his face out of handsomeness, "I wouldn't think so."

"We have some pretty good restaurants in Charlotte now," Marcus said.

"Bojangles?" said Simon.

"I mean real restaurants," Marcus answered. "High end."

"And don't be knocking Bojangles," I added.

Marcus grinned at me.

"My shoulders ache," said Kristen, stretching. "I suppose diving is more of a workout than I thought."

"You're using different muscles," said Brad.

"It's more about using the muscles you always use differently," said Simon.

"I'd kill for a massage," said Kristen. "When I'm on set, the studio has a masseuse on call to keep everyone relaxed. Raul," she added with a mischievous grin, "plays my spine like a grand piano."

"Does he indeed?" said Melissa.

"You wouldn't believe it," said Kristen. "Shooting is so stressful. Everyone running around, new pages to learn, the director racing the light . . . so stressful. Not sure what I'd do without Raul."

"Raul," said Melissa again, tasting the word in her mouth like it was ice cream.

"We have masseuses in the office," said Simon. "Neck and shoulder only. Very professional."

"There's a spa we use in Buckhead, isn't there, honey?" said Brad. "When you don't have Raul, of course."

Kristen smiled and looked down. Maybe I was imagining it, but I thought she was on her guard. There was something about the way Brad fixed her with his gaze that seemed . . . not predatory exactly, but proprietary. Like he'd just had his car detailed and was checking it over to make sure he'd gotten what he paid for.

"What about you, Jan?" asked Marcus abruptly.

I gave him a disbelieving stare. He knew as well as I did that neither of us could afford regular massages.

"You still go to Charlene every Wednesday?" he said.

To my amazement, he smiled fractionally and, sure that no one else was watching too closely, winked. Needless to say, I knew no one called Charlene.

"Regular as clockwork," I said. "Couldn't get through the week without her. And you?" I said, turnabout being fair play. "You still going to Oriental Elegance?"

He almost laughed but managed to nod seriously.

"It's handy," he said, "being right over by Thai Palace. I can get a massage and then go downstairs for some Prik King."

My turn to look down, hiding my grin.

"Oriental Elegance?" said Simon. "Full service, huh? Sounds like you're the *Prick King*!"

Brad laughed loudly, but Melissa rolled her eyes.

"So juvenile," she said, smiling. "What are you, thirteen?"

"I thought you loved my boyish charm?" he said.

"Oh, I do," said Melissa, grinning at him. I caught Marcus's eye, and we exchanged a private smile. I'd only had one glass of wine, but I felt myself flushing happily. I looked away bashfully.

"I can't believe I'm saying this," Gretchen remarked, "but I'd go diving again tomorrow if I had the chance."

"We have the gear all week," said Simon, tearing his gaze from Melissa and Brad. "Totally could. At the other end of the island, there's a submerged city. Ruins of temples and stuff. Roman or whatever. Greek, I guess. We'd need to get started pretty early but . . ."

"Let's play it by ear," said Melissa. "Gotta get some shopping in, right, ladies?"

Kristen said, "Oh, I think so," and reached over the table for a high five. Gretchen hastily added an "Absolutely!" and half reached for the high five, but slid her hand under the table when she realized she had been a moment too late. Again I looked quickly away.

"Maybe another day," said Marcus, whose curiosity was obviously piqued.

"Yeah," said Simon. "I thought you'd like that, professor."

"Not a professor," said Marcus, smiling, humble. "Just a lowly high school history teacher."

"Public school too," said Brad. "How's that for dedication?"

I saw Marcus's eyes harden a little, but he made the best of it.

"Lots of great kids," he said. "Smart. Capable. Just because they can't afford—"

"You have, like, metal detectors and stuff?" said Brad. "Keep the gangs under control."

"No," said Marcus.

"Maybe they build them in shop class," said Simon, grinning. "They still have shop? Woodworking? Car mechanics? Cooking classes?"

"Bojangles has to get its staff somewhere, right?" said Brad.

"I teach history," said Marcus, his jaw tight. "AP and IB courses. We get some of the best college placement in the state . . ."

"Oh, no doubt," said Melissa. "They didn't mean anything by it, did you Simon? Brad?"

"Just kidding around, man," said Simon.

"Yeah," said Brad. "Don't tell me you grew out of your sense of humor, professor."

"My sense of humor is well intact," said Marcus, putting his knife and fork down and meeting Brad's skeletal grin with something like defiance.

"That's so cool," said Gretchen, apparently missing the shift in the tone of the conversation. "You guys have such cool jobs."

I tore my eyes from Marcus, who was still staring Brad down, and tried to use what she had said to redirect the group, but it wasn't easy. My job was far from cool.

"Not really," I said. "I mean, they have cool jobs," I added, nodding expansively to the others, including Marcus. "I'm one notch up from your basic salesclerk."

"That's not true," said Marcus loyally. "You're a team manager for a major retail chain."

Just not an executive team leader . . .

"See?" said Gretchen guilelessly. "That is cool. Might not be doing CGI trolls or dinosaurs or whatever, but it's still better than answering phones for lawyers."

I felt my heart leap into my throat and forced myself to look at my plate, where the remains of fish skin and bones were congealing in a little stream of olive oil.

"I'm sure there's more to being a legal secretary than just answering phones," said Marcus, smiling. The kindness of his tone struck me as familiar, and I couldn't help but look up just as Kristen said,

"Who does CGI dinosaurs?"

"Jan's sister," said Gretchen. "Right, Jan?"

Marcus didn't look at me but he went very still, his blank gaze locked onto the table, fork suspended in the air, as if he'd forgotten about it.

"Oh, right," I said quickly. "Yes. So what are you guys hoping to shop for?"

I kept my eyes fixed on Melissa as she started to talk, but I didn't hear a word of it. All I could hear was the blood singing in my ears. All I could feel was the force of Marcus not looking at me.

⌒

We got to Knossos late. The upside of that was we had the place largely to ourselves, the tour buses at the entrance loading up and pulling out as we were buying our entry tickets. The downside, of course, was that we only had forty-five minutes to do the entire site.

"I'm just going to sit here," said Melissa.

"Really?" said Marcus. "It's an amazing site. There's so much to see."

She shrugged and flipped her shades down over her eyes.

"I can see it from here," she said. "I don't need to really look. I'll just . . . absorb it from where I am. If you see anything really cool, take pictures. You guys can tell me about it later."

Marcus gave her a look of true perplexity, then shrugged and smiled. He hadn't spoken to me since our late lunch, and I felt his silence like a cloud. I had gotten into the car, deliberately leaving a seat open for him, but he went to the bathroom as we were leaving the restaurant, so Gretchen got in next to me. I tried to pretend he hadn't done it on purpose, but the way he stared quietly out of his side window, never engaging the rest of the group or turning in my direction, suggested otherwise.

The archaeological site of Knossos was a baffling mixture of fragmented walls and exposed foundations made from pale sand-colored stone on the one hand and, on the other, monumental reconstructions complete with bright-red painted columns. There were information boards displaying two-headed axes and bulls engaged in some kind of sport in which people ran from or vaulted over the massive horned animals—practices supposedly connected to the legend of the Minotaur which had, in myth, roamed the labyrinth below the palace itself on this very spot. This was the monster killed by Theseus, who then found his way out of the labyrinth using the thread given to him by . . . Arachne? No, that's the spider lady who challenged Athena to a weaving contest or something. Ariadne? Maybe. Anyway, Theseus slew the Minotaur, then retraced his steps by following the thread he had spooled out when he first went in. The information boards had precious little to say about the mythology connected to the site, however, as if the place's more fanciful associations were a bit of an embarrassment, despite their domination of the souvenir shops. In other circumstances I would have been disappointed.

But I had other things on my mind.

I kept a watchful eye on Marcus, but he did not look at me, so I drifted around the ruins, not sure what I was looking at, further disappointed when I saw that the spectacular frescoes of dolphins and women with distinctively braided ringlets were all reproductions, the originals having been moved for safety to a museum in Heraklion. The sign said so. I wouldn't have known otherwise, and I found myself resenting the little information I was being given for somehow deflating my sense of the place.

Gretchen, looking prematurely drunk, wandered equally aimlessly, while Brad, Simon, and Kristen stayed together in a group, chatting about work and food and exercise and cars, as they always seemed to. They could have been anywhere. I felt uninformed and ashamed to be so. They didn't seem to feel anything at all, and within minutes I could hear Gretchen complaining that her feet ached and there was nothing to see, as if it was the place's fault that they were bored.

Only Marcus treated the site with the kind of scrutiny it deserved, but he kept his distance from me, and after a while I started wishing I was more like the others for whom the place and its ancient historical significance was, at best, irrelevant to them, their lives, and the things they valued. The idea depressed me and made me seek out Marcus, whether he wanted to talk to me or not.

"Pretty cool, huh?" I said.

He gave me a sidelong glance, then returned to what he was looking at—a stone-flagged chamber labeled as the Throne Room, with red painted walls, stone benches, and an impressive chair facing a pale basin, both carved from single pieces of rock.

"Yeah," he said. "Too bad we've been given, like, ten minutes to go through one of the most important sites in the ancient world."

"It's pretty confusing," I said, trying to give him an opening. Marcus loved to explain things. He was a natural teacher.

"It's a controversial site," he said, not looking at me.

"The reconstruction," I said.

"There's a lot of guesswork," he agreed, nodding. "Evans—the excavator—gets a lot of flak for it, but the guy basically found the oldest city in Europe, the center of an entire culture quite different from Mycenaean Greece, and with its own distinct writing systems. I say we cut him some slack."

"The reconstructed bits are pretty impressive," I said, urging him on. "I mean, to people like me who don't know anything."

"You know some," he said. "And you care about it."

Unlike others, he didn't actually say, though his eyes flashed to where Gretchen and the guys were laughing loudly.

"What are those animals?" I said, nodding at the wall paintings, creatures that were half bird, half lion.

"Griffins," he said. "It's not clear if the room was actually a throne room for the king or queen or if it was a religious space, though the bathing bowl suggests some kind of ceremonial or ritual function. What did you tell Gretchen about your sister?"

He said it just like that, with no segue, no pause, just moving from the tour-guide stuff to the question that had been on his mind for at least two hours.

"She was anxious about the dive," I said, my voice unsteady, the explanation stupid and implausible even in my own ears. "I was just trying to make her feel better. She latched onto something I said and it just happened."

He gave me a level look, unmoved.

"It just happened?" he echoed.

"Yes."

"What did you tell her?"

I hesitated, then swallowed.

"I made something up," I said. "Said she lived in Portland and worked in CGI. There was an article about the industry in the in-flight magazine . . ."

"Jesus, Jan," said Marcus.

"I know! I just . . ."

For a long moment, Marcus said nothing and went back to staring fixedly at the high-backed stone throne. At last he shook his head.

"Ever heard of Epimenides?" he said.

"No," I whispered.

"A philosopher, lived right here around 600 BC," said Marcus conversationally, though I suspected this had been circling in his head for a while and the speech was at least partly prepared. "You should know him. He's famous for one thing, the Epimenides paradox. It's very simple. He said, 'All Cretans are liars.'"

I swallowed and looked away.

"Marcus——" I began.

"No, listen," he cut in. "You'll like this. All Cretans are liars, right? But he was a Cretan. So the paradox is that since he was a Cretan, what he says must be a lie, but since he said that all Cretans are liars, it's actually true, a truth that confirms a lie and vice versa. It's like a Möbius strip, you know, turning back on itself: lies, truth, lies, truth, lies——"

"I see."

"Lies, truth. Lies, truth. Like every conversation you ever have, Jan. I'm sorry," he said, taking in my gasp of shock, "but that's right, isn't it? I thought you were over it. I thought you were better. But you're not, and it means I can't trust you. No one can. And what's crazy is that you know I'm right. You know that this is why you are so stuck, personally and professionally, why you can't move forward in any part of your life because people don't trust you."

"That's a bit unfair . . ."

"Is it? When we were coming back on the boat from the dive, and everyone was talking about the fish they'd seen and you said you'd seen a squid or a cuttlefish or some damn thing, and I thought, yeah, but did you really?"

"I did!" I said. "I mean, it was at a distance and it might not have been, and I was thinking about one of the pictures Archimedes had in that book of things we might see . . ."

"So you made the leap. You decided it was possible and it would be cool to see it, so you said you had. You see, Jan? People learn the hard way that you're not reliable, that everything you say is . . . *unstable*. It might be true, and it might not. People can't live like that! You can't be around someone who you never know for sure is telling the truth. I can't, anyway."

"I know," I said, a pleading note creeping into my voice, as I reached for his hand. "Marcus—"

"Don't," he said, snatching his hand away. "Just . . . don't."

"I'm sorry. I didn't mean—"

"No. You never do," he said, and if there had been frustration and hurt and anger in his voice only a moment before, it was all gone now. Now he was hard, implacable as the stones all around us. "It's like the Wilmington thing all over again."

"Marcus, I said sorry for that so many times—"

"I know. And I'm not looking for another. I'm just saying . . ."

"That you don't trust me. Yeah, I heard."

"Don't do that," he said. "The woe-is-me face, like you're the victim. Like I'm being unreasonable."

"I didn't say you were."

He looked away again and took a deep breath, as if he were about to dive into a pool and swim the entire length underwater, then he turned back to me.

"The thing about Epimenides, Jan—your great Cretan ancestor—is that the only thing we can deduce with any certainty from his statement is that he's a liar. Right? Because either not all Cretans are liars, in which case, what he's saying isn't true, or they are, therefore so is he."

"OK," I said. "I get it."

"Do you?" he said, giving me a quick, hard look. "I mean you say that, but how would I know?" He hesitated, then took an abrupt step away. "I'm going to go get back in the car."

I turned to go after him, but he stopped me with a gesture.

"Just . . . ," he said. "Give me a little while, OK?"

And he walked away.

PART 2

THE CAVE

Furious, Rhea resolved to save her newborn son, Zeus, by replacing the infant with a large stone which Cronus swallowed whole. She then took the baby, bathed him in the river Neda, and took him to a certain cave on Mount Ida in Crete. She then had her other children sing and clash their spears against their shields at the cave mouth so that Cronus would not hear the crying of the newborn within.

—*Preston Oldcorn*

Chapter Fifteen

"What was the first lie you ever remember telling?" asked Chad.

Sorry. Mr. Hoskins. *My occasional therapist.*

"I was eleven," I said. "I told the girls at school that my baby sister was training to be an Olympic gymnast."

"Which she wasn't."

"I didn't have a sister," I said.

Chad smiled in spite of himself.

I don't know what makes me think of that now as I work my wrist around in the manacle, trying to feel if any part of the iron feels weak or thinned by rust. I hold it carefully with my free hand, turning my left slowly inside the cuff, concentrating like some TV safecracker.

You told Gretchen you had a sister who worked in film effects, said *a voice in my head.* CGI or something. Marcus heard . . .

And wouldn't speak to me.

I stop what I'd been doing with the manacle, momentarily elated by the memory coming back to me, as if I have found a button and the chain has snapped away. The relief lasts less than a second before the implication of Marcus's angry disappointment settles on me, and I remember that I am chained in the dark, at the mercy of some nameless, bull-headed monster . . .

No. That's absurd. He's a man. Possibly, I suppose, a woman, and my strange sense that his head was too large was just my terrified imagination. He's a man, just a man.

And he will come back. He will ask the questions I can't answer, and then . . . I don't know, but it won't be good. Anxiety and dread build in my chest. I have to do something. If I sit here in the dark waiting for him to come back, I'll go insane.

I turn the manacle to the left and then—when my arm won't go any farther—to the right. It feels solid, uneven and certainly chewed by rust, but not so that it feels likely to crumble. Despair is stealing in on me and I have to push past it. I think of Marcus and try to recall his anger at the lie I told, and I find myself thinking back to when we were here before and the tense return to our shared apartment in Charlotte five years ago. We were tired and stressed with travel and each other, and Marcus went straight to bed before I noticed the light blinking on the answering machine. I remember playing the message and then sitting there, staring at nothing.

Marcus had applied for a place on an intensive teacher-training course in Wilmington: the last month of the summer before classes restarted. It was a government-sponsored program working through the UNC system, and if he committed to doing three of them, along with supplemental online assignments and the construction of a writing portfolio, it would earn him a master's degree. This was in the days when that meant an automatic pay raise in the Charlotte-Mecklenburg school district.

But it meant a month away, followed by him tethered to the computer in what little free time he had. Wilmington was a three-and-a-half-hour drive, and with my work schedule . . . we wouldn't survive that. Not then. I knew it with the kind of certainty of things beyond thought: that water is wet, that fire is hot. It was a given.

I knew it as clearly as I knew that it was wrong to delete the message, though that was what I did, as wrong as lying about it when he got more and more restless about not hearing from them. And he knew, with exactly the same kind of surety, that I had lied when he finally reached the school—too late to be admitted to the course—and was told that they had indeed called and left a message to get back to them. It could have been a mistake, of course, a wrong number or a faulty answering machine, but he saw through those possibilities right away and called me on it.

Maybe I should have kept on denying it, but I always know when the jig is up, and I had never wanted to lie to him. So I told him the truth, and then I said the worst thing I could have possibly said.

"I did it for us."

And while that was true, in a way, it was what killed us. How's that for irony? Not the Alanis Morissette kind, but the real deal, hard and bitter, like the sword you drew to defend yourself turning into a snake in your hand. I swore I'd never lie to him again, but that didn't matter. It was over. He moved out the following week. My biggest, most reckless, most desperate of lies had backfired, as they nearly always did, and secured the very thing it was trying to prevent. Marcus walked out and never came back.

Not helping, *I tell myself.*

I sit up with my feet on the concrete floor, feeling along the edge of the bed platform under the thin mattress. In parts the cement edge is almost sharp. I pull my left hand down toward it, thinking that if I can strike the manacle hard against the edge, it might break, but the chain isn't long enough. I shuffle down the bed, as close to the ring in the wall as I can get, and try again. I've bought myself two, maybe three extra links of chain.

It's just enough. With care, I can move my left arm in a short arc that will bring the iron cuff down on the edge of the bed platform. I push the thin plasticky mattress aside and, when it snaps back into place, fold it back and sit on it. I practice the movement, raising my left hand to shoulder height, then moving it down till the manacle meets the concrete lip. I do it four, five times at quarter speed, then I brace myself.

The manacle is everything in your life that is broken, *I think.* It's your job and your loneliness and your stupid impulse to lie, to wreck whatever you have that is good . . .

I take a breath, holding my arm out, my teeth gritted, then I slam it down, hard as I can.

The pain screams through my wrist, where it meets the concrete, and I know that I cry out even as I hug it to my chest, cradling it in my right hand. I missed the manacle entirely, and the full force of the blow seems to have caught my radius. I can't tell right away if it's broken, but it feels like it might be.

Stupid.

I hug my wrist against my breasts and rock silently back and forth, trying not to sob, the heavy chain stretched to its limit. After a moment like this, with the initial agony draining away, turning to an insistent ache that spikes with the slightest movement, I start to test the wound with the cautious fingers of my right hand. I feel no bloody slickness, no obvious tearing of the skin and flesh. The pain is all in the bone. I twist my left hand minutely, and for a moment it feels like it might be OK, but then it blazes, and it's like a light comes on in my head, a hard, burning light, impossible to look at.

I go still again, and now I realize that the tears I have been resisting are running down my cheeks. I let them fall, sitting motionless for perhaps as much as five whole minutes, and then I lift my injured arm carefully, feeling the way the tug of the chain makes my wrist groan. Bracing myself with my good hand, I lift my feet up onto the mattress and kneel as close to the wall as I can, facing it. I find the most neutral position I can for my left hand and begin to feel along the chain with my right. If I can't break the manacle, maybe I can find a link that could be twisted apart, or a gap in the ring mount on the wall.

My fingers work slowly, methodically, inspecting every surface, every inch, working my way from the wall up the chain to the manacle.

"What did you do?" my captor had asked.

I keep thinking he, but it could be a woman. The voice was being altered. I am sure of that. But the English sounded good. So not a local Greek. I think back but the memory of the voice in the dark is like the memory of the house, and I can't home in on its specifics. But then a detail comes back to me.

"What did you do?" he had asked. But then, the next time, after I said I didn't know what he was talking about, he had added, "What did you see?"

Strange. I search my memory of our last visit to Crete, but all I can think of is sun and drinks on the beach and laughter and, of course, Marcus, wonderful, diffident, brilliant Marcus, slipping slowly away from me. I had known it by the end of the week, days before the fiasco of the phone message. There was something in his manner, something weary, drained, and sad, like a lost child. I had felt it, even if I denied it to myself, lied about it. It was the best week of my life, but by the end of it, something was wrong, broken.

And now that I think about it, it hadn't just been him and me. We had done everything together, the six of us, for five days, but on the last day, the day after the cave, things had been different.

The cave.

My hands have been working along the links of the chain, probing, checking, but I stop, suddenly chilled. The half memory of the cave sends a ripple of unease through me, though I don't know why. My hands are still as my mind tries to focus.

It had been our one excursion, a tour to a little monastery in the mountains, followed by a visit to the cave where, in mythology, Zeus was born. The ride had taken ages, and we arrived tired and irritable, wishing we had stayed on the beach. The cave itself was at the end of a hike. Melissa had rented a donkey to ride and then complained how much it smelled. It was a deep cave, full of connected caverns, whose stalactites and draperies were lit with specially positioned flood lamps. It had been chilly and atmospheric and . . . what?

Unsettling. Creepy. Something.

We split up. Explored separately, but when we got back on the bus, everything was different. Tense. Quiet. We went back to the beach at the hotel, but it wasn't the same. That afternoon Simon ran his Jet Ski aground on the beach and got into a huge shouting match with the guy in charge of the rentals about where he had been and how fast he had been going, and Melissa went to bed early. The whole week had ended under a cloud that I, obsessed with my souring relationship with Marcus, had managed to forget.

What had happened in the cave, and how can I not remember? All my other vague amnesia is about the last few days. This was years ago. I remember the rest of the trip perfectly. Why not this, and why do I think it is what my captor wants to hear about?

But that makes no sense. Our mood that day had just been about boredom, tiredness, and a little sunstroke that triggered some petty domestic disputes. What could any of that matter to anyone else? It's not related. It can't be. And even if it is, I have nothing to offer my interrogator that might make my situation any better. I remind myself of what I already know.

You have to get out.

I feel cautiously around my wrist. The wound is still not bleeding, but it is beginning to swell, and that will only make the manacle tighter. I finish checking the chain for damage. Nothing. It's all quite solid, and the chain itself doesn't seem to have any of the rust-bitten characteristics of the ring or cuff.

New, then. Set specially.

I don't like that, but I can't think about it, as I can't think about the pain in my wrist. The chain feels strong, solid. The ring is older and more weathered, but it is thick and crude and solidly embedded in the wall. That leaves the manacle on my wrist. The hinge is simple: one half of the cuff fastened through a hole in the other. The workmanship feels rough, almost certainly handmade rather than done by machine, and I wonder just how old the manacle is.

Ottoman. Venetian, I think, remembering the age of the house.

Is that where I am? Some ancient cellar of what was once a fortress? Images come to me: a bedroom window looking out over the cliffs, stone countertops in a long kitchen, a spacious living room, its windows dark and rain streaked . . .

The dark red pool on the floor.

Something lying behind the overturned armchair. Someone. Hair matted with blood, face streaked with black and red, thick and awful and . . .

I stiffen, the horror of the thing stopping my heart. A memory? I can't be sure. Everything is too confused, though the other flashes of the house seem real, other sleeping parts of my body and mind stirring to them in recognition. But the blood? The body? I force myself to look closer at the image, but I feel only dread and a kind of awestruck revulsion.

I do not know who it is.

I have been sitting very still as these things go through my mind, and the pain in my wrist has ebbed out of my consciousness, but after the initial paralysis, the impressions of what I may have seen remind me of how badly I need to get out of here. I push down the throbbing tenderness in my wrist and refocus on the manacle.

The lock is crude, barrel shaped. Perhaps with a pin or something similar, I might be able to trip it.

Better chance of that than of shattering the cuff against the concrete bed, even if you don't break your arm in the process.

I feel around for my solitary sandal and inspect it with my fingers, hoping for the prong of a buckle or something I might use, but it's all soft parts. I feel my bra, but it has no underwiring, and the clasp at the back is tiny and plastic.

No use there.

I scoot carefully to the edge of the bed, doubly cautious now about overtesting the length of the chain, feeling its weight starting to wake the ache in my wrist, and drop my feet to the floor again. I stretch out my left arm to give myself as much range as I can, bite back the mounting pain, and reach down with my right hand.

Maybe there's something—a nail or discarded screw—that I might use . . .

The floor feels swept clean, and I can reach no more than a few square feet before the angle of the metal cuff against my wounded wrist becomes more than I can stand and I have to stop.

I sit up again, nursing my wrist, my breathing rushed and uneven, and I try to decide how much more floor I might be able to cover if I push through the agony a little more.

Not much. The chain is less than a yard long, and my reach is not just about pain. If I ignore the agony and stretch as far as is physically possible, I'll get a few more inches at best. The chance that those inches will contain my lifeline seems slim.

But it's possible, so I have to try. I find myself wishing that I could somehow detect a usable object with some sci-fi device, like the kind they use on Kristen's show, something that would light up and show me exactly how far I have to get to reach it. Going through the pain I am about to inflict on myself without even knowing if there is anything out there to be had is maddening.

But I climb back down onto the floor, this time twisting the chain carefully to make sure it doesn't knot in on itself, and I think I have bought myself an extra couple of inches right there. For a moment I squat where I am, my right hand tracing the places I have already been, lightly, as if smoothing someone's hair, trying not to think about what else might be there in the dark, the bugs and rodent droppings . . .

Rats?

Even there, with all the other horrors crowding in on me, the prospect of rats sends a visceral shiver of revulsion through my body. I hate rats. I saw two back in Charlotte only a few weeks ago in the dumpsters behind the store: long and brown, furtive but unafraid.

I swallow, then put my hand lightly, palm-down, on the ground, fingers splayed, feeling for something, anything, tracing a rough, expanding oval on the floor.

Then farther, the pain mounting.

Farther.

The manacle is lodged against the heel of my hand—bone, muscle, and sinew roaring in protest as I strain against it, right hand sweeping. I pull harder, and my oval expands another half inch. And another. A cry rises in my throat and comes out of my mouth, a long, teeth-set, relentless wail of fury and desperation. It comes out of me as a shout and keeps going as I reach and claw for whatever might . . .

There!

I touch something. Small and hard and long.

A nail?

But the pain is making me move too quickly. I brush it, and I hear it shift, a thin tinkling sound as it rolls out of reach.

Chapter Sixteen

"There was this guy during the war," said Marcus. "A Brit called Jasper Maskelyne. Good name, huh? He was a stage magician in the thirties and forties."

We were sitting on the patio at the back of the villa while Simon and Brad hovered over the burgers, chicken, and bell peppers sizzling on a charcoal grill; and Melissa carried a bottle of chilled white wine, topping off everyone's glass whether they wanted her to or not. It was a beautiful, warm evening, but the clouds were gathering again over the sea, so Brad and Simon, conferring like surgeons planning someone's bypass, had opted to fire up the grill as soon as we got back from Knossos. Their focus seemed to open up a space for Marcus, and he had launched into his story without preamble or explanation.

"Maskelyne figured he could put his knowledge of sleight of hand and illusion to work for the war effort," he said. "So he joined the Royal Engineers. Studied camouflage techniques and added his own stage trickery. He didn't want to just hide stuff from the enemy—he wanted to mislead them, right? They say stage magic is all about misdirection, about drawing attention to one hand while the other one does all the real work."

"So what did he do?" asked Simon, moving to the burgers with a spatula only to get a headshake from Brad.

"I already flipped them," he said.

"The German invasion of Crete was a nightmare for both sides," said Marcus. "Heavy casualties. The Allies were massively undersupplied and only had a few aircraft, while the Germans had to come in by glider and parachute and then consolidate their position. There were brutal attack and counterattack moves for the next two weeks, but the Nazis had massive air superiority in the region, and the Brits, Aussies, Kiwis, local partisans, and other ragtag imported troops didn't really have a chance. There's a monument in Rethymno commemorating them. The fighting was all along this coastline. Awful stuff, and after the Nazis won, they led reprisal raids against the nearby villages, rounding up people, imprisoning them, executing them—"

"Well, this is cheery vacation chat," said Melissa.

"What was left of the Allied force limped off to Alexandria on the Egyptian coast," said Marcus, ignoring her. "Ferried at night by whatever bits of the Royal Navy survived the German air assault."

"What does this have to do with your magician?" asked Brad, nibbling something he had fished off the grill with a long-handled fork.

"He was in Alexandria," said Marcus. "Which was the Allies' only toehold in the region. It was the spot they used to launch their counterattack against Rommel and the Italians in North Africa, then the Allied assault on Sicily and the backdoor into Germany. After the Battle of Britain, take the Russians out of the equation, and holding Alexandria becomes the Allies' most significant achievement in the war. Without it, they lose, plain and simple."

"Is this what you're like in class?" asked Simon. "I feel like I'm in school again. It's freaking me out."

"Shhh," said Kristen. "I want to hear."

Marcus smiled. It probably was, I thought, what he was like in class, and that was why he seemed so at ease, so in control of his story.

I liked watching him, hearing the way he built the narrative, laying it out like one of those Greek myths I had so loved in college. It was sexy.

"So there's Jasper Maskelyne," said Marcus, "and he knows—everyone knew—that if they lose Alexandria, they are toast, so he puts his mind to using all those old sleight of hand tricks he had learned, and he comes up with this amazing idea: make the enemy think that the Allies are stationed somewhere else and, to make sure the city doesn't get flattened anyway, hide it."

"What?" exclaimed Simon skeptically. "How?"

"Well, the first part of the misdirection is to draw the eye to the stuff that doesn't matter, right?" said Marcus. "So he gets the army to lay out big painted sheets that, from the air, look like buildings. They add plywood aircraft models and inflatable tanks, all stuff the Brits would do again in southern England in 1944 before the D-day landings so that the Germans wouldn't know where the attack was going to go. He makes sure Alexandria is in full blackout at night, and then sets up fake lights farther down the coast, including a lighthouse, so that when the Nazi night raids come, they bomb the wrong place. He claims he even used a complex mirror system so that when you looked at the city in daylight, it appeared to be several miles from where it really was."

"Claims?" I said, getting a sinking feeling.

"Yeah," said Brad. "What does that mean?"

"Means it almost certainly wasn't true," said Marcus, smiling. "Maskelyne was a deceiver by trade. A liar. And like a lot of liars, he was ultimately feathering his own nest, building his reputation by claiming responsibility for stuff that was done by other people or that never actually happened at all. He got a lot of press, made some money, but came under more and more critical scrutiny and eventually died a poor and embittered drunk."

There was an odd, baffled silence. I got up.

"Excuse me," I said.

I went back inside at the closest thing to a walk that I could manage but then ran up the stairs, locked myself in the bathroom, and vomited into the toilet.

～

I had retreated to my room and, like the first night I had spent in this place, burrowed under the covers, prepared to sleep out the long evening till breakfast time, but I was still awake when the knock came at the door.

For a moment I lay still, saying nothing, but when it came again, I flung the covers aside and went to it. I was still dressed, but I only opened the door a crack, ready with speeches about how I wasn't hungry and just wanted to rest.

It was Marcus. He looked abashed.

"Hey," he said.

"What is it, Marcus?" I said, not opening the door any wider. "I'm really tired and—"

"I just came to check on you," he said.

I didn't know what to say to that.

"Yes?" I said, defiant.

"Yes," he answered. "Look, I'm sorry about that. It was a shitty thing to do. I was angry and—"

"It *was* a shitty thing to do," I said. "It was a dick move. Totally unworthy of you."

"I know," he said. "I just said that. And . . . can I come in?"

"No," I said.

"Jan . . ."

"You made me look like an idiot," I said. "And it was cruel."

"You didn't look like an idiot. No one knew it was . . . that the story had anything to do with you till you marched out."

"It was still cruel."

"Well, yes," he said. "It was, but as I said, I was angry and—"

"Did you come to apologize or to explain?" I said, laying the question out so he knew that he had to pick one and one only, that the wrong one, or any attempt to pick some kind of middle ground, would result in me closing the door. He seemed to consider this.

"To apologize," he said. "Now can I come in?"

I didn't say anything but walked back inside, leaving the door slightly ajar so he had to push it open to follow me. I sat on the bed. He looked like he was going to begin some long, wheedling apology or—in spite of what he had just said—another classroom explanation, and suddenly I couldn't handle either.

"You think I don't know?" I said.

"What?" he replied, genuinely confused.

"What you think of me?" I said. "That was clear five years ago. Well, four. But maybe you felt it the year before too, and I managed not to see it. Or rather I hid it from myself. I am, as you know, good at that."

"Jan, I didn't mean—"

"You did," I said. "You meant what you said, and I don't blame you. Actually, I've always . . . *respected* you for it," I said, finding the word at the last moment, "for your honesty. Ironic, isn't it? But it's true."

"I know."

He was still standing up, looking lost and sheepish and very, very young.

"Oh, sit down, for God's sake, Marcus," I said, shoving along the bed so he could take a seat beside me.

I looked at the wall, feeling his presence, his eyes on the floor.

"Do they know?" I asked, still not looking at him.

"I told them I was just checking on you," he said. "The food is ready and—"

"I mean, do they know about . . . all of it? Why we broke up? My . . ." I was going to say *fibbing* but couldn't. "Do they know I'm a pathological liar?"

He shifted uneasily at that and shook his head vigorously.

"You're not—" he began.

"Don't," I said. "I don't think this room can hold more than one liar. You're the American here."

"The . . . ?" He looked at me, puzzled. "American?"

"I'm the Cretan," I said.

He flushed.

"Fuck, Jan, I'm sorry," he said, ashamed of himself. "I shouldn't have said that either. I was just taken aback and—"

"You weren't wrong," I said, turning to face him. "And I learned something new. The Epimenides paradox. Never knew that before. So there's that."

He blew out a sigh and squeezed his eyes closed.

"That's me," he said. "Always teaching."

He gave me a sad smile.

"Do they know?" I asked again.

He shook his head, frowning.

"I think from time to time, there have been questions about . . . inconsistencies in things you've said," he answered carefully. "But I've never heard any real suggestions that . . . you know."

"Yes," I said. "I guess that's something. But . . . they've probably figured it out. Hell, I lied to Simon within minutes of seeing him. In the car coming from the airport."

"What did you say?"

He was hearing me out. He didn't really want to know, but he thought I wanted to get it all out into the open, so he was helping, like he was rinsing out a wound.

"I told him I saw the Colosseum," I said. "From the plane."

He gave me that look I'd seen on his face a hundred times: kind but puzzled to the point of incredulity.

"Why?" he asked.

"Well, there's the million-dollar question," I said. "I don't know. Because . . . because, unlike Simon, who probably goes there for lunch,

129

I have never been to Rome. I've never seen the Colosseum, and I really wanted to, and I thought that if I looked really carefully out the window as we came in to land, I'd spot it, and that would be, you know, something. But I looked, and I looked, and I had to lean across this guy who had taken his shoes off and they stank, and he kept looking at me like I was going to steal his wallet if he fell asleep or something, and I couldn't see it. I don't think we came in over the city at all. Or if we did, I was on the wrong side of the plane and . . . anyway. I didn't see it, and I was disappointed, so I started imagining what it would look like from above and—"

"You liked that version better than what had actually happened," he said.

There was a weariness in his voice, but he still sounded compassionate, like he was indulging a child, and when he smiled it was a real smile that made me want to throw my arms around him and hold him forever . . .

"It just slipped out," I said. "I was talking to Simon, and somehow the made-up version of my flight sounded better, more real somehow, though I know that sounds stupid. *Is* stupid. And before I knew it, I'd told him I'd seen the Colosseum from the air. Then I told him I had recently been to Vegas and he asked me about the hotel . . ."

"You've never been to—"

"*I know.* I think he knew I was lying. If I got away with it, it was because he would have asked himself why anyone would lie about anything so ridiculously unnecessary and obviously untrue and, therefore, wouldn't have reached the logical conclusion: because Jan is a pathological liar."

"You're not," Marcus cut in.

"I am, Marcus. You know it more than anyone."

"I shouldn't have said—"

"I'm not looking for an apology," I said. "You were right. Especially about Wilmington. That was unforgiveable."

"Nothing is unforgiveable. I started the course the following summer."

"No thanks to me."

"You were upset."

"That's no excuse for anything and you know it."

"Yeah, but—"

"Marcus, don't let me dodge what I did. I have to face it."

"Four years later?"

"If that's what's needed, yes."

"I could have made the point more constructively," he said. "Less publicly."

I shrugged and breathed out a voiceless laugh.

"Yeah," I said, "but I had it coming."

Neither of us spoke for a moment and then I, gazing around the room and out through the great picture window, said, "Jesus, Marcus. How did we get here?"

He shook his head.

"Damned if I know," he said.

"And you're the professor," I said mockingly.

"Don't you start," he remarked with a wan smile, like we were old allies against the world. "I wish they would . . . I mean, is it intended to make me feel small and irrelevant, to remind me that I'm *just* a teacher, not some big-shot academic and certainly not anything interesting like a fucking hedge fund manager or whatever the hell it is that Simon does? Jesus."

"Maybe it's a kind of jealousy."

Marcus laughed, a short and single bark without a lot of amusement in it.

"Seriously," I said. "They have money, but I don't really know what they do with their time when they aren't working. They don't seem to have interests, hobbies, do they? Work, gym, clubbing, mixing with the fashionable . . ."

"With celebrities . . ."

"Going to parties . . ."

"Buying fancy cars . . ."

"Made of gold . . ."

"With platinum tires."

"What was my point again?" I said.

He laughed again, for real this time.

"You were saying how shit their lives were and why they'd be jealous of a high school history teacher."

"Right," I said. "Got a bit off track."

He put his arm around my shoulders and gave me a little squeeze.

"For real though," he said. "I'm sorry."

"Yeah," I answered. "Me too." I hesitated, then asked the question that had been on my mind since I arrived. "What do you make of Gretchen?"

"Well," he replied, seriously, "she's down with OPP."

"Oh my God, that was excruciating."

"That would be the word."

"She seems quite taken with you," I ventured. "Did you know her before?"

"Met her the day we got here. You know as much about her as I do."

I decided to leave it at that, merely nodding thoughtfully.

"Come on," he said, getting to his feet in a showy way. "Come get something to eat. If Brad is to be believed, they have created the Mona Lisa of burgers."

"I don't know what that means," I said, but I stood up.

"No one does," he said.

"Marcus," I said, taking his hand on impulse.

"What?" he said watchfully, even warily.

"I don't lie to you, you know," I said. "Not anymore. And I won't. Ever."

The wary look deepened, complicated; then he nodded once and smiled.

"Food," he said.

132

So we ate. It was good too, and with Marcus giving me encouraging smiles between bites, I managed to put my little meltdown aside and enjoy the evening for what it was. The burgers were half beef and half lamb, and Simon had mixed garlic and oregano into the meat, serving them with tzatziki sauce on the side, while Melissa had whisked up a Greek salad with fresh local cucumbers, tomatoes, and kalamata olives, topped with the best feta cheese I had ever tasted.

"Gotta say," said Melissa, "Greek cuisine is kind of limited, but what they do, they do well."

"Hey, what's with the *they*?" said Simon. "This was all us."

"OK, we do it well," said Melissa. "I guess we're honorary Greeks."

"Cretans," said Brad.

I shot Marcus a look, but he didn't react, merely laughing as Simon exclaimed in mock outrage.

"Who are you calling a cretin?"

"I never even thought of that!" said Gretchen, delighted. "Is that where the word comes from? Is it, I don't know, *racist*?"

"Cretans aren't a race," said Brad.

"Neither are morons," said Simon.

"I thought it was pronounced *krehtin*," said Marcus.

"Really?" said Kristen, making a face.

"Yes," said Marcus. "You've never heard that?"

Kristen shook her head, and Marcus gave her a puzzled look that lasted a fraction longer than the moment merited.

"Check it out, Brad," said Simon. "We beat the professor on vocabulary!"

"Yes!" said Brad, pumping his fist. "*F* for the teacher! See me after class, young man!"

Marcus acknowledged the joke with a self-deprecating smile, but I noticed the way his gaze slid back to Kristen. It was an odd look, appraising, watchful.

"So tomorrow: shopping?" asked Gretchen.

"Shopping!" Melissa sang out, raising her glass. "There's supposed to be some really cute leather stores in Rethymno."

"Ooh, leather," said Simon. "Looks like my lucky night."

"Shut up," said Melissa.

"It's so great that we're seeing more of the island," said Kristen. "Last time we barely left the hotel, apart from looking for bars and that one trip to the cave thing. What was that place called?"

I happened to be looking at Melissa as she said it, and I saw the change, the way her shoulders clenched and her spine stiffened, the freezing of the smile that had been so genuine only a moment before. And it wasn't just her. There was a momentary stillness, as if the time had stopped and I was in a weird little bubble, as I had been in the scuba gear, a world unto myself. It lasted only a second, the spell broken by Marcus saying, "The Dikteon cave, where Zeus was born and hidden from his father, Cronus."

"That's right," said Kristen, seemingly oblivious to the odd tension in the air, the way Melissa was studying her drink without actually seeing it. "You know I saw an old painting a couple of years later, Cronus eating his children. Awful thing. All dark and bloody, and he has this baby with no head, and he's got these wild, mad eyes. Totally freaked me out."

"Goya," said Marcus. "It's pretty horrible. He actually painted it on the wall of his living room."

"In his house?" said Kristen, aghast.

"It wasn't transferred to canvas till after he died."

I remembered the myth. The Titan Cronus—Saturn—had been warned that one of his sons would take his throne from him and rule over a new order of gods, so he destroyed them all shortly after they were born, eating them. Zeus's mother fed Cronus a stone in place of the child and hid the god in the Dikteon cave till he was old enough to fulfill his destiny, cut his siblings from his father's belly, and imprison him in the underworld dungeon called Tartarus. The memory sent a tremor of discomfort through me, though I wasn't sure why.

"To think we actually went there . . . ," said Kristen with a shudder.

"More burgers?" said Brad, getting up and moving to the grill. It was a kind of joke, I guess, but no one laughed.

"I'll get some more wine," said Melissa, rising and heading to the kitchen.

Kristen looked up like a startled bird, vaguely aware that something had happened, but shrugged it off when Gretchen, who still looked a bit starry-eyed around her, said, "So tell me about filming. Do you get to write your own lines at all, or do you have to stick to the script?"

The atmosphere still felt just a little off, and when I looked around I thought Simon was watching Brad with unusual attentiveness as he moved the meat patties onto the cool part of the grill with a long-handled spatula. He felt my eyes on him and turned, snapping on a smile like a mask.

"More wine, Jan?" Marcus asked.

Before I could respond, Gretchen said, "Did I just feel a raindrop?"

It's funny the way unimportant things can annoy you. It was a perfectly innocuous remark, and it quickly became clear that it really was starting to rain—hard, as it turned out—but it felt like she was pulling the conversation back to her, as if no one had been paying her enough attention, and all this talk of our last visit was getting on her nerves.

"I'll take some of that wine," she said to Simon as she got up. "But I'll take it inside, I think. You coming, Marcus?"

I turned to her sharply, on the brink of saying "he was talking to me," or something equally unwarranted, but managed to keep quiet. And in truth what I really wanted to say was "Why are you here? Who are you?"

Stupid.

I watched the way she trailed her hand as she walked past Marcus, grasping his and pulling him jokily up. He bumbled and went along with it, but I felt the blood rise in my face.

"Come on," said Simon, giving me a look that was as close to compassionate as I have ever seen from him. "Let's get inside before we get soaked."

—

We did get soaked. At first it was just a few fat, oily raindrops, but the heavens opened before we could get all the food inside, and we went from a clear, if overcast, evening to a full-on storm in under three minutes. The rain washed away the lingering strangeness, pulling us together as we laughed at our saturated summer clothes and marveled as lightning flickered through the floor-to-ceiling windows of the living room. Our rediscovered happiness and exhilaration even survived the blackout.

We had been directly under the storm for maybe twenty minutes when the lights went out. The sky was just bright enough to see the way the trees bent in the wind, but the last glow of the sun was fading fast and the storm was, if anything, intensifying, rain lashing the windows so that great sheets of water ran down with each gust. The silence was almost as alarming as the darkness. Melissa had been shuffling through her nineties alt-rock playlist through the speakers wired to the villa's expensive, if old-fashioned, hi-fi, and when the sound (Blink 182's "I Miss You") died abruptly, taking with it the soft drone of appliances that you barely noticed, I actually gasped.

"Damn," said Simon. "Hold on. Let me check the breakers."

The box was in a wall closet at the foot of the stairs to the tower, and he made his way there while the rest of us sat in expectant silence.

"Ooo," said Gretchen. "Spooky."

We heard movement from the kitchen, then the snap of switches.

"Anything?" called Simon.

A chorus of *no*s.

"No worries," Simon proclaimed. "We are prepared for all eventualities. Brad, you wanna help me with the generator? There's a flashlight in the cabinet under the kitchen sink."

"Because of my experience as a professional mechanic, you mean?" said Brad. "What the hell do I know about generators?"

"I'll come," I said.

Even in the gloom and with my dreadful vision, I registered Simon's hesitation.

"I know a bit about generators," I said. "The store carries them."

I was glad it was dark because even though I spoke with a hint of defiance, it felt like a confession. I was reminding everyone that while they worked with their brains, their talents, while they had money and glamour or a sense of purpose, I checked invoices and filled shelves and reported Joey Mansetti to HR for missing his shift, and was in bed by six in the evening.

"OK," said Simon. "Though all I really need is for you to hold the flashlight while I pour the gas."

"I'll stay here and protect the womenfolk," said Brad.

"My hero," said Kristen beside him.

"Be quick, there's a love," said Melissa. "Sitting in the dark is going to get pretty fucking tedious fast."

Simon made a noise that might have been a sigh and might just have been a breath. I felt my way into the kitchen, located the sink, and dropped to the cupboard beneath it. My eyes, already bad, were exponentially worse in the gloom, but my hands found the heavy rubberized barrel of the flashlight. I snapped it on, a good bluish brightness that made the shadows around me leap.

"This way," said Simon, reaching for it.

I gave it to him and followed close as he led me round to the tower steps at the end of the open foyer.

"There's a stairwell down here," said Simon, opening a door I had assumed was a cloakroom or closet on the wall opposite the tapestry hanging. It looked like it should lead to a tasteful little half bath, but inside was only a cramped hallway with a stone floor and a bare light bulb hanging from the ceiling. It was dingy inside, and the corridor was less than ten feet long, ending in a much heavier and unfinished wooden door that gave the impression of having been there a very long time. It was barred with iron, and its joints were reinforced with large square-headed nails, black with age.

Simon gave the flashlight back to me and worked the bolts free while I guided its beam, and then he shouldered the door open. Behind it was a spiral staircase down into darkness, the steps a mixture of old stone and concrete. A heavy rope running through rings set into the walls provided a handrail. The stairwell smelled old and musty. I wouldn't have liked it even in daylight.

"This is the less classy part of the house," said Simon.

"No kidding," I said, trying to mute my unease.

"It's OK," he said. "There's some pretty extensive cellarage for a house this size, but the genny is just round this corner."

He led the way down a dozen steps that turned slowly like a corkscrew into the ground. At the foot of the stairs, before you entered the room proper, was the scuba gear, the air and oxygen tanks carefully stacked, the masks and fins hanging from hooks on the wall.

"Through here," said Simon.

We emerged in a low-ceilinged chamber piled with old crates, gardening implements, and rusty tools. Coiled around a stand of ancient mattocks and shovels was a bright new garden hose, green and glinting like a python. It was the only thing down there that looked less than half a century old. I played the flashlight around the room, which was maybe fifteen feet square, the walls and floor stone and draped with cobweb. At one end were five or six steps down to a metal-framed door made of heavy wire mesh, like a cage.

"What's through there?" I asked.

"Unused storage rooms," said Simon. "Cellars. The place was closer to a castle than a house, once upon a time."

Something about the antique door sent a cold thrill through my back, so I turned my gaze to the opposite corner. The generator—new, cartoon yellow, and shiny, as if just out of the box—looked like an alien device by comparison.

I didn't know the model, but I had seen similar units. It was the size of a couple of stacked suitcases and sat in a purpose-built cage with wheels at one end. There were four gas cans next to it: two plastic and two old metal ones mottled with rust that looked vaguely military. As Simon checked the manual, which he removed from a plastic sheath, and examined the exhaust tube that ran up and through a hole in the external wall, I unscrewed the cap from the generator's gas tank. We filled it, draining two of the four jerry cans, watching the level rise to almost full, then checked the oil.

"The owner said it's only tied to the kitchen and living room circuits," said Simon, checking the connections. "So we'll still have no power upstairs, and I'll shut it off over night to conserve fuel. There's candles and some battery lanterns in the kitchen, though. Look right to you?"

"You have to open up the fuel line first," I said, reaching in. "And disconnect the battery charger. OK. You're good to go."

He flicked the red power switch, then pushed the starter. The generator rumbled to life. It was lawnmower loud in the tight basement, and I didn't hear what Simon said as he plugged in the main cables, but he gave me a thumbs-up and we went back upstairs, closing the doors behind us, and cutting out most of the noise, though you could still sense it buzzing through the stone foundation, part sound, part vibration.

In the little hallway between the cellar and the living quarters, Simon closed the door to the stairs but didn't bolt it, and he turned to me before he got the other door open.

"Thanks," he said. "Knew you'd be able to get the job done."

The remark struck me as odd, and for a second I felt uncomfortable with him so close in the tight, windowless corridor. It felt like the airlock on a submarine. He stood there, as if waiting for something or trying to decide whether to do something or not. I gave a kind of dismissive laugh and reached for the door handle behind him but, for a split second, he didn't move, and the smile on his face, distorted by the inconstant beam of the flashlight, looked . . .

What? Menacing? No.

Just . . . not like him.

He half opened his mouth to say something, thought better of it, and grinned amiably.

"Better join the others and see how we did," he said, as if nothing had happened.

He opened the door and I stepped out quickly, breathing in the air as if we had indeed been trapped in some kind of airlock, leaving him to close the door behind me as I moved swiftly back to the others.

I found the kitchen and living room lit up as if nothing had happened, Melissa bent over the stereo and Gretchen toasting us with her wineglass, looking impressed and happy. The others turned to applaud us, and Simon bowed in the doorway.

"Actually," he said, "Jan did most of the work. I was ready to blow us all up."

"Yay, Jan!" said Kristen. Marcus beamed at me and I smiled back bashfully, like an underappreciated schoolgirl singled out for praise by a teacher. Of the strangeness I had seen in Simon, there was absolutely no trace, so a minute or two later I was sure I had imagined the whole thing.

Chapter Seventeen

I try twice more to reach the nail or whatever it was I had touched before, but I can't find it and the pain in my wrist has become unbearable. I reinspect the sandal and find it as useless as before, the misery of which makes me throw it—stupidly, pointlessly—against the far wall, but the soft flop of its impact on the wall tells me nothing. I try to sit on the ground, but the awkwardness of having to hold up my left arm is too much, so I climb back onto the mattress and sit with my back to the wall and my knees drawn up to my chest, tears running down my face. I am still scared and confused, but now I also feel defeated, and that drains all the energy and will to resist out of me.

As I imagined some sort of sensor pinpointing the nail I couldn't reach earlier, I now imagine a stopwatch ticking down to the moment the door will open and my captor will return, questions and blade at the ready, snorting from huge bullish nostrils, his great horns spread wide as the door . . .

Stop it.

He's a man, not a monster.

The two may not be mutually exclusive, *I think.*

After all, those myths grew out of something ordinary, something human. Maybe the Athenian tribute to the Minoans in Knossos involved some form of gladiatorial combat or bull fighting forced upon slaves or war prisoners. Maybe the root horrors of the labyrinth were military, economic, and political rather than supernatural, but they probably still involved bloodshed and people behaving like beasts, even if they didn't actually look like the bull-headed Minotaur that Theseus slew. We don't need to look to mythological creatures to find terror and brutality. People can do that all by themselves.

Stop it, *I tell myself again and this time, I do. I have other things to think about.*

I can't unlock the manacle, and I don't think I can break the cuff itself. The chain feels strong, and the ring in the wall seems both solid and well anchored. That leaves getting my hand out.

The manacle is old. I'm sure of that. That means the mechanism is simple. There's no adjustable ratchet that clenches the cuff to the wrist so that it fits snugly regardless of who is wearing it. Once, a year or so after Marcus and I had started dating, we were at a party and won a pair of handcuffs as a gag gift. They were real enough and came with a pair of little keys on a ring. One night a week or so later, we decided to take them out for a test run. I can't say either of us really enjoyed the experience. It was thrilling for a while, but Marcus wasn't comfortable as either the captor or the captee—if that's a word—and we both got embarrassed and started giggling.

Anyway. I know how handcuffs work, and the one I am chained to now is nothing as sophisticated as those with which we had played. It is locked in a single position and, I think, designed for wrists slightly thicker than mine. I can work the forefinger of my free hand under the cuff all the way to the second knuckle. The whole thing slides over my wrist as far as the heel of my hand, but when I try to move it all the way off, it lodges hard against the spur of bone at the base of my thumb just below the joint. I pull at it experimentally, and my swollen wrist groans again, as if the pain is something alive that has been sleeping but now wakes and stretches.

I stop, and almost immediately I hear movement beyond the door. Footsteps. Then the door creaks open, and for a second I see a vague gray halo around the silhouette in the doorway. My eyes are too bad to make out details, but there's no doubt that the figure looks strangely misshapen, its head too big for its frame.

I gather my knees up and shrink as far away as the chain will let me, and then the door is closing again and the darkness thickens. For a whole minute or more he does nothing and makes no sound so that I can almost believe he didn't come in, but then I hear his strange, magnified breathing.

He does not speak.

"Listen," I say, "there's been some mistake. I don't know what it is I'm supposed to have done five years ago, but I really can't think of anything. Just tell me what I can do. What you need to let me go . . ."

He sits as before, slumped forward and still, so that almost immediately he could be a trick of the darkness—a piece of furniture, a pile of old clothes. I can hear my heart thudding fast and hard. He makes no sound at all except for the sibilant hiss of his deep, regular breathing, and then the little light comes on again: first red, then green.

"Jan," he says again.

The voice is as before, heavily distorted and slowed down so that the sound seems dragged up from a pit deep below the floor. It's an electronic sound, but it feels liquid and thick as tar.

"Yes," I say. "Who are you? What do you want?"

"Five years ago—" he begins, but I cut him off.

"I told you, I don't know!" I say. "I don't remember. I didn't do anything!"

"Five years ago," he says again, as if I hadn't spoken, "you came here. You saw something. Something you shouldn't have."

The last two words were almost sung, the first high, the second low, like the tail end of a nursery rhyme. My skin tightens and creeps. My eyes widen. My hair stands on end.

He is playing with you.

"I . . ."

My voice is unsteady and the words won't come.

143

"I . . . I didn't . . ."

"Come on, Janice," sings the voice, as before. "You can tell me. You have to. After all, you have been very naughty, and we can't have that, can we?"

Still the lilting clownish tone. It drives the breath from my lungs and threatens to stop my heart. I can't speak or move.

"All kinds of trouble you have caused me," says the voice, unwinding out of the darkness like a snake. "Not acceptable. Not permitted. This is your last chance to say sorry. Tell me everything: what you saw, what you know, and whom you told. That last one is very important. Who did you tell, Jan? Tell me and, if you are a very good little girl, I might still let you walk out of here."

My breathing is back now, but it's rapid and shallow, a thin panting that sends tremors through my whole body.

"I'll tell you everything," I stutter. "But I need to know what it is you think I know. I'm sorry, I really am, but I don't know what you are referring to and . . ."

I sense his sudden movement a fraction of a second before I feel the gloved hand that thrusts me against the wall. My head bangs against the stone, and fireworks go off under my eyelids. I lash out with my free hand and connect with something hard and unyielding where his head should be, but then the blade I felt on my thigh is against my neck and I go very still.

His dragging, hissing breath is all around me, but I smell only oil, gasoline, and something under it that I can't immediately place.

"This," he whispers, "is very disappointing."

And suddenly he has let go, and I'm free and breathing again. When the voice comes next, it's from the door, which is opening.

"Think about it, Jan," he says. "This is your last chance. When I come back, you tell me what I want to know, or—and I promise you this is true—my voice is the last thing you will ever hear."

Chapter Eighteen

Simon was right about the generator. It ran smoothly and quietly, and the lights in the living room didn't so much as flicker as the storm outside gathered and eventually blew itself out. Even so, it was a short evening. Whether it was the lingering effects of jet lag, the swimming and walking around, or the heavy food and constant drink, we all faded fast, particularly after Simon and Melissa decided to call it a night.

"I've got some reports to read," said Simon, following Melissa to the stairs on their side of the house. "I'm beat, but my body's not quite ready to sleep. I'll give it an hour and then come shut the genny down before I crash."

"I can do it," I said. "Save you coming back down."

"Nah," he said. "I promised the owner I'd take care of it. He pretended he was worried we might burn the place down, but I think he's more concerned I'll mess up his shiny new generator. If you're all in bed by the time I come down, I'll see you in the morning."

We said our good nights and then dealt with the sudden realization that the five of us would now have to deal with each other without the couple who was the social glue holding us all together.

"So, Gretchen," said Brad. "Who are you exactly?"

We laughed a little crazily because we had all thought it, but Gretchen just smiled and shrugged in a way I had already started to see as familiar. When she looked abashed, as now, she lost all her superficial resemblance to Melissa, who could show every emotion but embarrassment, and she shed at least seven years, maybe more. She was still pretty, but she looked lost and vulnerable in ways I found disquieting, and I found myself wondering again how someone so conventionally good-looking could, beneath the occasional party-girl persona, seem so insecure.

There's trauma there, I thought. *Somewhere in the past.*

"I told you, silly," she said teasingly, like she was reprimanding a toddler, "I'm a friend of Simon and Mel's."

"Well, yeah," said Brad. "And I'm a Beatles fan, but I've never met Ringo."

"Ringo?" said Gretchen, befuddled. "That's a person?"

"How did you meet Simon and Melissa?" said Kristen before Brad could say anything else.

"I went to high school with Mel," said Gretchen.

"Really?" said Marcus.

Gretchen gave him another look of innocent puzzlement—she had a sack full of them—as the rest of us processed this. For all the physical resemblance, Gretchen and Mel were different in the way that animal species were different: Mel a jaguar, all grace and presence and power. Gretchen was . . . I don't know. A stick insect. A fruit fly. Something from another continent entirely. A different planet.

"She was older than me," said Gretchen. "Two years."

"Still is, I assume," said Brad.

"What?" said Gretchen. "Oh. Right. You're funny. You should be on stage."

"I am," said Brad, reaching for the wine bottle. "And my club has an eight-drink minimum."

"So, high school, huh?" said Kristen.

"We weren't really close," said Gretchen. "Not like now. You know how it is at that age. A couple of years is like . . . a really, really . . . a lot. But we got back in touch after college."

"You're a legal secretary," said Marcus.

"Office administrator," said Gretchen, correcting him with a hint of pride.

"Right," said Marcus.

"And I'm taking night classes for my paralegal certificate," she added with feigned casualness. "So . . . you know."

"What?" I said.

"Sorry?"

"You said, 'You know,'" I said. "We know what?"

Marcus shot me an uncertain look.

"Oh, just a figure of speech," said Gretchen. "Should be a big step up when I get there."

"Next stop, Supreme Court," said Brad.

"Oh, I don't know about that," said Gretchen.

"I think he was kidding," I said. Another look from Marcus, with a touch of warning this time.

He was right, of course, and I colored slightly. Why was I being such a bitch? The girl was not that bright, but she was pretty, pleasant enough, and seemed to be doing OK for herself.

At least as well as you. Maybe better. Perhaps she's handling whatever trauma you're so sure is buried in her past rather more skillfully than you are handling yours . . .

I dug my fingernails into my palms. I remembered Marcus's throwaway crack about me being the goddess of underachievers. I was smarter than Gretchen. I'd put money on that. But I wouldn't have much money to put on it, not much more than she would, anyway, because while Gretchen's aspiration to be a paralegal seemed a pretty decent living that fit her talents, my "career" was hampered by my own self-sabotage. She drifted, smiling through life, did her job, took her classes, took her tests, and moved up in the world. I sat on the sidelines, wallowing in my own fantasies, my own lies, the very things that constantly and irreparably fucked me over time and time again . . .

There's a handy little passive construction, said my inner English minor. *You were fucked over by your lies. Couldn't be helped. Circumstances beyond your control . . .*

OK, I fucked myself over through lies. Happy?

"That's great, Gretchen," I said, shamed into being a person.

"And you reconnected with Mel, how?" said Brad. He was watching her keenly.

"Well, it's a funny story, actually," she said.

"We will brace ourselves for the inevitable hysteria," Brad shot back, still motionless as a lizard. Kristen nudged him into silence.

"I was in a bar with some girlfriends," said Gretchen. "It was close to campus but I hadn't been for years. Not since I graduated. A place called O'Flaherty's. It was an Irish bar."

"Astonishing," said Brad.

"And I turn around, and there's Mel, looking just like she always did! Older, of course. This was only two years ago, after all. But still. Same old Mel. And she was by herself and looking kind of blue, so I went over to say hi. I don't know that she remembered me right away, and she had already had a few little drinkies and wasn't in the best mood, and I was worried about her getting home OK, so I stayed with her and we just talked and talked. And drank. And drank. And after that night, we've been inseparable."

"Well," said Brad in the vague, smiling lull that followed this. "That was gripping. Wouldn't you say, Jan? I was right there with her. I could see the barstool, the sawdust on the floor, the smell of spilled beer, and the burly red-headed barkeep called, I'm almost certain, Pat."

Kristen thumped him hard on the shoulder and said, "Be nice," but Gretchen seemed oblivious.

"Why was Melissa so sad?" I asked, still trying to be the good person, a better person than I really was—which is to say that I was, in my usual way, lying.

"Well," said Gretchen, leaning in conspiratorially, "she'd had a bit of a fight with Si and had come to get away, have a few laughs and a few drinks . . ."

"Go home with a strange man," said Brad.

The look Kristen gave him this time had no humor in it at all, but again Gretchen rode the wave right through.

"Between you and me," she said, "if I hadn't been there . . ."

She made a face to suggest what she wasn't prepared to say, eyebrows raised, eyes almost shut, held tilting to the left.

"Good thing you were, then," said Marcus.

"Must have been quite a fight she'd had with *Si*," said Brad, putting inverted commas around the nickname.

Again, the look from Gretchen, secretive, loving being in the middle and able to perform her closeness to our dazzling hostess, but as she opened her mouth to reply, something flashed through her face. She actually brought one hand up to stop her mouth and she flushed pink, her eyes going round with something like shock, or panic. When she did finally speak, it was in a lower, uncertain tone, and she looked down primly.

"Oh, you know. Just couples stuff. Ordinary. I mean, everyone fights from time to time, right?"

A lie, and a big one. It was written all over her face. She'd blundered into it, like she was reversing a car and slammed into a telephone pole she didn't know was there till the second she hit it. Then she'd hit the accelerator and set the tires spinning, screeching, burning in her haste to get away.

Clumsy.

The look in her eyes was panic and a sudden desperate need to be gone, and I mentally adjusted my metaphor. It wasn't like she'd backed into a telephone pole. It was like she'd run over a body.

"Sure," said Brad. "We all have our little squabbles, don't we, dear?"

"They don't usually lead us to go out looking for a new bloke," said Kristen. "But yeah."

"Well, no," said Gretchen. "Obviously. I didn't mean that . . . and from time to time, everyone . . . I mean, I'll bet you . . ."

"You'll bet I what?" said Brad, no trace of friendliness now.

"Nothing," said Gretchen, who now looked like she wished she had gone to bed. On cue, she checked her watch, her hand visibly shaking. "Is that the time? Boy. I need to hit the hay."

The room was suddenly loaded with a tension so electric, you could almost hear it humming like cables stretched between pylons, like the heaviness of the air before a storm. For my part, it was just awkwardness, embarrassment, and maybe Marcus felt the same way, though it was hard to be sure at this distance. From the others I felt a swelling anger and hostility that I couldn't completely explain. Brad got to his feet, teeth gritted and eying Gretchen as if he were going to start yelling questions or accusations; Kristen got up quickly, taking his hand and gripping it even as he tried to shrug away.

"Us too," she said. "You want to use the bathroom first?"

Gretchen blinked, catching up.

"No," she said. "You guys go ahead. I think I'm just going to crash."

Gretchen fled, and after a deliberately staged bit of business with glass washing and tidying to make sure she was safely out of the way in her room, Brad and Kristen went up after her in steely silence.

"What the fuck was that all about?" said Marcus in a whisper.

We both got the giggles, then sat back with our drinks, shaking out heads.

"There are some weird-ass tensions in this group," I said. "Was it always like this?"

Marcus shook his head.

"Gretchen wasn't here last time, of course," he said. "But no, I don't think so. It's different now."

I was suddenly self-conscious. It was different for us, at least, because *we* were different.

"Just older, I guess," I said. I had wanted to be alone with him like this, and not simply because I had meant to ask him about the cave, but I was suddenly weary beyond words, and I didn't think I was alert enough to get into anything even vaguely difficult with Marcus. Not now. I had caught some of the strange tension off Brad and Gretchen's exchange like it was contagious, and now I just wanted to go to bed and wake up in the light and warmth of the Cretan sun . . .

"What do you suppose Mel told Gretchen?" said Marcus, almost to himself.

"What do you mean?"

"She might be delusional about just how close she and Mel really are," he replied. "But she really knows us, have you noticed? All kinds of little things. Personal history. How I take my coffee! She had it all ready for me this morning, and when I asked how she knew I took it . . ."

"Black with one sugar," I inserted.

"She just gives me this knowing smile and says, 'Oh, I'm an expert on all Mel's little buddies.' It kind of freaked me out."

"That is weird," I said.

"It's like she's been studying us in preparation for coming, while we know nothing about her. We just asked, and we still know nothing about her. She went to school with Mel years ago and they met in a bar after college? It's bizarre. And did you see how she reacted when Brad . . ."

"Also weird."

"Granted, but when he asked what Mel and Simon had been fighting about, she freaked, like she'd given something away. It's fucking strange. She comes to a reunion for people she doesn't know. A *reunion*, for fuck's sake. What's that all about?"

I was starting to giggle again. His hushed earnestness, combined with the fact that he was saying things I had been thinking, seemed incredibly funny.

And you were pleased that he wasn't as charmed by her as you thought.
That too.

"She even looks a bit like Mel," Marcus went on. "Have you noticed? I've mistaken them for each other twice. *Twice!*"

"I don't think she can help that," I said, cutting the girl a little slack. It felt good to be her defender while Marcus took aim. "It's not as if she dresses like her or something."

"Oh my God!" said Marcus, delighted and horrified. "How weird would *that* be?"

We laughed some more and for a warm, bright moment it was like we had gone back more than 1999 days and it was, as it had once been, the two of us against the world, together.

"Come on," I said, getting up and offering my hand. "Bedtime."

I realized my mistake as soon as I saw his face.

"I didn't mean—" I said, but he cut me off, grinning and nodding and not quite looking me in the eye, so I pulled my hand away before he could take it.

"Of course," he said. "I know. Sleep time."

I lay awake much longer than I expected to, so I heard the sound of someone moving in the corridor, a strange, stealthy movement that set old boards creaking, then silencing, then creaking again. I kept still, trying to determine whether the sound was coming from the hallway outside my door or the floor below.

Yours. Pretty sure.

Which meant what? That Marcus—the only other person with a third-floor tower room—had decided to go to the bathroom or gone down to make himself a sandwich, or . . .

That Gretchen had come up to apologize some more? Or he was paying her a visit . . .

No. I didn't believe it. I got up and stood motionless by the door but was suddenly so tired that I felt wobbly and light-headed. After a minute or two, standing there, listening to nothing, I forgot why I was there, and when I remembered again, I decided that I had been asleep after all and had dreamed the creaking of the floorboards. I went to the window and peered out and down, though I didn't know what I was looking for, and my gaze found the gate at the end of the drive. It was open. Not thrown wide and fastened back like it would be to let a car in. Just cracked in the middle, as if someone had slipped through on foot.

The doors and windows were all locked downstairs. There was no alarm system, but the house was secure. It had once been a kind of fortress, after all.

Still . . .

I made a mental note to mention it to Simon. Maybe there was something wrong with the latch. He'd want to look at it.

I shuddered, feeling suddenly and inexplicably unnerved by the depth of the darkness around the house, the lack of street lamps or the familiar ambient glow I was used to in Charlotte, even when the lights were out. I took it for granted. Without it, up here in the mountains where the only light was the moon and stars overhead, the darkness felt strangely ancient, primal, a darkness that led the mind to invent monsters. It filled the great window like a pool.

I didn't like it. It made me feel scared, exposed.

I stumbled quickly back to bed and pulled the covers up around me like a shield, my head thick and throbbing from all the wine, though why it had kicked in so abruptly then, I had no idea.

Chapter Nineteen

He will be back soon. I know it—and I will not be able to tell him what he wants to hear. I try to make a picture of the fragments he has given me. At first I thought he wanted to hear about something I did, but now I think differently. He thinks I saw something and then did something bad in response.

Naughty.

It was a strange word and thinking about it again raises the hairs on my neck as his voice had done, that singsong tone of his . . .

It wasn't me who had done something bad. It was him. But I had found out about it and then—afterward—had been naughty. What had I done or tried to do?

Blackmail.

Yes. That felt right. That would be naughty, wouldn't it? He did something, and I caught him and tried to milk him for it . . .

Except that I didn't. My momentary elation dies like a sputtering candle, and I feel the full dread of what is going to happen next. He thinks I have tried to hurt him, but I don't even know enough to negotiate some kind of deal, some way out . . .

I am going to die for someone else's crime. I am going to be murdered by mistake.

It is almost funny, and if I thought I might be able to convince him of his error, I might still find it in me to laugh. But there is no mercy in that voice, no understanding. He might be giving me one last chance to speak, but he is also toying with me, enjoying my misery, my terror.

He isn't going to let me live, no matter what I say, no matter what I know or don't know.

Manos.

The word floats up like driftwood surfacing from some deep, unseen current. It bobs on the surface of my consciousness, rotating in the flood, but I can make nothing of it. It sounds Greek—and familiar, which doesn't help—and as I try to puzzle it out, a new possibility occurs to me. I have been assuming my captor has the wrong person, that his questions are absurd because he thinks I know something I don't. But what if I do? Or did? What if I really did stumble upon some crucial truth, the core to everything that is going on, but have forgotten it?

Again the idea strikes me as darkly funny. Dying over something I've forgotten is, if anything, worse than dying for something I never knew. Now it's not just an accident—it's another study in my dazzling ability to fuck things up.

Manos.

The word continues to spiral on the currents in my head, but it's already being carried away, and I no longer feel sure that it means anything.

There has to be more I can remember. It is maddening to still have these dark holes in my mind where the last few days have been, though, now that I think of it, the vague amnesia began before I woke up down here, and it affected all of us. We were all tired, listless, forgetful. I hadn't thought anything of it at the time, but now I wonder if it was more than sun and jet lag and overindulgence.

Drugs?

God knows we were drinking constantly, and anyone had the chance to slip something in our glasses. But that would mean it had been someone there. One of the group . . .

That couldn't be. Surely. I have decided that my interrogator was not a local, but I haven't seriously considered the possibility that the person who chained me up here is one of those I was laughing and drinking with only days ago. One of my friends.

Or is that me sidestepping reality again, just another lie?

No, I haven't put a face to my captor, but then I haven't tried to, have—in fact—avoided even thinking about it, because a part of me knows that it is at least possible that the face in the dark is one I know all too well. The thought settles on me like snow, freezing me in place, heaping up around me. It is paralyzing. Unhelpful. Instead of dwelling on who my captor is, I need to focus on escape. If I am going to think about him at all, it is to come up with something I can use against him.

I think over our last encounter again.

A scent blew in with him. It lingers in the darkness still, a sharp, familiar smell—gasoline and motor oil—and it takes me back to the tire and lube place beside the Great Deal employee lot. There are other memories too, some much older and too dark to look at . . .

Night and silence and blood and gasoline all combining to hiss, You have been here before . . .

and one memory that is new and fresh: the generator in the basement of the villa.

That's where I am. I'm sure. When Simon showed me the generator, there had been another door; I saw it quite clearly in my mind, pulled out of forgetfulness by the scent of the oil. A wire-mesh door to storerooms and cellars . . .

Simon?

No. I just can't get my head around the possibility. The fact that I am down here close to where he was working—if that's where I am—doesn't mean it has to be him. Anyone could have gone down into the cellar, track-ing a little oil and gas in as they did so . . .

The oil and gas prove nothing. I try to remember if I had smelled it the first time he came in to question me, but I can't remember it. It strikes me as I compare the two visits that his demeanor felt quite different that first time, more reserved, less coldly playful. I don't know what to do with that and come back to the smell, remembering that I noticed something else under the odor of oiled machinery. I reached for it with my mind and came up with, Rubber.

I frown to myself, pushing at the idea, but it holds up. Yes. Some kind of pliable rubberized plastic. And when I tried to hit him—more a pan-icked reflex than a real strike—I made contact with something hard where his face should be. That had felt familiar too. I put the two together, the plasticky scent and the stiff, resistant something around his head that had made it seem too big for his body: like the bull head of the Minotaur. But suddenly I am sure, though my certainty leaves me almost as bewildered as I had been when I didn't know.

He is wearing the scuba mask.

Chapter Twenty

The power was still out. I wasn't sure why that pissed everyone off so much, but it did.

"We'll have to get more gas while we're out," said Simon. "Maybe pick up some more cans too, in case it doesn't get fixed in the next few days."

"Few days?" said Gretchen, dismayed. "Why does it take so long? It's not even raining now."

"Because it's fucking Greece," said Brad darkly. "The glory days of this island civilization-wise were like five thousand years ago, right, professor?"

Marcus smiled tightly and nodded.

"Well . . . something like that."

"In some forgotten grave," said Brad, "King Minos is probably still waiting to recharge his bronze age iPad and leaving himself voice mails saying, 'As soon as the lights come back on, don't forget to feed the Minotaur.'"

"Funny," said Marcus.

"Just trying to keep things light, professor."

"I really wish you wouldn't call me that."

"And I really wish I could turn the fucking TV on," said Brad. "But as Mick Jagger once said, 'You can't always get what you want.'"

"God, I'm tired," said Kristen.

"Me too," said Marcus, still looking sourly at Brad. "I feel like I didn't sleep at all, but I was totally out the moment I put my head down."

"Me too!" said Kristen. "I don't even remember getting into bed. But now I feel like I was run over by a truck."

"Maybe ease off on the booze today, hon," said Brad, looking out the window.

She shot him a quick, injured look, then gave Marcus and me an embarrassed smile.

"Might not be a bad idea," she said. "One can have too much vacation."

Brad snorted at that, a nasty, knowing laugh, though I wasn't sure what—or whom—it was directed at.

"I had bad dreams," said Gretchen. She looked distant, troubled, and I didn't think it was about the awkwardness of last night's spat with Brad. "People asking me questions in the dark. Monsters. It was weird. I think I was tied up or something . . ."

"Ooh," said Brad. "Kinky."

Gretchen shot him a look so savage and hostile that she looked, for a moment, like someone I'd never seen before.

"It was horrible," she said. "It went on and on, and then . . . I guess I woke up. In my bed."

"Best place to wake up," said Brad, unmoved.

"What were they asking about?" I said.

"What?" she said, turning to me as if just realizing I was there.

"You said the monsters were asking you questions. What about?"

"Oh, I . . ." She hesitated and seemed to fade for a second, her eyes narrowing as she tried to remember, then widening suddenly, as if something unexpected had swum into view. Something unsettling. "I don't remember," she said, her face suddenly closed.

Now, I've told a lot of lies. I'm good at it, and I'm good at spotting when others tell them too. I wasn't sure if it was because she wanted the attention, suddenly becoming the center of our glittering little circle as she had been the night before, but Gretchen was lying. If I had to guess, I'd say that it hadn't begun as a lie but it had become one out of necessity as she blundered about in her own head, finding things and covering them up. I had done the same thing many, many times.

I watched her as she put her coffee cup down, and I thought her hand trembled slightly. I was almost sure it wasn't the tremble of someone caught up in the thrill of misleading other people, the giddy rush of having secret knowledge no one else has. Gretchen was afraid.

Must have been one hell of a nightmare.

I must say, I didn't feel great either. Like them, I had slept like a log, but now I felt wearier than ever. It wasn't just physical tiredness either. I felt slow-witted and a bit out of it. Marcus had asked me what I wanted for breakfast, and I had just stared at him, knowing he was talking to me but somehow not able to process what he said, and I had already taken three Advil for a headache that rumbled in the front of my skull like a tractor trailer. Maybe Brad was right. It was time to lay off the vino and whatever-the-hell cocktails Mel kept producing.

"I need some air," said Marcus. "This place is fantastic, but it doesn't exactly circulate, does it?"

"Fancy a walk?" I suggested.

"Morning, people!" called Melissa, appearing from the other wing of the house and showing none of the half-awake misery that the rest of us were laboring under. "No walking off by yourselves. We're heading into town for brunch. All of us. Won't that be fun?"

She said it beaming and in defiance of our mood, though she couldn't bring herself to look at Brad, who was glaring at her. But once Simon and Melissa put their minds to something, it would take an act of God—or at least a major fight—to derail it, and twenty minutes later we were boarding the Mercedes in compliant, if surly, silence. Where we were going, however, had not been determined, and our fearless leaders were not in agreement.

"Come on, Simon," said Marcus. "For old times' sake."

"The Diogenes?" said Simon. "No. There's a dozen restaurants in a two-block radius. We never thought the food was that good there. We just kept going back because it was familiar."

"Exactly!" said Marcus. "We have to go at least once. Back me up, Kristen."

"Absolutely," said Kristen. "For old times' sake."

"Really?" said Simon. "Souvlaki and fries for brunch? Tomato salad drenched in olive oil? This is how you eat these days?"

"Of course not!" said Kristen. "Which is why I want to do it here."

"I always kind of hated that place," said Simon, and he wasn't joking now. He meant it.

Simon had always had a tendency to push minor irritation into belligerence. Little things might stay little—meriting no more than a raised eyebrow or a resigned sigh—or he might dig his heels in and fight his corner like there was something real at stake. Still, I tried to remember him bitching about the restaurant before, but couldn't recall him ever saying anything of the kind.

It was called Taverna Diogenes. It sat on the bus route from the hotel we had stayed in to Rethymno, though we had always walked there. It was less than five hundred yards from the Minos's concierge desk, and it was someone there who had first recommended it to us.

"Probably his brother runs the place," Brad had observed, not unreasonably. The local community seemed tight and interconnected. It was like a hundred other tourist-oriented Greek restaurants on the island, but it had become our place, and we'd eaten most of our meals there.

"You know, Si, it really might be fun," said Melissa. "As they say, for old times' sake."

They exchanged a look that said anything but fun, then Simon shrugged and turned away.

"Fine," he said.

As we drove over there once more, Simon grew quiet—"just focusing on the road, Mel," he snapped when his wife asked him what was wrong—and the rest of us, as if to compensate, seemed to wake up. Our mood lifted, and even my headache went away as the ibuprofen kicked in, so that by the time we reached the Diogenes, I was feeling much better and had developed a serious appetite.

There were a few tables inside, but most were out in a flagstone-paved area by the road, surrounded by a low stone wall and canopied with a roof that was half thatch and half real grapevine. That had been a selling feature when we first arrived, the fruit hanging from the rafters above the table. It had seemed so exotic. Marcus told us some story about Diogenes wandering the streets at noon with a lantern. "Claimed to be looking for an honest man," he said.

The food was standard Greek tourist fare—a dozen or so main courses, a handful of predictable sides, retsina, wine, ouzo, and pints of Mythos beer served very cold. It was still run by a boisterous middle-aged woman called Maria and staffed by her children and their cousins, some of whom also worked around the hotel and the beach. One of the boys, a teenager who had taken an obvious shine to Melissa, had appeared in Marcus's slide show. He led tourists on snorkeling and paddling expeditions around the bay, and I remembered him badgering us to join him, though we didn't go. Mel had flirted with him till he promised to bring us all fresh local sponges recovered from the sea by his own hands. There had been a rack of them, bagged in cellophane, beside the counter, and a couple of baskets of larger ones that looked like great ocher corals. I had bought a small one from the hotel and used it religiously for the next two years till it finally disintegrated. But the kid had said he knew where the best ones grew and would bring one as big as his head for Melissa. I remembered his boyish pride, his determination to prove himself worthy of Mel's glamorous favor, though he never delivered the sponges—not to the rest of us, at least—and he wasn't around at the end of the trip. I think Simon got tired of him buzzing around and may have said something to Maria. Or to Mel, for that matter. Still, I remembered his boyish grin, white teeth in a deeply tanned face, black hair and eyes to match, an exuberant, good-looking kid.

Waiter boy, Mel had called him teasingly. I smiled at the memory.

"You think they'll remember us?" said Melissa, looking around.

Sometimes that lighthouse smile of hers seemed designed to attract attention to herself as well as to shed her beatific light on the less worthy. She was doing that now, being conspicuous as she scanned the seating area.

"Why should they?" said Simon sourly. "We were here for a week five years ago, and these tables have been full of people who looked and behaved just like us ever since. Oh, for God's sake, Mel, just pick a table."

She chose the one we had always chosen, and I found myself surprised by the realization that she wanted to be recognized, that she wanted Maria and her kids to flock to her as to an old friend or to some princess or celebrity who had graced their humble establishment before. It reminded me of the first time I realized that Melissa's glamour was not as effortless as she made out, when I caught her touching up her makeup in the ladies' room after she came out of the sea. Annoyed that I had seen, she had snapped something catty about how it must be nice not to have to worry about how you looked.

Perhaps this was the source of Simon's irritation. He had anticipated some rerun of what Marcus and I had occasionally and privately called *The Melissa Show.*

Starring Melissa! With special guest . . . Melissa! Written, directed, and edited by Melissa!

We could go on for quite a while on that score. It was all in good fun—mostly, at least—but it contained a kernel of truth. Melissa liked to be the center of attention, and the only reason that no one minded was that the rest of us liked to be her adoring audience. I wondered if Simon had started to find that wearing, and I remembered Gretchen's tale of the cataclysmic fight that had sent Mel to a bar by herself.

Mel slumped into her seat, pouting at Simon, and we took our designated places. If Gretchen realized that she was, once more, butting in on a ritual reenactment from half a decade ago, she showed no sign of it.

"God," muttered Simon, studying the menu. "It's exactly the same. Nothing has changed."

"Prices have gone up," said Kristen.

"A response to austerity measures," said Brad wisely.

In truth, we had seen very little of the much-touted collapse of the Greek economy, but that was because we were visitors with money and had been confined to tourist areas and activities. Perhaps if we spent more time in the local grocery stores and shops over the next few days, we'd see more. We'd also seen precious little of the waves of desperate immigrants coming across from North Africa and Syria, of which I had read so much about before leaving the United States. That, I'm ashamed to say, was something of a relief. I knew there were people in the world whose lives were exponentially harder than mine, but I didn't want to be confronted with the evidence this week. Not while I was on vacation.

God, I thought, *what awful people we are.*

But then that wasn't fair either. Maybe it was just me. And let's not forget the maxim carved in the stone of the oracle at Delphi: "Know Thyself." If I was an asshole, at least I knew it and, from time to time, tried not to be. Even so, my momentary relief at having dodged the poor and desperate shamed me, and I found myself wondering how much the locals, underneath the welcoming smiles, the necessary hospitality, really hated us. I wouldn't blame them if they did.

We ordered what amounted to "the usual," even though we hadn't been there for five years, but no one recognized us, something that clearly deflated Melissa, though Simon gallantly attempted to cheer her up by saying that the moussaka, kebabs, and grilled chicken were better than he remembered. In fact, none of the waitstaff looked familiar, and we discussed the possibility that the restaurant had changed hands since our last visit. We were counting out a stack of colorful euros when Maria herself finally appeared, looking notably older and clad in layers topped with a shapeless dress with a faded floral print and a stained apron. Marcus gave her a half smile and Melissa turned to her, standing to give her the full lighthouse effect.

The older woman looked baffled at first and half turned away but then rotated back again, very slowly. She pointed squarely at Melissa and began jabbering in furious Greek, bearing menacingly down on us and gesturing with her hands. I couldn't catch anything she said, though I knew she spoke decent English, but it was impossible not to read her face, her tone, her hands.

Get out! they said. *Get out now. And never come back.*

∿

Melissa was distraught. The woman's anger—it was fury, really—was terrifying to see, and I think that if Brad and Marcus hadn't shielded Mel with their bodies, the restaurant owner would have attacked her physically. The woman's fists had been balled and, crazy though it sounds, I found myself watching to see if they would stray to the cutlery on the tables. Her rage was volcanic: hot and sudden and capable of all manner of violence.

As we got back in the car and sped in the direction of Rethymno proper, we struggled to make sense of it.

"She must have confused us with someone else," said Simon. "I'm sure tourists come and duck out on the check all the time."

"Seemed like more than that," said Marcus. "It was . . . I don't know. Personal."

"They're a fiery people," said Brad with a grin. "Hotheaded. Like the Sicilians."

"I don't understand," said Melissa, wiping her eyes. "I was so glad to see her . . ."

Melissa was sitting in the back, Simon driving, Brad in the passenger seat. Kristen took her hand and gave her a soothing look. We were all trying to turn our shock and confusion into sympathy, but it felt odd, off balance, like we had started watching a movie halfway through and couldn't make sense of the plot. We had also been drinking—it seemed we had been drinking constantly since we had arrived—and were feeling slow and a little buzzed.

"Did any of you catch what she was yelling about?" asked Simon as he drove.

We shook our heads, and he checked our faces in the rearview mirror, scowling.

"Shouldn't have gone," he muttered, flashing a fierce look—somewhat surprisingly—at Melissa. For a split second Melissa's face hardened and her lips drew back from her teeth as if she was going to turn on him, but then Gretchen was reaching forward and patting her shoulder vaguely, and she turned back to us.

"I just said *hello*!" she said. "I smiled at her. I didn't think she'd remember us, but . . . I don't understand . . ."

She sobbed.

"It's OK," said Simon, conciliatory now. "A misunderstanding. It's over."

"We'll go shopping," said Gretchen. It was offered as something that would cheer her up, but a mean-spirited part of me thought she also just wanted everyone to forget the incident because it didn't involve her. How could it? She hadn't been here last time.

"She was so mad," said Kristen to no one in particular. She looked stunned still, like she'd just been slapped awake. "It was . . . weird. Irrational."

"Maybe she has mental problems," I said.

"She didn't use to," said Marcus. "Not that we ever saw."

"It doesn't make any sense," said Melissa, her voice quavering, tears running down her face. "How can people be hateful?"

"We're gone now," said Kristen.

"But I loved that place!" Melissa blurted. "It was *our* place. We were there all the time. And now it's ruined."

"You can't think like that," said Kristen. "So the woman has issues. You can't let that spoil the past."

"Too late," said Melissa, her grief turning sulky and resentful, as she turned to stare out the car window. The traffic was heavier as we got closer to the town proper. "She spoiled it."

"No," I said, trying to sound breezy. "It wasn't the same place, any-way. Not really. We'll keep our version of the way it was in our heads."

"And it's not like we would have gone back again," said Brad. "Psycho lady or no psycho lady. The food was only . . . *meh*."

I saw the flicker of irritation in Simon's face as he half turned, look-ing for a place to park.

"I wonder why she—" Kristen began musingly.

"Oh, come on," muttered Brad to himself. "Who cares? Leave it."

Kristen turned to stare at him, but Simon was starting to reverse into a parking spot.

"Down in back, please," he said. "Thanks."

We were a couple of blocks from the town center.

"I don't know if I want to do this now, Simon," said Melissa. "Maybe I should wait in the car. Take a nap."

"No!" said Gretchen. "Let's get out, get some air. Clear your head. Spend some of Si's money!"

Melissa gave her a weary half smile.

"And no one made any sense of what she said?" said Simon, putting on the hand brake. "The Diogenes woman. No one understood any of it?"

Again we muttered our *no*s and shook our heads.

"All Greek to me," said Brad with his trademark grin, clambering out.

"Dude," said Simon. "You wanna be a person for a minute?"

Brad stared him down.

"You said it yourself," he said. "We shouldn't have gone."

"Yeah, but we did, and she's upset so . . ."

"You're making a fuss over nothing," Brad replied. "So some crazy Greek woman throws a fit because she thinks Mel is someone else? So what? Get past it."

"Jesus, Brad," muttered Kristen.

"What?" he demanded, rounding on her. "This is our holiday too, Kristen. Crying over some lunatic who runs a crappy restaurant isn't my idea of a good time."

"I'm sorry if my wife's distress isn't sufficiently fun for you," snapped Simon.

"Oh, whatever," said Brad. "Look, if you're gonna play support group to the Wounded Warrior there for the rest of the afternoon, count me out. I'm on vacation."

"Then maybe you should go do something else for a while, bud," said Simon, putting a protective arm round Melissa.

For a second, I thought Brad would climb down, nod, say he was sorry, but there was something about Melissa that needled him.

"Fine," he said. "You know, I keep casting my mind back, and I'm pretty sure that this wasn't how anyone partied in 1999. I'll meet you back here in two hours."

"Four," said Simon. "The girls want to go shopping."

"*Four?*" said Brad, incredulous.

"Four," said Kristen quietly but firmly.

Brad stared at her, his face reddening at the betrayal.

"Fine," he said again. "Whatever. See y'all later."

⌁

He stalked away, not looking back. His anger gave his speed the appearance of purpose, like he knew where he was going, and for a moment the rest of us just stood there watching him in awkward silence, like he'd taken the needle of our compass with him and we were suddenly lost.

"Don't mind him," said Kristen. "He's just . . . Brad."

She shrugged and smiled in a way that was both knowing and apologetic, so I reached out and touched her shoulder sympathetically.

"Now he's spoiling everything," Melissa whispered to Simon. "First that woman, now him."

She sounded like a child whose Christmas had been canceled, but when I caught a look at her face, the teary pouting contained something else entirely. Her eyes were hard and fierce, her teeth set. I thought Mel had revealed a vulnerable side I hadn't seen before. She had, after all, always seemed so *together*. But now I saw that she wasn't just upset—she was angry, indignant that her plans had been disrupted. Shocked, and just a tiny bit scared by the intensity of her look, I stepped back.

"OK," said Gretchen. She made a series of odd, wavy gestures over Melissa's head, like she was washing her hair. Some weird, New Age ritual thing that might or might not have been a joke. "And we're rinsing away the past," she said, "all negativity and cruddy experiences, and now we're clean and ready for . . . *fun!*"

She beamed, eyes wide and delighted, like she was leading a toddler to her birthday party. Melissa's returning smile was small and wan but it didn't last, and Gretchen's exuberance stalled. So we walked through the tangled, cobbled streets of Rethymno quietly at first, Simon with his arm around Melissa, sometimes almost pulling her along. All the light had gone out of her face, and she looked both sad and sullen. Every time he asked her if she wanted to go into such and such shop or stop for a coffee or gelato, she would shrug and look away, as if the day was already ruined and she was just marking time before going home to bed.

But it got better. Simon, knowingly, wisely, didn't force the issue, but he guided her around, and gradually the little streets of artisan shops dotted among the souvenir T-shirts and assorted kitsch began to work their magic on her. Gretchen helped too, I was mildly annoyed to note. Having failed with the frontal attack, she tried a more tangential approach, taking her free hand and chattering girlishly as if nothing had happened, ignoring Melissa's sourness and very gradually drawing her into talking about the clothes and jewelry in the shop windows.

Rethymno was quaint, but its narrow carless medieval streets weren't some kind of walkable museum. It was a real town with real people living recognizably regular, modern lives, and the contents of the store windows wouldn't have been wildly out of place in Charlotte, even if the stone facades were several hundred years older than anything there. There were stores full of artfully arranged mannequins in trendy clothes—some of them well outside my budget and others selling appliances and cell phones. There were pharmacies, banks, law offices, and everything else you would expect in a place where people actually lived all year-round, though everything was on that smaller, slightly huddled, European scale. I was mildly surprised by it, and I started to find the day-to-day stuff more interesting than the stores of faux Greek statuary and painted ceramics aimed at the tourists.

"Ooh!" cried Gretchen, pointing. "Let's check this out."

It was a leather goods store, nothing like as shiny as most of what we had just passed, and the heaped purses, the bins of wallets, and the hanging bags on the walls all suggested a cottage industry. The place had that unmistakable leather scent, warm and fragrant and comforting as baking bread. I drank it in, picking up a satchel and inhaling its musky, outdoor earthiness. At the back was a workbench, where an old man sat with a set of slim carving tools, shears, stacked sheets of hide, and spools of leather thong, working quietly while the woman I assumed was his wife ministered smilingly to the customers.

"These from factory," she announced, indicating the brand names stamped into the polished leather. "These made here."

She must have said it a million times, but her eyes still flashed with pride.

"I love this," said Kristen, picking up a tiny boxlike purse, whose rough leather was contrasted by fine chain. She wobbled a little as she considered it, leaning back as if trying to get her eyes to focus, and I wondered how much she'd had to drink at lunch.

"What about that!" said Gretchen, pointing to one of the hanging bags.

The shopkeeper broke off her conversation with another customer—a woman in stretch pants and heavy gold jewelry—bustled over wordlessly, and reached up with a hook on a pole to lift it down.

"You have these in red?" asked Melissa.

And she was back. Whatever sadness and bewilderment had been coiled around her since the episode at the taverna fell away and was forgotten. I caught Simon's watchful eye and gave him an appreciative look.

Well handled.

He smiled back in acknowledgment, though there was, I thought, no joy in it. Melissa considered the bag critically, then nodded and set it down on the pile to look over another, a rich teak-colored thing with heavy leather lacing. The woman in the heavy gold jewelry was at her elbow, scrutinizing the purses with a predatory air. As soon as Melissa turned away from it, the woman reached for the red one, but Melissa turned on her, all weepiness swept away by a hard and instant ferocity.

"That's mine," she said.

The woman snatched her hand away as if it had been scalded.

"There's a Venetian fort by the harbor," said Marcus. "Sixteenth century. Who's up for it?"

Bored of shopping, he was getting antsy, walking a bit faster than everyone else, standing and looking back at the rest of us like he was leading a dim and distracted school group. I couldn't say I blamed him. Being in retail—albeit at the unglamorous backside of it—I've never been much for window shopping. It starts to feel like work.

"Me," I said.

"Yeah," said Kristen lazily. "That might be a novelty."

She had been quiet, insular since Brad left, and I think Gretchen's glee was starting to wear on her nerves.

"I think I'll stay here," said Melissa. "Drift. Buy some stuff. Get a latte or something."

"I'll stick with you," said Simon to her.

"To protect me from the Greek randoms," said Melissa.

"Absolutely," said Simon.

"Thanks," she said, tipping her face up to his and kissing him quickly.

"I'll stay too," said Gretchen, ever the third wheel.

Melissa hugged her, then turned back to Simon.

"You know," she said, "you should go with them. You don't want to go traipsing around a bunch of stores while I try things on."

Simon hesitated.

"Well," he said, "no, but . . ."

"Go ahead," she said. "I'll be fine. Gretchen and I can do a little girl talk."

"Yay!" said Gretchen, like she'd won a prize in some low-rent sideshow.

"You sure?" said Simon.

"Positive," said Melissa. "Go do some history."

"OK," he replied, giving us a wry grin. "More history. Lucky me."

Marcus looked very slightly pissed off, but he glanced away so they wouldn't see.

"OK," said Simon. "Back at the car at five. If we get done sooner, I'll text you."

In town we had a decent signal, and everyone had been glued to their phones for the first ten minutes of our visit. It felt like some cautionary meme about the decline of Western civilization—the six of us huddled over, blind to the ancient beauty of the town around us.

I reached over and gave Mel a parting squeeze, and she smiled gratefully.

"I'm fine," she said. "Have fun."

⸺

We bumped into a group of Americans outside the imposing entrance to the fort—college students, perhaps, or just graduated.

"Christ," said Kristen. "It's us, five years ago."

It kind of was. You could spot the couples, the shining ones who ran the pride, the quiet ones who followed after . . .

"Oh my God!" exclaimed one of them, a girl in a top cut almost to her navel. She was staring at Kristen, and for a split second I thought we were going to be the target of another arbitrary attack. "You look *exactly* like Kar Gohen!"

That was her character's name. I was amazed. I had almost forgotten that Kristen was a star and didn't think anyone would recognize her behind those massive Sophia Loren sunglasses. She raised them, smiling, and said simply, "Hiya."

The group broke into raptures, grinning like kids, all fighting to announce how awesome she was, telling her she had short hair—in case she might not have noticed—and listing their favorite *End Times* episodes. It was quite endearing, watching them geek out, and I confess that some of her glamour seemed to coalesce around the rest of us, like we must be amazingly cool to be hanging out with her. Several of them eyed us cagily, as if trying to figure out if we were castmates or actors from other shows. Their eyes lingered particularly on Simon, who might easily have been a movie star or the kind of basketball player who got invited to the same parties.

"I know you're on vacation and all," said one of them, "but if we could maybe get a picture with you . . . ?"

"Absolutely!" said Kristen, as if they were doing her the favor. "Brilliant."

"Her English accent gets stronger when she's talking to fans, have you noticed?" whispered Marcus to me.

I grinned at him, but his gaze was still on her and it was thoughtful.

"What?" I asked.

He shrugged.

"Nothing," he said, though I didn't believe him. Kristen was smiling for cameras and signing hastily produced notebooks, showing no trace of the silent irritation that had clung to her since Brad had stormed off. "Tell you one thing," Marcus added. "She's a better actress than I thought she was."

It hadn't been long since I thought the same thing, and for a second I wondered how much of the real Kristen I had ever really seen. Not much, I suspected.

I confess I had rather hoped to have some time alone with Marcus, if only to solidify our newfound friendship, though I also still wanted to ask him about the cave of Zeus. There had definitely been an odd vibe when Kristen had mentioned our trip there, and I felt sure that there was something I was missing, probably something I had missed five years ago as well. Whether Marcus would know more than me or not, I couldn't say, and it seemed odd that he had never mentioned it if he did, but then maybe the strangeness of whatever the cave meant involved him somehow. It had, after all, been the beginning of our unraveling, though maybe that had been an accident of timing. I couldn't imagine what might have occurred at some random tourist outing that made him like me less than he had the day before, but with Kristen and Simon on hand, I wasn't about to ask him about it now.

I had expected the fortress to be more compact, like the castles in *The Lord of the Rings* or *Game of Thrones*, with rings of walls and towers with the occasional Disney spire and Hogwarts decor, but it was more like Fort Sumter: big and open, with lots of ramps and platforms for guns. There were no towers at all to speak of, though the perimeter wall was dotted with little turrets that bulged out over nothing but the long drop to the shore, where turquoise water deepened fast. There was a single domed mosque and, close by, some rusted cannons overgrown with weeds, where a solitary tortoise nestled. On the lower level was a long, dark tunnel with a barrel roof, iron gates, and heavy wooden doors leading into storage rooms, barracks, or cells. It gave us a nice break from the sun—the top side of the fort was almost entirely without shade—but I was glad when we left. It was starting to give me the willies.

The place was largely deserted. When Marcus and Simon wandered off to inspect the gift shop, I found Kristen on the main platform, gazing out over the coast.

"You OK?" I asked Kristen.

"Yeah," she said. She smiled wanly, then shook her head. "Not really."

"Brad will be fine," I said. "Just one of those things."

She nodded but looked unconvinced and a moment later said, "These things happen a lot lately." She backtracked immediately, as if keen to make sure I didn't get the wrong impression. "I mean, he's fine," she said. "Just stressed. Really stressed."

"Work?" I said.

Again the silent nod, and this time the silence was longer and deeper. Out over the sea a pair of gulls rolled and dived, screaming at each other. Eventually she gave me a sideways look, took her shades off, and slipped them into her purse.

"Don't say anything to the others, OK, not even Marcus," she said. "But he lost his job."

"What? When?"

"Two months ago."

"God. I'm sorry."

"Yeah."

"He'll find another, though, right?" I said. "All those deals he did. Companies must be lining up to get him."

"Not an option," said Kristen. She gave me a steady look, then gazed out to sea. "He lost his real estate license."

I gaped at her, feeling suddenly out of my depth, not because I don't know anything about business—though that is also true—but because I didn't really know her. This was personal stuff, and we were little more than strangers. I didn't know what to say, but she spoke anyway, something of her usual poise returning to her, as if a weight had already been lifted from her shoulders.

"I mean it about not telling the others," she said.

"I promise," I said, wondering how much my word would carry with her. What had Marcus told her? Or Simon? What had she deduced for herself about my occasional fibbing?

Occasional . . . ?

"The way Brad's business works," she said, "is that companies who are looking to expand send his agency locations where they want to go, and I don't mean towns or regions. I mean coordinates. Latitude and longitude. Often they've already identified the site themselves."

"Why don't they just buy the property themselves?" I asked.

"Something about retailers not wanting to also be in real estate," she said with a shrug. "It never made much sense to me either, but apparently it's about showing their investors that they are staying within a particular area of business expertise and subcontracting for related services. Anyway. So a company like yours—Great Deal, right?"

"Right."

"Great Deal says they want three stores in metro Atlanta in these locations and they'll pay between one and three million per lot. Brad goes in, negotiates the deal with the property owner through a broker, ensures the land is suitable, then purchases it for Great Deal. But say he finds out that the seller will part with the land for only a few hundred thousand? He knows Great Deal will pay way more than that so . . ."

"He convinces the seller to ask for a higher price and gets a cut of the extra?" I suggest.

"Worse," she said, and now her previous despondency settled back into her body so that she sagged and, for a second, squeezed her eyes shut. "He buys the land himself. Sets up a shell company under some-one else's name, then tries to sell it on to Great Deal at the markup he knows they'll pay. A million plus profit per site."

"Oh," I said. I knew how lame and stupid that sounded, but I couldn't think of anything else. I knew nothing of such stuff, but even I could see that this was bad.

"Great Deal finds out, reports him, his agency fires him, and sus-pends his license for five years."

"So . . . he's out of work?" I wasn't sure where the conversation had moved from the hypothetical to the factual.

"To say the least, yeah. It's not Great Deal, of course, but otherwise the story is . . . yeah, he's out of work and lucky not to be banned for life."

"Oh, Kristen, I'm so sorry."

"Thanks. I mean, it's his own stupid fault but . . . yeah."

"Will there be criminal charges?" I asked.

"I don't think so. It's a matter of professional ethics, but I don't think he broke any laws. Not that that matters. He had to pay back what he had earned and now has no source of income."

"Is that why he is so keen to get Simon to invest in his wine-shipping idea?"

Kristen sighed.

"A pipe dream," she said. "He knows it won't work, but he won't give it up. And he won't stop spending money, living like he's pulling in millions a year. Right now we're living off my income, which is crazy. No TV show lasts forever. I figure we have another two seasons, maybe three. Tops. I might never work again."

"Oh, I'm sure you'll get snapped up by—"

"It's not that simple. Especially for someone in a role like mine. Not many shows are looking for someone who reminds the audience of the alien they played on another show every time they appear on camera. But that's not the point. He's living off me, which I'm not thrilled about, and there's a very good chance that I'll be out of work before he can go back to work in commercial real estate. I'm sorry to tell you all this," she said, smiling sadly, as if remembering whom she was talking to. "I'm just so sick of carrying it round in my head."

"Brad doesn't want anyone to know?"

"God, no. He's living this trip like it will set the clock back. Take us all to where we were five years ago. I don't understand it."

"Things were good five years ago," I said.

"They were OK," she said. "We had fun. But for me, in all honesty, life is way better now."

I said nothing, again lost for words. That was certainly not something I could say for myself. Five years ago I had been poised to do so many things. My collapsed college career notwithstanding, I had thought there were all kinds of possibilities on the horizon. I had still been thinking seriously about going to med school. I still had Marcus.

"You remember when we went to that cave?" she said suddenly. "Last time. The one where Zeus was born?"

It was as if she had seen into my head. I blinked.

"Yes," I said, cautious now. "Why?"

"I don't know," she said, gazing out over the sea. "Everyone is so weird about it. Like something happened that no one wants to talk about. Have you noticed?"

"Yeah," I said. "I don't know why."

She looked at me then, shading her eyes from the sun and fixing me with a steady, appraising gaze that made me suddenly sure someone *had* said something about my not telling the truth.

"Honestly," I said. "I don't know. I had been wondering the same thing. I noticed the way the others responded when you mentioned it before but . . ."

"I asked Brad," she said musingly, "and he got . . . defensive. Hostile. It was not like him, even with all the work stress and everything. Scared me."

That I had not expected.

"I could ask Marcus," I said. "Not sure he knows anything about it, but . . ."

She nodded vaguely, looking back out to sea.

"Not Simon though, OK?" she said. "Not Mel."

"OK," I said.

"Something else," said Kristen. "You remember the word we saw in the leaves back at the villa."

"Or imagined we saw," I said, not sure where this was going but feeling a tug of unease. "We thought it said *Nanos* or something."

"Right," she said. "I think it was *Manos*."

I thought for a second, then nodded noncommittally.

"Could have been," I said. "Why? What does that mean?"

"I don't know," she said. "But I'm pretty sure the woman at the restaurant said it. Maria. The one who yelled at Mel. I didn't understand what she was saying, but among all the screaming she said it. Twice."

Chapter Twenty-One

I don't know why the scuba mask bothers me so much, but it does. It feels . . . macabre. Horror movie stuff. I try to convince myself that it's just because my captor wants to hide his face in the same way he's hiding his voice, but that doesn't help because it reinforces the possibility that he is someone I know.

If there's an upside to the mask, it's that concealing his face means he's not decided for certain that I will die in this little stone box, chained to the wall. I might get out. I might walk away from this dank little cell and walk under the sky once more, and when people ask me who held me captive here, I won't be able to tell them. If that wasn't at least possible, he wouldn't care whether I could recognize him or not. I wasn't dead. Not yet.

So why don't you believe it, this 'upside'?

I'm not sure, but I don't. It smells like a lie, a sour, deathly tang like rotten meat that I, old expert liar that I am, can detect at a hundred paces. He's going to kill me, mask or no mask. I feel it. So the hiding in the dark, the voice concealer, really is just to scare me? To make me think I'm in some kind of nightmare from which there is no waking up?

Working pretty well, then.

I test the chain again, as I have a thousand times. I stand and stretch and inspect the floor with blind, crawling fingers, as if there is something I might have missed, but I sit down again with nothing: no progress, no discovery, no hope.

I know what I have to do. I've known it for a while, I think, but I wanted to believe there was an alternative, something less desperate, less awful. There isn't, but I keep looking for it, like when you misplace your keys and you keep re-searching the same spot over and over, knowing they won't be there, but half believing in something like magic, something summoned from despair and driving, animal need that will change the laws of the universe and set the ring of keys where you knew it should be but knew just as well it wasn't. But I have searched my cell over and over, and the keys are not there. There is only one possibility left to me. It almost certainly won't work, and the attempt will bring new levels of pain and misery, but it is all I have.

A year or two ago I caught some soft news piece about a woman who had been ravaged by her friend's pet chimp. She had visited the house having had her hair cut in some new way, and the animal didn't recognize her. It had ripped most of her face off and—and, for some reason, this was the part that had given me nightmares—torn her hands off. It had simply taken hold of her, one hand in hers, the other on her arm, and pulled her hand off, first one, quite deliberately, then the other.

I hadn't believed that possible, or at least, the possibility had never occurred to me and not just because I didn't know chimpanzees were that strong and aggressive. I just hadn't imagined that with sufficient force and savagery, you could yank a hand right off at the wrist.

I feel my swollen wrist with my free hand, working the manacle as high up onto my hand as I can, pushing it back and forth, tilting it from side to side till it will move no farther. It lodges at the knuckle. There's softness between my thumb and forefinger and actual space beneath the crevice at the base of my palm and the cuff. With my right hand, I squeeze the fingers and thumb of my left as hard as I can, gasping as the pain roils and swirls, reaching a steady simmer, and then I press the edge of my hand against the concrete of the bed platform, stand up, and push down on it with my other hand, using all my weight. The pain comes to a rolling boil, but the cuff shifts another half inch. It won't come over the core structures of my hand, the bones that give it shape and form, but it needs to move no more than another inch and a half for me to be free.

Now it's just a matter of the pain. And the sacrifice.

I'm sweating. My breathing is thin and ragged. My heart is throbbing. My eyes have begun to stream. I think of the chimp tearing the woman's hand off, then push the horror away.

I consider stepping out of my dress so I can use it to staunch the blood, but I don't want to wait any longer.

I'm satisfied that the manacle can be made to move no farther, not without altering those structures in my hand, the spur of which is where the rusted iron is most clearly stuck. I'm light-headed as I stand, and the pain swells and kicks as I let go with my right hand and lean out into the darkness, all my weight straining against the chain. I rock on the balls of my feet, tipping first toward the wall, then away, building force and speed with each agonizing pull, like a gymnast on the high bars, working up the momentum for an acrobatic maneuver. I take deep, rapid breaths through bared teeth, a weight lifter bracing, then I lean into the wall over the bed so that my hair brushes against it, and then slam hard away, trying to hit the opposite wall.

Once.

Twice.

The pain is bright as a flare, hard and sharp as glass. I feel the sinews pop, the muscle tear, the bones break.

Three times.

I fall heavily against the far wall, clutching my wounded hand and sobbing.

Free. Broken, but free.

Chapter Twenty-Two

"Well, Mel is the lead singer, obviously," said Brad, toasting her with his glass of red.

"Obviously," said Gretchen.

"What about Simon?" said Melissa. "He's got *rock star* written all over him."

"I'm the unspeakably well-paid manager," said Simon. "I found the rest of you playing seedy nightclubs and made your careers. You're welcome, by the way."

"I'm lead guitar," said Brad, putting his glass down and doing a little air guitar solo.

"Yeah," said Melissa. "The bad boy of the band."

We were all pretty drunk. We had eaten, but dinner had been heavy on Greek salad and phyllo pastries with spinach and feta, served by candlelight in the villa's formal dining room: good, but light. I was still hungry, which meant I shouldn't be drinking, but I was. We all were.

We had moved back to the living room, since its circuits were on the generator's power supply, and were lounging around after abandoning a game of charades because Melissa was weirdly crap at it. She was fine at guessing other people's clues, but when it was her turn, she either couldn't think of any suitable hints and just sat there fretting and complaining or made unintelligible hand signals and then got mad when no one could figure out what the hell she was doing. It had been funny at first, hilarious in fact, but when it went on for a while, she got irritated and sour, which pretty much killed the fun of the game. I was disappointed because I'd been paired with Marcus and it was, for a moment, kind of like old times, but once Melissa has decided she's not having fun anymore, that's pretty much it, and if you insist on continuing you can expect to be on the receiving end of all the passive-aggressive weapons at her disposal. If she could harness that creativity for other things, she'd be a lot better at charades.

Anyway, we had abandoned the game, which was already getting fuzzy with drink, and had somehow fallen into this nonsense conversation about what we would all be doing if we were a band. I hated stuff like this. It always made me feel inadequate and unwanted. People with strong personalities love this kind of shit because everyone immediately knows how to peg them in ways that remind everyone how cool they are. Of course Melissa was the lead singer. Of course Brad was lead guitar. What about me? The Pluto of the group. The black hole. Everyone would forget me until the end and then pretend it was really great to be the band's accountant or ticket taker or some damn thing.

I felt the heat in my face. I really shouldn't have accepted another glass of whatever precious wine Brad had insisted on bringing with him.

"Kristen's backing vocals and bass," said Brad. "All sultry and hot."

"See?" said Melissa. "Bad boy."

"She is my wife," said Brad.

"Oh, like that matters," said Simon. There was a fractional, shocked hesitation, as if time had stopped, and then he added, "Bass and backing vocals sound good to you, Kristen?"

"I'll take that," said Kristen, not missing a beat. Since our chat at the fortress she had gone right back to being her old self, composed and easygoing, so I thought it again: she really was a better actress than I had assumed. "What about Gretchen?"

There was quite a different kind of hesitation, which Gretchen pretended not to find embarrassing. We didn't know her and, frankly, there didn't seem like there was that much to know. And that's coming from the group's black hole.

"Drums," said Melissa, seemingly at random.

"Yeah!" said Gretchen, delighted, starting immediately to bang away sloppily on the edge of the coffee table.

"Careful," said Brad. "You'll spill the bottle."

Gretchen looked crestfallen, but Simon came to her rescue.

"What about Marcus?" he mused aloud. "Roadie? Producer? The guy who gets the sound just right . . ."

"Sitting in the booth in the dark with a headset," said Brad, liking this more and more.

"Sure," said Marcus. "Fine."

"And then there's Jan," said Brad.

"Can we just play cards or something?" I said. "Something grown-up, like poker?"

I'm a good poker player, but then you'd expect that, wouldn't you?

"No, little Janice," said Brad. "Everyone is in the band. You wouldn't want to be left out, would you?"

I braced myself. There was something sharp in his face, something wolfish that made me want to disappear. When he was drinking and dropped his sardonic guard, he could be like a kid on the playground: maybe not the gang leader, but its principal enforcer, a master of minor cruelties, even if they were only manifested in comments and sneers.

"Rhythm guitar," said Marcus quickly, "*and*," he added before anyone could comment, "songwriter."

"Huh," said Simon. "Yeah, that'll work. I think we're all set to play the Grammys."

"Woo!" said Gretchen, raising her glass predictably.

I shot Marcus a sideways look and smiled, but I couldn't help noting the way Gretchen had squeezed up next to him on the couch. And the way he didn't seem to mind.

"Oh my God!" exclaimed Gretchen. "I didn't show you the bags we got!"

She leaped to her feet and began rummaging in a holdall behind the couch.

"Wait, wait!" said Melissa, also getting up and mouthing something at Gretchen, who dutifully stopped what she was doing and stood there, grinning about whatever was about to happen.

"You bought a bag," said Brad, deadpan. "How shall I contain my excitement?"

"Wait, Mr. Snarky," said Gretchen in a little-girl voice. Melissa had ducked out of the room at a run and was now shouting, "Hold on! I'll be right back," from somewhere upstairs. We waited. A door banged. You couldn't hear her footsteps because she was barefoot, and the floors were ancient and solid, so her breathless reappearance was a minor surprise. She was dangling a boxy red leather purse like a runway model, her face a mask of haughty indifference for a posed second.

"Oh, that's cute!" said Kristen.

"Wait, wait," said Gretchen, frustrated by how Melissa had upstaged her moment. "See?"

She stood up, arms outstretched in a version of Melissa's model pose. It was the same purse. Exactly the same in every respect. Gretchen scuttled over to the doorway and arranged herself next to Melissa to make the point, the two purses suspended side by side.

"Besties forever!" said Gretchen.

This was too much. I turned an eye-rolling look toward Marcus, but he was smiling at her and didn't see me, though I wanted to grab him and shake him and say, *"Oh my God, now she IS dressing like her! She is so fucking odd!"*

Instead I looked away and, by way of cover, said the first thing that came into my head.

"So, Brad, what did you get up to this afternoon?"

"What do you mean 'get up to'?" he said, giving me a hard look. "I didn't get up to anything. Why do you ask?"

"No reason," I said, backing off hurriedly. I had assumed he was over whatever snit he had gotten into after the restaurant fiasco, but I was clearly wrong. "The fortress was pretty cool."

"I'll bet," he said, his tone mocking and dismissive. "Got yourself a personal tour from Professor Marcus, no doubt. Next thing, you'll be writing his name with little hearts around it in your exam book. You know, you two really should get together. Oh wait . . ."

He stared unblinking at me, his eyes showing none of the smile that pulled at his lips.

For a second I just looked at him, keeping my own eyes open in case blinking would release a tear.

"You can be a real son of bitch, Brad, you know that?" I said.

"Yeah," he said. "That's quite the popular opinion of late. Still, I'm going to open another bottle of this rather excellent Shiraz and just for that remark, Janice, you won't be getting any."

*

I went outside. Though the power was still out, the storm had not come back, and the night was cool and crisp. Besides, I needed some air, and not only because the villa, with its locked-up windows, was stuffy, the air developing an old, recycled quality. I couldn't wait to get out and clear my head, which frequently and inexplicably felt thick and slow when we were in the house.

I stood on the patio where Kristen and I had seen the pile of leaves swept, it seemed, to form the nonsense word *Manos*. I looked at the spot now, but there was no trace of it nor any sign of the telltale leaves.

I scowled and looked around for more signs of cleaning up, wondering vaguely if the villa had a janitor or gardener who had never been mentioned. Ever since we had arrived and Simon mentioned that someone had left the front gate open, I had been fighting the sensation that there had been someone moving around the grounds just out of my line of sight. I kept stopping to look out, without any clear sense as to why, beyond the size of those floor-to-ceiling windows that made us feel so conspicuous when the lights were on and the world outside was dark. I didn't feel watched exactly, just exposed, and Gretchen's tales of nightmare inquisitors, combined with my own confused sense of people moving around the house at night, added to my unease.

"Jan."

I turned, startled, spilling my wine. It was Marcus.

"Oh God," he said. "I'm sorry. I didn't mean to . . ."

"It's OK," I said. "It's white."

"I thought you didn't like white."

"I don't," I said. "Brad poured it for me and I just took it because . . . who the hell knows. I swear to God, Marcus, I find myself looking around all the time and thinking, *Am I having a good time?*"

He laughed at that.

"Yeah," he said. "I know the feeling."

"Right? I mean, is this something I would have chosen to do if I'd known what it was? Are these people I would have chosen to be friends with if we hadn't bumped into each other on a beach five years ago?"

"I was wondering the same thing."

"I don't mean I dislike them or anything—though, I'll tell you that Brad is getting on my last nerve—but I'm not sure we have anything in common except a kind of historical accident, you know? We met, and now we're friends. Kind of. I don't know how they vote or what they believe in. I don't know if they have interests, hobbies. Not really. But then, maybe friendship is always like that: coincidence that becomes history. You're friends because you're friends."

"I'm almost scared to ask," he said, "how they vote, what they believe. When they reveal anything at all that isn't about their jobs or their damn health clubs, I kind of want to run or cover my ears like a kid, you know?"

"La-la-la, I can't hear you?"

"Exactly," said Marcus. "I feel like I'm tiptoeing around, always one false step away from the kind of fight you don't recover from. I don't really know why. And we should be able to talk, shouldn't we? These are smart, successful people. So why do they seem so deliberately, willfully ignorant? I mean, we're in Crete, for Christ's sake. The place is stuffed with art and history from every period, philosophy, religion, mythology . . . and no one cares."

"I do."

"I know."

He nodded, the darkness and my terrible eyes conspiring to make him little more than a brown face with glasses.

"Come closer," I said. "I'm not being weird. I just can't see you properly."

"No contact lenses, I take it," he said, smiling ruefully.

"Of course not," I said, glad to finally say it. "I lost my fucking glasses in the fucking sea on the first day. I've been blind as a bat ever since."

He tried to look sympathetic, but then he was laughing, doubling up, tears streaming down his face at the absurdity of it. I couldn't blame him, and if it wasn't so fucking infuriating to be almost blind all the time, I'd have been laughing too.

"Sorry," he said at last. "Why didn't you say? We could have found an optician's in Rethymno . . ."

I waved the thought away.

"I'm not spending my vacation at the goddamned eye doctor being tested for a prescription that will arrive—if I'm lucky—on the last day. I have things to do. Lampposts to walk into."

"I have a spare set you could borrow," he said.

"Those huge Harry Caray things? No thanks."

"Might help you get around. Jesus, Jan, we went sightseeing! Knossos. The fort! Did you see any of it?"

"Lots of stone, right?" I said very dryly. "Looks like the Colosseum? I haven't seen that either."

He gave that familiar laugh of his, something between a snort and a sharp exhale.

"God," he mused, gazing up at the night sky. "What a strange little trip this is. Still, we're seeing more than the beach—those of us who *can* see, at least."

"Oh, you're hilarious," I said. "But, yes. Last time we saw almost nothing." The opening presented itself in my head, though I hesitated to explore it. There was, I felt, a risk, though I wasn't sure what it was. "Marcus?"

"What?"

"What happened in the cave?"

"The cave?"

"Last time. On the last day, we went to see . . ."

"Oh, the Dikteon cave where Zeus was born," he said. His voice was flat, the words coming out slow and thoughtful.

"Yes."

"When you say 'what happened' . . . ?"

"Something happened," I said. "I don't know what it was, but I sense it, and I think you know. It changed things. Not just between us, but in the group. What was it?"

He hesitated and looked down, then shook his head.

"I don't know—" he began, but I cut him off.

"Marcus? Come on. Lying isn't your thing."

"I wasn't going to lie," he said, meeting my eyes. "I was going to say that I don't know if we should talk about it. It's all water under the bridge, and I don't think it's my place to share other people's secrets."

I considered him closely.

"Whose?" I said.

"Jan," he warned.

"Who am I going to tell?" I said. "Everyone knows but me. I feel left out."

"Not everyone."

"Kristen," I said. He gave me a quick look. "Kristen doesn't know."

"You know that for sure?" he said. It was a real question, one that came from surprise.

"She says she doesn't."

"That's not the same thing."

"In this case," I said, "I think it is."

"Well, that makes telling you even more awkward," he said.

"Because it's about her?" I said.

He looked away.

"Or it's about Brad," I said, knowing that was it. "What did he do?"

Marcus looked back to the house. You could see every detail of the brightly lit living room, the people inside moving soundlessly around, laughing and drinking, like characters in a movie.

"There's a bench at the end of the garden," he said. "Let's sit down."

There was something ominous about his manner, as there was about walking out of the pool of light on the flagged patio and into the deep shade of the garden, the edge of which was lined with tall black cedars. They loomed, and in their deep shade the temperature dropped a few degrees. I stayed close to him, my shoulder brushing his so that I would have to rely less on my dreadful vision, and as we walked, he started to speak.

"I don't know what you remember," he said. "We all went in pretty much one at a time. It was a long and tough hike up the hillside, and it was already late by the time we got there. The crowds had gone. I remember feeling weary and thirsty before we even went inside. You and I were . . . well, we weren't getting on very well. I don't recall what we were fighting about, or even if we were really fighting, but we went into the cave separately. Melissa had come up on the donkey and was complaining, so Simon left her. I don't know what was going on with Brad and Kristen, but I think he was walking faster than her on purpose . . ."

"On purpose?"

He hesitated, indicating an old wooden bench, and sat down heavily with a sigh. I settled next to him, gazing back toward the house and its TV window, where our friends—if they were our friends—were acting out their silent little party.

"The cave was creepy, remember?" he said. "It went deep into the mountainside, and you had to follow this roped-off stairway, but it was huge, and every time you thought you were at the end, you'd go round some massive stalactite and there was more cavern, more little greenish lanterns set into the rock. Parts of the path were steep, dangerous."

I remembered. The whole place was eerily silent, dripping coldly as it had for centuries off those ancient folds of stone hanging like swags of fabric. It was beautiful, but it was the kind of beauty that felt hard and primal, a beauty in which people are irrelevant and unwelcome. The cave had known history and myth. It *was* history, and in it, you felt insignificant, like one of those bugs that is born, mates, and dies all in one day. And it *was* dangerous, the path punishingly hard and slick with the constantly dripping water of centuries past. Then there were the formations themselves, bulbous and strangely organic-looking; some of them polished like bone; others spongy like vegetables or brains, split open. *Creepy* was right.

"So we're all in there by ourselves," said Marcus, "and I won't lie: I'm a bit freaked out and looking to leave as soon as I've done the basic circuit of the caves. So I'm walking as fast as I dare, and I lose my way, miss a turn or something. But then I think I hear someone around a bend in the passage, so I figure I must be able to get out that way. I go round the corner and there's Brad and Melissa."

He floats it out there like that's all I need and goes quiet.

"Doing what?" I say. I wasn't sure what I had expected, but it wasn't this.

"I don't even really know," he said. "It was dark, and I'm surprised—and they are surprised—and at first I don't even recognize them, and then they break apart, and it's clear that they were doing something they shouldn't, and I apologize and try to get the hell out of there as fast as I can, but the damage is done. On the way out, I bump into Simon, who is looking for them, and he knows—I can just tell that he knows—and I get out of the way before he finds them, but I'm still in the cave when the shouting starts. It echoes back, you know? I couldn't hear what they were saying, but yeah. That was it. That was the end of the holiday, pretty much. The next day everyone was pissed off and quiet. Simon wrecked his Jet Ski. And in the end we all just went home. In a heartbeat, it was all over. I was amazed when I heard from Simon a month or so later, more so when he talked about seeing Brad. I figured they had all worked it out, that it was just some vacation flirtation that got out of hand, and it was all done and mended. But I also figured Kristen knew. I guess not."

I wasn't sure what to say, so for a moment we just sat there. Was I surprised? Not really. Melissa flirted with everyone. It was her basic mode of being. She made people love her, or at least she made them want to be around her. Like that kid at the restaurant. Waiter boy. He couldn't have been more than sixteen, but he positively swooned over her, and we went back time and time again because she liked it. Was I surprised that she had had a bit of a thing with Brad? That it seemed to have gone further than flirting? No. I was only surprised that she had been caught. Mel was careful, and she usually walked a fine line between playfulness and anything that might spark real jealousy in Simon. Maybe Brad had forced the issue. That seemed possible. He still seemed to watch her with a kind of fascination. Maybe that was why no one had told Kristen. Because it wasn't really over. The incident was past and everyone had moved on, but who knew what the hell Brad thought—felt—in his heart of hearts? Kristen deserved better.

Not that my opinion mattered.

"What was Plato's myth of the cave?" I said.

"Not really a myth, more a metaphor," said Marcus. "The people who live in the cave and have never been outside see shadows on the walls cast by the sun. Animals and stuff. Because they've never been outside they think the shadows are the real thing rather than just, you know, shadows. Plato thought life was like that. That all we saw were shadows, but that the real things—the ideal forms of them—existed somewhere else."

"Huh," I said, remembering. I try to decide if it's relevant to what I've just been told and decide it isn't.

"We should go back in," he said.

"Yeah. You know, Marcus, that was very professorial of you just now. The Plato bit, I mean."

"Ha. Is that a compliment?"

"Well, I know you don't like being called professor, so . . ."

"I don't mind it from you," he said.

I smiled up at him and almost—*almost*—went to kiss him. For his part, he dithered as only Marcus can and then haltingly started to walk back to the house, each step closing our window of opportunity a fraction till we were back and had to be part of the group once more.

I thought of that window for the rest of the night, wondering if it was steadily closing as the week came to an end. I didn't know why the possibility of getting back together with Marcus seemed more likely in Crete than it did in Charlotte, where we both lived, but it did, as if the foreignness of the place, its ancient monuments, glorious scenery, and storied towns made everything more exotic, more alive with possibility.

Here, I was vacation Jan, not the Great Deal flow team leader who had so disappointed her friends. It also occurred to me that Marcus was looking better to me here too. I didn't come back intending to rekindle those old, long burned-out fires. Being here had made me consider the possibility.

I wondered if that last part was true or if I was still lying to myself, if I came expressly to be with him and take him home to my apartment like some souvenir statue.

I snorted to myself, and Simon shot me a look as if he thought I was laughing at him, so I smiled and chatted until it was time to go up to bed, and I made a point of not looking at Marcus while Gretchen hung on his every word, of keeping my *good night* to him brief and non-chalant, even as I felt the window closing a little more, so that there was only a crack of light above the sill. I was considering this overwrought metaphor in my room when the screaming started.

Chapter Twenty-Three

"You said the first lie you told was about your sister," said Chad. "Any idea why that would be?"

"No," I said. "I mean, it was a long time ago. I don't remember. I just liked the idea of having a sister."

He considered me in that shrewd way of his that was almost mockingly smug. I didn't like it. I liked it when he listened to me. He was a good listener, and that, in a weird kind of way, was sexy. But his appraising, therapist watchfulness got old fast. He reached for a folder and flicked it open.

"But you did have a sister, didn't you?" he said.

I sat very still. I had not seen that folder before.

"Where did you get that?" I asked.

"Gabriella," he read aloud. "Two years younger than you. Yes? Jan?"

"Yes," I said.

"And you've never mentioned her before."

"No."

"Why not?"

"I didn't think it was relevant," I said. "She died a long time ago."

"In a car accident," he said, consulting his notes, as if just spotting the detail for the first time. "With your mother."

I wanted to be somewhere else now, but the longer I sat there, the steadier his gaze became. I considered getting up, screaming some outrage about his nerve in requesting my old medical records, then storming out and never coming back.

"Jan?" he prompted.

"Yes," I said.

"Your mother and sister both died in a car accident when you were ten."

"Yes."

"And your father . . . ?"

"I never knew him. After my mother died I was raised by my grand-mother till I went away to school."

"That must have been very hard."

"Not really," I said. "I mean, in some ways, I guess. But it was OK."

I don't know why I am thinking about this now. To take my mind off my situation, I guess.

My situation.

It's a grotesquely inadequate phrase.

The pain in my hand is so great that I have to feel to make sure it is still there, that I didn't just tear it out at the root, like the chimp, leaving the hand lodged in the manacle on the wall while I sit here bleeding to death from my ravaged wrist. But it's still attached, though I can barely touch it to be sure.

The brutal surgery had been about as simple and rough as I could imagine. I had just pulled—yanked, really—till enough bones broke that I could drag what was left out of the manacle cuff. It took all my strength, and now I'm horrified by the results. I can move my fingers, just, but my thumb is badly dislocated and probably broken. It hangs loose, resting at a distressing right angle to my palm. It hasn't bled as much as I thought it would, but the skin around my knuckles and the heel of my hand where the damage to the thumb begins has been peeled away. The muscle beneath feels smooth and soft as raw chicken breast.

I have found the sandal I threw away and now sit there beside it in the dark, clutching my broken hand to my breast, waiting for the pain to subside and wondering why now, of all times, my desperate mind keeps straying back to my dead sister.

And Mom.

My memories of her are astonishingly brief and few. I have photographs that I used to get out from time to time in an effort to remember more, but the pictures have eaten all other memories, like the last fat fish in the tank, so that now all I can remember are the pictures. A couple of decades later I still weep for her, but I don't know what exactly it is that I'm missing, and it is the idea of the loss itself that drives my grief. Of my sister Gabby, there is even less.

I sit there, listening to my breathing, trying to decide if the pain in my useless hand is subsiding, and I decide eventually that it isn't. I'm going to have to function without it. I did this to myself to get free. It was crazy not to use that freedom now that I had it.

I get unsteadily to my feet, wonder briefly if there might be any use in holding on to the sandal, and decide there isn't. Too flimsy to use as a weapon. Even considering that is alarming, and as I move quietly to the door, I find myself wondering with a new and different dread if I am going to have to fight my way out.

"Where were you when the accident happened?" asks Chad in my head.

Not now, *I say to myself.* I don't want to do this now. I can't. It's not relevant.

"Are you sure it's not relevant?" says Chad, and this is not memory anymore. He's in my head talking to me now.

"I was at school," I say, the words actually coming out in a rough whisper.

Stop thinking about this, *I insist to myself.*

I am at the door now. I don't think it is locked. I have been trying to escape for what feels like hours, trying to get away from a man who will certainly kill me if he finds I have gotten out of the manacle.

Focus!

The door is cold to the touch, solid and wooden. I hold my crippled left hand behind me and reach for the handle with my right. There's a metal latch, the kind with a lever you press with your thumb while pulling the handle.

It will make noise.

No, *I think.* It won't.

He has come in twice now, and I didn't hear the door latch either time. I make the decision, take a breath, and push the lever. It moves so smoothly and silently that for a second, I don't realize that the door has opened.

Oiled, *I think, and that gives me a moment's pause because it suggests deliberation. Whoever has done this to me planned it.*

For almost a minute I listen for footsteps, movement, breathing. Anything. When I'm as sure as I can be that there's no one standing on the other side, I pull the door open. It should feel good, this escape from the cell, but any relief that action brings stalls immediately as I find the darkness as thick out there as it was inside.

I have no idea where I am.

I move forward, right hand out in front of me, bare feet sliding along the floor, feeling as they go. It feels like stone flags, old and a little uneven, gritty and unswept underfoot.

The villa's cellar.

That still makes sense. I try to orient myself but have no idea which way I'm facing. I take a step, then another, and my outstretched hand runs into something cold and solid.

Another stone wall.

For a second I feel panic and despair rising. My cell was inside another small locked room? But then I move to my right, my left shoulder brushing the wall, my wounded hand pressed softly to my chest, and there is space.

Not a room, then. A corridor or passage.

That's better, at least until the word passage *settles in my head, combines with the darkness and sense of being underground and emerges, less comfortably, as* labyrinth.

Chapter Twenty-Four

It was a woman's voice, and it sounded like it was right outside my door, the sound a high and rising wail that chilled my blood. It was wordless, an abstract keening, and as I blundered out of bed and pulled a robe around me, I tried to decide if the root of the sound was fear or pain.

I had the door unlocked and was through it and into the night-black hallway before I stopped to think of my own safety. The power was still out, and I had come upstairs by the light of a stuttering candle that I had blown out as soon as I got into bed. It sat, cold and forgotten, on my nightstand now as my fingers flicked stupidly at the light switches and got nothing. The cry came again, but it wasn't right outside my door. It was one flight down.

I stumbled down the tower staircase, hand on the bannister for guidance in the gloom, and rounded the corner. The screamer was on the landing, a pearly ghost in the dark, shrieking like a banshee.

Gretchen.

Almost immediately another door kicked open, and someone came out with a flashlight, its beam flitting around and making the darkness wherever it wasn't seem all the deeper.

"What the fuck?" said someone. Brad, I think. The person with the flashlight.

"Gretchen?" said Kristen's voice, soothing and calm. "What's wrong, honey? You have a bad dream?"

She might have been talking to a three-year-old. In the leaping and uneven flashlight, I could just make out Gretchen, her hair down and ragged around her shoulders, clad in a faintly Victorian nightdress, staggering away from her open door and throwing herself against the opposite wall, as if trying to get as far from her room as possible.

Marcus appeared on the stairs behind me, an old-fashioned hurricane lamp held above his head, its amber glow lighting the hall. He was wearing only boxer shorts and glasses but looked wide awake.

"What's going on?" he said.

"Gretchen!" said Brad sharply. Gretchen's wail had dwindled into a feverish sob, but she was still saying nothing. "What happened?"

In answer, like some Gothic specter crouched in the angle of wall and floor, she stabbed a finger in the direction of her bedroom, pointing wordlessly. Marcus strode in, radiating irritation, as Kristen dropped to her and put an arm around her shoulders. The sound of Marcus's commanding footsteps falling suddenly silent was unnerving, like a thunderclap. For a second there was a loaded stillness, and then, his voice low, he said, "Who did this?"

"Did what?" said Brad, pointing the flashlight and moving into the doorway to see. There was another momentary pause, and then he whispered, "Jesus."

"What?" said Kristen, vague anxiety turning quickly to panic. "Brad, what is it?"

Brad said nothing, but I heard him moving around, and then he was back in the doorway, the flashlight splashing the hallway, and in his hands were pieces of colored fabric, mostly very pale—cream and ivory and satiny silver—and other bits of navy and pink and black, some trimmed with lace, some no more than thongs . . .

It was underwear. Gretchen's, presumably. I frowned, baffled, and then I saw. Brad held a sample out in one hand and fixed them in the beam of the flashlight in his other hand so that everything else seemed to dissolve into blackness and there were only Gretchen's ravaged panties, every pair cut to ribbons.

"We have to search the house," said Marcus.

We were all downstairs now. Brad had roused Melissa and Simon from the master suite on the other side of the house, and they had joined us, bleary eyed, caught between bafflement, irritation, and alarm. The last of those quickly won out. Simon put the generator back on, and the rest of us buzzed around Gretchen like bees jarred from their hive and unable to settle.

"The doors are all locked," said Simon. "I checked."

"So he's still inside," said Marcus, as if that proved his point.

Simon looked away. He glanced at Melissa and something passed between them. I caught her puzzled frown and the minute shake of her head.

"What?" Marcus demanded. He was as close to losing it as I had ever seen him.

"No one could get in," Simon muttered, shaking his head and still not meeting his eyes, as if he didn't want to talk about it.

"Meaning what?" said Marcus.

"Nothing," said Simon, his voice low, his gaze wandering to Gretchen.

"You think she did it herself?" said Marcus, incredulous.

"That, or one of us did it," said Brad, as close to nonchalant as he could get. Kristen had gathered Gretchen onto the couch, and Brad had flopped heavily into an armchair, his watchful face unreadable. The rest of us were still standing awkwardly, not knowing what to do or say.

"Is that what you think?" asked Marcus, fixing Simon with a defiant stare. "That it was one of us?"

"I don't know."

"You don't know?"

"No, Marcus," Simon shot back, his voice rising. "I don't know. You have a problem with that?"

"You two want to save the pissing contest for another time?" said Melissa.

"All I'm saying is that we should look around," said Marcus, "rather than, you know, assuming one of us is a colossal asshole."

"Or a liar," said Brad.

I stared at him. His gaze was on Gretchen, but it was impossible not to feel like he was talking about me.

"Gretchen, hon," said Kristen, and it struck me that Marcus was right. Her British accent vanished when she wasn't thinking about it. "Tell us exactly what happened."

Gretchen groaned and turned her face into Kristen's shoulder like a weary toddler.

"Come on," Kristen coaxed. "It will help to get it all out, and then we can get it all sorted."

Gretchen gazed at her, her watery eyes huge, then moistened her lips.

"I took a shower before bed," she said. "You all crashed, but I was still awake, so I took a shower. Then I thought I would choose my clothes for tomorrow, you know? Lay them out. Something cute, and . . . anyway, I opened my suitcase. And there it was."

She dissolved into tears.

So I hadn't been asleep, or not for long, when it happened. I frowned, trying to get my head round it. I felt dazed, half-asleep, and almost as taken aback by the idea of someone laying out her clothes for the morning as I was by what had been done to those clothes.

"So it happened while she was in the shower?" said Marcus. "Gretchen, when did you last look in your case? When was the last time you saw that everything was . . . OK?"

Gretchen shrugged and shook her head wearily.

"This morning, I guess," she said. "When I got up."

"So it could have happened anytime today," Marcus concluded.

"Why would anyone do this?" she said. "What did I do to them?"

As she said it, her gaze strobed across the room, found me, and lingered. I stared at her. For a second I tried to ignore it, but as she continued to stare, the silence became awkward, accusatory.

"Wait," I said. "You think that I . . . ?"

"Did you?" she said, and suddenly she was quite together, quite calm, and both her wet eyes and her cracked voice had a touch of steel.

"No!" I said. "Why the hell would I do that?"

"I think you know why," said Gretchen.

Everyone was looking at me. What had been a dull, smoldering anxiety in my head had suddenly roared into bright, hot flame.

This can't be happening.

"What?" I said. "You can't be serious!"

"You're jealous of Marcus and me," she said.

I was so stunned that for a second I just gaped at her. No one else spoke.

"What?" I demanded.

"You know," she said, snakeskin quiet.

"Marcus," I said. "Tell her!"

"Tell her what?" he said. He was quiet and still. Wary. His manner gave nothing away, and his uncertainty turned my smoldering anxiety to anger. It flared white hot in my chest.

"Tell her I wouldn't do that!" I shouted. "You know I wouldn't. Marcus, you can't think . . . I didn't. I wouldn't! Why would I . . . ?"

"You didn't like me near him," said Gretchen. "I could tell. Everyone could tell."

I felt the sudden embarrassment in the room and knew she was right, they had all thought it, discussed it . . .

"No," I said. "You're wrong."

"Jan," said Melissa. "I get it, but this is really not the way . . ."

"Shut up!" I shouted. "All of you. I said I didn't do it, OK?"

"Now, Jan." Simon this time, also still and quiet but deliberate, like some guy in a movie defusing a bomb. "This isn't the time for one of your stories."

I stare at him, breathless, tears starting in my eyes, and then I look to Marcus, who had said they didn't know about me, not really. He looks down, ashamed, though whether that's about me or him, I can't tell.

"I didn't," I manage, crying openly now. "I would never . . ."

And I mean it. I didn't do it. I swear to God, I didn't.

"We can fix this," said Melissa, turning between Gretchen and me and smiling. "Tomorrow we can head into town, buy you some new things, Gretchen, and then we'll have a little chat, just us girls, maybe a few drinks, and then—"

"No," said Gretchen. "I need to call the airline. I'm leaving."

Melissa protested, of course, said it would all be better in the morning, but Gretchen stuck to her guns, watching me from under her bangs as if I might attack at any moment, and at last the call was made on the ancient rotary phone in the foyer. Kristen sat with her on the tower stairs as Gretchen talked, but she met my eyes and shrugged with noncommittal exhaustion.

So the jury is still out on me.

Simon and Melissa huddled in the stairwell to their room, then went through the motions of searching the house for intruders while I stood at the bottom and stared, unseeing, at the large tapestry that hung in the foyer, all faded birds in threadbare green and gold. Having found nothing, Brad, who had gone with them, armed with a knife from the kitchen, went back to bed—something of a relief to Kristen, I think, since his patience was already worn thin—and Marcus drifted apart like a satellite in high orbit, just barely connected to what was going on. Once I caught his eye and took a step toward him, but he shook his head minutely and I stopped, trying to decide if he wanted to keep whatever conversation we might have for a more private moment, or if he was just done talking to me.

It was impossible not to feel betrayed by the world and him most of all, and the look I gave him was less imploring than it had been and more accusatory.

You'd think that tales about boys crying wolf would make me immune to this sort of thing, but it didn't. It was an obvious downside of being a known embroiderer of the truth, a distorter, a misleader, that even when you were being absolutely honest, the best you could hope for was a kind of wary détente, a truce between battles while everyone waited for independent confirmation that you weren't, in fact, lying your ass off. So I should have known better than to be hurt by Marcus's careful distance and by the way no one had really come to my defense. It shouldn't have been a surprise that my word counted, apparently, for nothing, but it still hurt.

It hurt like ice pressed deep into my heart. Like fire. Like rejection.

As to the offense itself, anyone could have done it. We had all had the opportunity to slip into Gretchen's room—she apparently didn't keep it locked—at any number of times after we got home from Rethymno or even before we left this morning. If someone had broken in, it could have been done while we were out, but no one seemed to be taking that possibility too seriously. Nothing was missing, and the attack—if that was what it was—felt specific. Personal. There was nothing I could say. The more earnest I was in my denials, the more I looked like a stone-cold lying bitch. After a while, I just stopped talking.

I sat on the stone steps to the tower, caught between wanting to flee to my room and wanting to be supportive of the woman who had blamed me, as if that would help. I knew I couldn't sleep, though I was weary to the point of exhaustion, and I was, ironically, more afraid than the others. They all thought they knew who had gone into Gretchen's room and cut up her clothes, an act that was more than malicious. It was voyeuristic. Pornographic. It was frightening, particularly for me, the only person in the house who didn't think they knew who had done it, the only one who knew for a fact that it wasn't me.

Because it wasn't. I had never even been in her room before. I certainly hadn't rooted through her things, cut them up, an act at once petty and deeply, troublingly sadistic.

I watched the others coming and going, avoiding my eyes. An hour passed. Maybe more. I spoke to no one, staying where I was, gazing into the foyer as the others murmured in the living room. I was still sitting there when Gretchen walked in, making for the phone. She had already changed her flight, so I hadn't expected to see her here, and I think she thought I'd gone to bed. She froze in the act of picking up the receiver, staring at me, though I couldn't see the expression on her face at this distance.

"I know you think it was me, Gretchen," I said. "And I know you think I'm jealous of the way you are with Marcus . . ."

"You are," she said, not moving.

I hung my head, not wanting to say this, not wanting to say anything, but then looked up and nodded.

"Yes," I said. "I am. But I didn't go in your room. I didn't cut up your . . ."

She started walking over to me, a sudden, brisk stride that got me to my feet in case she was going to take a swing at me. I braced myself, but instead of hitting me, she got hold of me by the shoulders and pulled me close.

"I know," she whispered.

I was dumbfounded.

"But you said . . . ?"

"Yes," she said, checking over her shoulder to make sure no one else was in earshot. "I'm sorry. I had to."

"You did it yourself?" I said.

"No!"

"But you know who did?"

She shook her head, but it was less a denial than it was a pushing away of the question.

"I have to get out of this house," she said.

"What?" I said. I couldn't get my head around how radically the conversation had shifted. "Why?"

"I can't be here anymore," she said. She was still quiet but was, if anything, even more hysterical than when she had first found her shredded underwear. She was trembling, her grip on my shoulders tight, each finger digging into my flesh like a clamp. "You don't understand, but I can't be here. It's not safe."

"Not safe?" I said. "What do you mean?"

"We're in danger. Not just me. All of us. You, I think, most of all."

PART 3

TARTARUS

Theseus and his companion ventured into that point of the underworld known as Tartarus through a secret way and came to the palace of Hades, who ruled that fearful place. They made their request to take Persephone back to the world of the living and Hades seemed to consider their request, but then the king of the dead suggested they sit down to rest themselves and they realized—too late—that the seats were the Chairs of Forgetfulness. Their skin immediately bonded to the chairs so completely that they could not get up again without tearing their flesh away. Snakes surrounded them and, with Hades looking on, Theseus was lashed by the Furies and mauled by the great three-headed dog, Cerberus, so that it seemed they would be trapped there in deepest pain and misery for ever.

—*Preston Oldcorn*

Chapter Twenty-Five

"Where were you when your mother and sister died in the car wreck?" says Chad.

Not this again. We don't have time for this.

"I told you. I was at school."

"Liar," says the Chad in my head. *"You were in the car. Weren't you, Jan? You were in the car."*

I start to deny it, then stop, suddenly unsure.

I keep very still, eyes shut, feeling for the truth like it is an old dog that cannot be relied upon not to bite. And then I see it, remember it, the darkness, the smell of oil and gasoline, electricity and blood. It all comes back and, for a moment, I'm stunned by the fact of it, as if I hadn't known till now, even though I had, however many fathoms deep I had buried it.

"Yes," I say to myself. *"I was in the car."*

"But you survived."

"Yes."

"Barely a scratch on you," says my imaginary Chad. *"Your mom was driving. You were in the back with your sister. You were both buckled in, but when the car came off the road, when it rolled down the ditch and into the tree, the left side took the brunt of the damage."*

"Yes."

"You were sitting on the right."

"Yes."

"Barely a scratch on you."

"What do you want me to say?"

"Nothing," says imaginary Chad. "I'm just wondering if what you say you told your first lie about . . . the reason you lied about having a sister—a living sister, that is—was because you felt guilty. She died. You walked away. Motherless. That can't feel right to a child. Kids. They always feel responsible for what happens in the world. Step on a crack, break your mother's—"

Stop.

I can't think about this. The pain and the fear and the cumulative exhaustion have gotten to my nerves. I'm losing it just when I need to concentrate, to be on my guard. He's out there, somewhere. The Minotaur, stalking the labyrinth. Hunting for me.

Focus.

I'm out of my cell, but I'm still underground and in the dark. I have to find a way out. I can't see, and I don't know what's there, but it feels like passages spreading in all directions, turning in on themselves like a great hard-angled knot, all blind alleys and long, winding false hopes burrowing back into the center. I think of Daedalus, who made the wooden bull for Pasiphaë and built the maze that housed her dreadful offspring, and I remember what James Joyce called him: the "old artificer."

Artificer.

I had puzzled over the word in a corner of the Wilson library one day, when I was in college, thinking of the strange way it evoked different but related things, combining them in a slippery gray fog that I instinctively—if unhealthily—liked:

Art.

Artisan.

Artifice.

Artificiality.

I wrote them out just like that, amazed by the neat way the words made a picture, a right-angle triangle like a half Christmas tree. I thought about the slim distinction between the base of the tree and the star on the top, between fiction and lies. It comes back to me now, and I think, wildly, perhaps still delirious from the pain in my hand, "I am the great artificer, Jan, the Cretan liar. I am Daedalus. This is my labyrinth, and I will find the way out."

I move blindly along the stone corridor, listening to the echo of my shallow breathing as it bounces off the stone. The air feels the same as the cell. Smells the same. Maybe a little more dank. The stone flags underfoot are irregular, their edges rounded with age, their surfaces coated with dust and grit fine as sand. And then, without warning, there's something else. I feel it with my foot, a metallic coldness. I drop to my haunches and feel with my good hand, registering the long iron strip set into the ground and feeling over to the right to find the other I know will be there.

Railroad tracks.

So I'm in a tunnel?

This throws me. I've seen no sign of a railway system on Crete. In fact, I'd swear there wasn't one. I run my good hand along the steel. The sides are furred with rust, but the tops are worn by use, though not, I think, recent use.

A railway.

My mind tightens around the idea, trying to squeeze the strangeness out of it. Some kind of minor mountain funicular for the tourists and skiers? It doesn't seem likely.

Or a mine.

It could be one of those old underground cart railways that I know only from Wile E. Coyote and Indiana Jones. I guess they are real things, but has there been much mining in Crete? I kick myself for not learning about the place before I came and wish Marcus were here. He would know. Not that he'd want to talk to me.

I am remembering more and more about the last few days. Awful though my imprisonment has been, it has somehow cleared my head. The longer I am down here—in this mine or whatever it is—the more I feel like myself in ways I haven't for hours, even if some of the memories that come with that clarity are things I'd rather not recall. I had made up with Marcus, gotten past the whole lying-about-my-sister thing, but then it had all gone wrong again.

Gretchen's underwear . . .

It should be funny, but even down here in the dark, picking my way along some underground railway line and listening for the return of my sadistic captor, it makes me shudder. I wonder if the two people—the one who chained me up and the one who ravaged Gretchen's clothes—are the same person.

I pause. I have just noticed that the rails beneath my feet are sloping gradually down. I am sure of it. If this is a mine, I am going deeper, and while that might give me somewhere to hide, it probably won't get me out. I need to go the other way.

I turn carefully, using the rails to orient myself in the dark. I am pretty sure my cell opens onto the track at a right angle, that if I follow the lines back the way I came, I might go right past it. I hold on to that idea as if it is a lantern so the prospect of turning back won't feel quite so much like failure, like a return to the place where I was entombed.

I pick my way back along the tunnel, my toes half gripping the edges of the deep-set rails so that I don't lose my way. It seems even darker here than it had in the cell, the kind of darkness where up, down, left, and right mean nothing. If I stumble and fall or spin around, I will have no idea which way I am facing without the railroad tracks to guide me.

Like waking up in the car, your cheek against a window smeared with torn grass and dirt . . .

I keep walking, slowly but steadily, deliberately, not knowing whether I am going away from my enemy or toward him, knowing only that I need to keep moving, to feel like I am doing something to get out. He could be back any moment, his bull-headed form looming in the blackness, muzzle wet, nostrils wide and flaring with each breath, horns spread wide as the hallway . . .

No. The railroad tracks might be my Ariadne's thread, but my Minotaur is just a man.

Simon.

Do I really believe that? It seems impossible, and the evidence is circumstantial at best. A whiff of oil and gasoline? A facility for scuba gear? That's nothing. It could be any of us, including the women, though that is harder to picture than, say, the idea of Brad as psychological torturer.

That is much easier.

But why? Unless this is all just some psychopathic freak-out and my captor has no rational motive, none of this makes sense. I can't make it look any more rational with Brad's face under that Minotaur-head scuba mask than I can with Simon's.

I think again of Manos. Or did I mean Minos, the king whose Knossos palace was the home of the Minotaur myth? Or Midas, the king whose touch turned everything to gold and whose name Melissa had confused with the name of our hotel so very long ago in some sunny, idyllic land when life had been so good and full of promise . . .

Manos, Minos, Midas. None of it helps.

The tracks beneath my bare feet arc sharply to the left. I press on, my right hand out in front of me, from time to time reaching out to the side to see if the tunnel is narrowing, but I can't reach the wall. My left hand continues to burn and throb with the slightest movement, so I keep it lightly pressed to my sternum and can feel the steady pulsing of my heart.

The ground underfoot changes. There is suddenly more debris, more fragments of stone, and twice I kick against loose metal objects. I stoop to one and test it with my fingers. It is a long metal bolt, its thread rough with rust. I stand up, take two more steps, and bark my shin against a hard barrier that runs across the track. Another meets my waist. I feel along it and find a pair of bulbous metal buffers directly above the rails that stop me going any further.

End of the line.

Chapter Twenty-Six

Gretchen's second phone call was to a taxi company. Simon offered to drive her, but she said that everyone had done enough and that she just needed to go. She thanked them. She took her suitcase, packed for her and brought downstairs by Marcus, and collected her brand-new leather purse from Melissa, and sat silently on the front step till the cab's headlights lit the driveway.

It was all weirdly fast. No one talked to me, and Gretchen pointedly left me out of the series of hugs she gave before running down to the taxi, but as she stooped to her case, she shot a look back to me. She held my eyes just long enough to show intent, to remind me what she had said, despite her apparent play acting to the others. Then she was climbing into the back of the car and roaring off into the night.

Simon closed the front door and it boomed through the foyer. He threw the bolts and turned the key, and then there was, after the flurry of activity that had filled the last couple of hours, a strained and empty silence. I wanted to tell them what Gretchen had said to me, if only the part about her not believing I was the one who had torn up her underwear, but I knew that would just sound like another lie, and anger flickered through my head, adding to all the other questions that centered on Gretchen. Why hadn't she told them? Why had she so deliberately misled them if she hadn't thought me guilty? It was OK for her, jetting back to the States, while I toughed out another three days as the pariah, the deranged obsessive out of a fucking Brontë novel. Maybe I should have gone with her.

For a second I considered the possibility, but paying change fees on three separate flights, assuming I could get them, wouldn't just stretch my budget to the breaking point, it would do a number on my finances for the next couple of months. It would also—and I couldn't believe I actually felt this—feel rude, walking out on the others, on Simon and Melissa, who had spent so much time and energy hosting the reunion. And then there was Marcus.

No. You can't leave yet. Not with things as they are. Get through this, and everything will get better.

But even with this half-assed resolve in place, I had caught something of Gretchen's fear and felt sure that someone in the house knew much more than they were letting on.

We're in danger. Not just me. All of us. You, I think, most of all.

I didn't know what to do with that. Maybe Gretchen was the deranged obsessive. Maybe she had felt thwarted in her attempt to bag Marcus and had staged the whole absurd pantomime for dramatic effect.

Maybe. But I didn't think so. The fear that had been writhing in my belly like a basket of snakes since Gretchen's strange confession on the stairs now hardened and chilled till it felt like a stone in my gut, weighing me down, a constant, pulling dread.

"I don't want to go upstairs," said Kristen. "Can we sleep down here? All of us?"

"What about Brad?" said Marcus.

"What about him?" Kristen replied. "Apparently, he's fine where he is. I'm not. Not there, I mean. I want to stay here."

"OK," said Simon, carefully, like he was setting down a fragile vase or pitcher. "We can do that. Everyone?"

Melissa nodded. Marcus shrugged and said, "OK." Simon turned to me, and everyone turned with him.

"Jan?" he said.

"If I'm welcome," I said.

If I had expected a chorus of encouragement, I was disappointed. No one spoke. Kristen frowned, uncertain. Marcus tipped his chin up, his face blank. Melissa looked hawkish.

"Of course you're welcome," said Simon.

I didn't feel it, but I also didn't think there was anything I could do about it. There was certainly nothing I could say. So I went up with Kristen and Simon to get my bedding, all three of us going into each bedroom, not talking, and then rolled out my duvet and pillows in front of the hearth in the living room. Brad came down with Kristen, but he didn't speak, merely throwing himself onto the couch away from her and covering himself with a blanket they had found in a hall closet, rolling to bury his face in the cushions. Kristen watched him, her lips so thin they seemed to vanish, then made herself a bed on the other side of the room. Marcus curled up in an armchair. He had always been able to sleep in almost any position. He did not look at me. I considered marching over to him, yelling at him, slapping him, but I didn't.

When you lie all the time, you get used to people losing faith in you, even the ones you want most desperately to believe you, and you know in your heart that it's your own fault. Not in the present, but in the past, where all those little evasions and misdirections burrowed into the bedrock of your relationship and left it prone to tremor, sinkhole, and collapse. I couldn't really blame him.

Except, of course, that I could and I did. I told him I never lied to him anymore, and I meant it. He knew me well enough. He should have trusted me.

I looked at him now, and he seemed more than sad and confused. He looked distraught. Bereft. Suddenly I wondered if I hadn't been the only one hoping to rebuild our friendship, our love, and a new impulse to speak to him, to make it all right, ran through me like fire. I was trying to think what I would say when he shifted in his chair, nestling, his face turned away from me, and I knew that the moment had passed.

Simon didn't want to run the generator just to keep a nightlight on, so he left the hurricane lamp burning on the stone counter in the adjoining kitchen, making sure there was nothing flammable close by. It lent the room a soft and shaded glow, like firelight, and might, in other circumstances, have been warm and evocative. Even romantic.

Not now.

"Should one of us . . . I don't know, keep watch?" said Marcus, stirring.

"It's not the *Lord of the* fucking *Rings*, professor," said Brad.

Marcus scowled and looked away, then turned quickly back and said to Melissa, "Did Gretchen spend the whole afternoon with you?"

"What?" said Melissa, who was already lying down.

"You went shopping together when the rest of us went to the fort. Did she stay with you the whole time?"

"No," said Melissa. "Just an hour or so. I felt like doing my own thing so . . ."

So she dumped her. That sounded like Mel.

"You know where she went? What she did?"

"No," said Melissa. "Why?"

"No reason," said Marcus. "Just wondering."

"Can we go to sleep, please, Nancy Drew?" said Brad. "Miss Marple, or whoever the fuck you are. Or would you like to arrest the butler?"

Marcus said nothing and shifted again, closing his eyes. Brad settled down and started snoring softly almost immediately, but I lay awake, eyes open, going over and over what I had heard and seen, listening to the house settling. Simon fell asleep next, I thought, and within another half hour or so, I was fairly sure I was the only one still awake. I kept quite still, watching the black cedars swaying through the tall windows, listening for footsteps upstairs, for the sound of a door opening or closing, for anything—*anything*—out of place.

There was nothing.

As I lay there, I tried to make sense of Gretchen's words but I couldn't. People were keeping secrets, I was sure of that, but I couldn't grasp how we might be in real danger. Even the underwear incident, nasty though it was in every sense, felt more like a mean-spirited and possibly deviant prank than a threat. Melissa had said as much to Gretchen as she tried to talk her into staying. Gretchen had been appalled, said Mel was blowing it off like it was just a kind of bad-taste joke. Melissa had abandoned the argument gracelessly, making it very clear in her slamming and banging around the house as she helped prepare for Gretchen's departure that she didn't approve of this running off to the airport. It was, unsurprisingly, Brad who added his own hard and dismissive brand of wit to the matter as he made himself toast the following morning.

"You know what I always say," he mused to whoever might be listening. "It's no good crying over spilled panties."

He grinned to himself. Kristen, still in her makeshift bed, sat up and glared at him for a long moment, then lay down again, teeth clenched, eyes fixed on nothing.

The rest of us got up slowly and quietly, all the energy and fun long gone, the weight of my supposed guilt hanging over the room like a storm cloud. It reminded me of the final day of our last visit, the day after the cave.

I went to the bathroom upstairs and checked my room, half expecting to find my suitcase ransacked, my clothes torn to shreds and patches, but there was no sign that anyone had been in, and with the window bathing the room in golden morning light, it was hard to believe that we had been too scared to sleep upstairs.

In fact I had barely slept at all. The floor, in spite of the comforter, had been hard, and with my mind as preoccupied as it was, and with one ear open for the sound of unwelcome movement in the house, I had hardly shut my eyes. Bizarrely, however, I felt less tired than I had the previous morning, and my mind was clear. I confess to hesitating before drawing the shower curtain, but there was no Norman Bates lurking, and I emerged comparatively refreshed and determined to do one thing.

I had to bide my time because Marcus was, predictably, avoiding me. This was an old strategy of his when there were problems or the possibility of confrontation. I used to call him Old Ostrich Face, because of his ability to bury his head in the sand when things got rough, but since my coping mechanism involved inventing an entirely fictitious version of the universe, I guess I didn't really have the high ground. In the end, I snuck up when he was taking his shower and ambushed him as he came out.

"I didn't do it, you know," I said to him.

"Jan, I don't know what to think right now," he said. "So I think it's best if you just let me be."

"I told you I'd never lie to you."

"Yes," he said. "You did."

It was almost an accusation, and I decided I couldn't be bothered arguing the point. Instead I got right to what I should have asked him the day before.

"What does the word *Manos* mean to you?" I said.

The question caught him utterly off guard. He blinked and leaned back, as if trying to refocus his gaze on me, then shook his head.

"Manos?" he said. "Never heard it. Why? What is it?"

"Not sure," I said. "Something I read."

"No," he said. "Means nothing to me."

You remember your firsts, especially where romance is concerned. First love. First kiss. First true sexual encounter. You remember them usually because you didn't really know what they were till they happened. They open up a rush of new thoughts and sensations, like you've stumbled on a world you hadn't believed in till you found yourself in it. The feelings that come with that new world may be the beginning of a long sequence that eventually becomes familiar and staid, but they begin as surprise.

It makes sense then that I could think of nothing else to say. Marcus had never lied to me before.

~

I returned to my room to breathe, though I knew the air would be stale and stuffy. I needed a moment alone to process what had just happened. I couldn't explain how I knew that Marcus had lied, but I knew it in my heart because I knew him. I knew his face. I knew the involuntary tic of his cheek, eye, and lip muscles. He had never lied to me before, not really, but he had tried to conceal a straight flush across the poker table, had pretended not to take notice when I remarked on a particular perfume three weeks before Christmas, and had tactfully buried any sign of disappointment when I made a less than successful meal or—exhausted from getting up before dawn—started to drop off during a date. Those were all long ago, but I remembered them like my arm remembered how to catch a ball, though I hadn't practiced it for years. Some things didn't change. The hesitation, the blank look, the slightly evasive gaze, the repetition, the stupid questions (*"Manos? Never heard it. Why? What is it?"*), these were his tells, and I could read them like headlines.

He was lying.

But why?

I snatched up the phone I hadn't touched in days and tried to find a signal, moving to the window and waving the thing around. No bars. No Wi-Fi. I opened a search engine and typed in *Manos*, but when I hit the "Go" button, it just cycled and cycled. I was staring irritably at it when I heard a shrill and distant tinkling.

A telephone.

The telephone. There was only one in the house that worked.

I left the bedroom and moved along the hall to the stairs and was halfway down when I heard someone pick up.

"Hello?"

Kristen. There was a momentary pause, and then all her quiet reserve was replaced with earnestness and concern.

"What? Slow down," she said. "What happened?"

In the silence that followed I heard other people coming from the living room to listen.

"How?" said Kristen. "And you spoke to the airline?"

Gretchen. It had to be.

"Let me talk to her," said Melissa in a low voice.

"Hold on," said Kristen. I wasn't sure which of them she was talking to. "She took the wrong bag. Those damn purse things you bought. She has your passport, not hers. They won't let her on the plane."

"Oh, for God's sake!" Brad said. "Have her change the name on the ticket to match Mel's passport. She can pretend to be you. There's no finger printing in immigration. She'll be fine."

"And what about me?" Melissa whispered back. "How do I get home?"

"On her passport! Easy peasy."

"That's massively illegal, Brad," said Kristen. "Hold on, honey," she said, brightly to Gretchen, "we're just kicking some ideas around."

"No one's gonna know," he said. "They even look alike."

"That's absurd," said Melissa.

"You have a better idea?" said Brad. I was still halfway down the stairs, paused now, for fear that if I suddenly appeared, it would look like I was eavesdropping, which, of course, I was.

"Better than illegal immigration?" snapped Melissa. "Er. Yeah. Reschedule the flight."

"She'd have to wait till tomorrow," said Kristen. "No more available planes out today."

"So she waits a day," said Melissa.

"She doesn't want to," said Kristen, quietly now. I suspected she had the mouthpiece of the phone pressed against her.

"Tell her we'll come pick her up and get her there in plenty of time tomorrow," said Melissa.

"I think she's happy to stay in a hotel in Heraklion," said Kristen.

"It's no trouble . . . ," said Melissa.

"I think she'd prefer to stay in a hotel," Kristen clarified.

"Give me the phone," said Melissa.

"Mel, she's upset," said Kristen.

"Give me the damn phone."

I heard Kristen sigh. There was a flurry of movement, and I should have known to go back up the stairs. Or down. Anything but stand where I was, where Kristen could see me as she came, her face flushed and annoyed, round the corner and up the stairs. Her eyes met mine, processed my lurking, then she kept coming, up and past me. I heard her footsteps on the landing and then the slam of her bedroom door.

I breathed out, only dimly aware of Melissa's cooing, sympathetic noises into the phone in the foyer below, then came down the rest of the way to find them all grouped around the telephone table like a collection of statues, straining to hear. Simon was leaning against the tapestry, Marcus against the door to the basement where the generator was. They saw me. Their eyes went back to Melissa and to the phone, as if I had intruded on something private.

⌒

"I'll go with you," I said.

It had taken Melissa twenty minutes to talk Gretchen into coming back. I hadn't listened so I didn't know what she'd said. In fact, she had urged everyone away so they could talk "properly," whatever that meant, and when she returned to the living room, it was with the look of someone who had just finished a long-distance run in a competitive time.

"Not sure you're the one she wants to see right now," said Melissa, her smile brittle.

"Perhaps not," I said. "But I want to see her. Give me a moment to talk to her and she'll come back a lot happier. She may not even want to leave tomorrow."

I'm not sure why I added that last part. It was instinct. My gut said that Melissa didn't want Gretchen to go: that it was important she stayed the whole allotted week. Maybe it was an ego thing. Mel, the perfect host, didn't want people fleeing her party . . .

"Why?" she said, hawklike again. "What are you going to tell her?"

I swallowed, conscious of everyone listening.

"Why I did what I did," I said.

It was as if the house itself had sighed, a collective breath, a little release of the pressure that had been building up overnight. Melissa gave me another calculating look, processing what I had said, then threw her arms around me.

"Oh, Jannie," she said. "It's OK, sweetheart."

I shuddered, suddenly overcome with real emotion, and squeezed my eyes shut as I buried my face in her neck. When I opened them again, I expected to see relief, contentment in every face, not just because the crisis was past but because their suspicions had proved correct, and that meant that all was right with the world. But that was not what I saw. Not from all of them, anyway.

Marcus looked as unsure as he had before. Kristen looked flat-out stunned and puzzled. And Brad was staring at me with fierce and terrifying malevolence.

Chapter Twenty-Seven

I explore the chamber where the railway line ends, but there's no way out, just a roughly cut wall of stone behind the buffer. I have to go back, though how far I have to go before I find another route, I have no way of knowing.

For a moment I squat between the steel rails, my back to the buffer, my hands clasped under my chin and my eyes squeezed shut like a child in prayer, which is, I suppose, pretty close to what I am.

I am Daedalus, the great artificer, *I think*. This is my labyrinth. I will find the way out.

It's stupid, and desperate, but it holds back the fear like the iron bracing of some great door as the ram batters against it, and from the stillness comes the beginning of a realization.

The curve. I remember the track suddenly curving this way. Perhaps if I got back to that point and go straight, I'll find that the room I am in now is a kind of siding, a place to store trucks or a small locomotive. Maybe going straight will lead me to a door, to stairs, to safety.

So I get up again and take three cautious steps, arms outstretched, toes feeling for the steel rails set into the stone floor. I can feel the gentle arc of the turn as I walk, but then . . .

What was that?

The tunnel is so silent that every movement I make seems to fill it with sound loud as thunder, the fractional skittering of gravel underfoot, the shifting of my dress, the roar of my breathing, my heart. But I am sure there was something else, something sharper that came from . . . where? Farther along the hall but also somehow above me. It echoed, furring the edge of the sound, but I feel certain that it had been short and crisp, like the snap of a door latch.

I listen, and at first there is nothing, so I eventually raise my right foot to take another step; but then it comes again and is followed by the short, staccato sound of shoes on stone steps.

I freeze once more, straining to hear, to pinpoint the source of the noise.

And then I see the flashlight bouncing crazily off the walls that are a mixture of soft-yellow stone and concrete block. The rails gleam where the light hits them some fifteen yards from where I am standing.

Whoever is holding the light hasn't appeared yet, and I am caught between hope and despair.

I open my mouth to shout.

Help! I was trapped but I got out. Show me the way up!

But I don't say anything. Instead, instinctively, I take several long, silent strides back along the track, still facing the person with the light. My feet are almost soundless, and I plant them carefully, exaggerating the downward movement so I don't inadvertently kick something that will make a noise. The buffer hits me in the small of my back. I grasp it with my right hand and hold on as I go round it and drop to my knees. The buffer is braced with diagonal struts, and I almost lose my balance as I get between them and press myself small and close to the gravelly stone floor, breathing fast.

The footsteps have not altered. The flashlight still feels unguided, almost casual. But then, abruptly, everything stops.

He has reached my cell. That was where he was going, and now he can see that the door is open.

Should I have closed it?

It doesn't matter.

He is perhaps twenty yards away. No more. I hear his uncertainty, his confusion in the uncanny stillness. Then there is movement again, urgent now, panicked, and the light stabs this way and that, so I bury my head in my hands and try to make myself invisible behind the buffer. I hide my hands and face and hope he won't make sense of what he can still see.

Keep still.

I do, and in my peripheral vision I sense the flashlight raking the tunnel. The passage is narrower than I had imagined and low ceilinged, no larger than the inside of a train car. Behind the buffer it stops, the blocks ending in a wall that looks like solid natural rock. For the merest fraction of a second, the light hits my skin and the hem of my dress. It's yellow, and I remember it immediately, though it is filthy now. The light moves on, and I can almost smell his furious alarm, his disbelief.

But then he calms, and the flashlight begins to move more carefully. There is almost complete silence again, and I realize slowly that he has seen something, something worthy of close inspection.

When I am sure the light is not turned toward me, I risk a look over the buffer. He has the flashlight aimed at the ground and seems to have dropped to his haunches. I can see the cell door open. It is one of three, though the others are closed. The light fixes on the floor and by the overspill I see, silhouetted and unfocused though it is, the size of him, the bulk of his body and head. All the old terror floods back at the strangeness of the sight as my hindbrain shrieks

Minotaur!

But then he moves, and I realize with another shock that his body above the waist seems so large because he's wearing something, something that goes with the mask on his face.

An air tank.

He's not just wearing the scuba mask to hide his face. He's wearing the complete breathing apparatus.

From my hidden vantage I stare, and that's when I realize what he's doing. He's seen something on the cell floor. I feel the slickness clotting around the thumb of my left hand, and I know what he's seen.

Blood.

Not a lot, but enough. I've left a trail.

Chapter Twenty-Eight

It was just Simon and me. I had hoped Marcus would come. Or Kristen. But for all Melissa's words of understanding and forgiveness, they were all still wary of me and I couldn't blame them. However much they might pity me, who would want to be friends with someone who might break into your room and cut up your underwear? They might tolerate me. They might even accept me, look after me, but you can't love someone this fucked up.

If Marcus had come, I told myself, I would have found some way to tell him my confession had been false, but that may have done more harm than good. It was probably just as well that we were apart.

So I rode with Simon, back through the mountain villages to the coast road past Rethymno to Heraklion, and it was only in that last stretch that we encountered any real traffic. In the hills there had been rockslides, and trees had come down in the storm. It wouldn't take much, I thought, to cut us off if the weather worsened.

Simon said little for the first hour. He seemed tense, focused on driving, and when I reached for the radio he said,

"I'd rather not, if you don't mind."

I snatched my hand back as if burned, but I smiled and said, "Sure, no problem," because that was what I did, those little lies that grease the wheels and make life bearable.

"Why did you come, Jan?" he asked without preamble.

"What?" I said, still smiling. "I told you. I want to speak to Gretchen . . ."

"No, not now. I mean Crete. The whole trip."

"What do you mean? You invited me and I thought—"

"Yes, but why did you come? I mean, we cover your costs and all, so it's a free vacation and you don't have a lot of spare cash, but . . ."

"Well," I began, about to counter that last remark and probably spin some stupid falsehood in the process. I didn't get the chance.

"No, but seriously," he said. "It's just us. Just you and me. So what's it all about? Why are you here?"

I blink, genuinely confused.

"You think this is about me wanting to get back with Marcus," I say.

"No," he says. "Maybe. Is it?"

"No."

"OK, so what is it?"

"I just wanted to see you all, relive our last trip . . ."

"And how are we doing?" he said. His eyes were on the road, riveted to it, but his voice was clipped, the words bitten off like meat.

"I don't think I understand . . ."

"Which bit of our last visit did you most want to relive, Jan?"

"Just seeing everyone and—"

"OK," he said, cutting me off.

"I'm not sure I get what you're . . ."

"I said, 'OK,'" he said. "Leave it."

"I'm sorry," I said, confused and uneasy. "Is it something I said?"

He laughed at that, a short, snapping sound without amusement.

I think to ask him about *Manos*, but I don't. His mood is too strange and Gretchen's odd warning is ringing in my head. We barely speak again till we reach the airport, and when I say I'm going to find a bathroom, he just nods.

The bathroom isn't as easy to find as I thought it would be, and I have to walk a ways. While I'm sitting there in the stall, I fish out my phone and take the opportunity of a signal to scroll through my e-mail. There are a few notifications from work, the announcement of who got the executive lead position—a woman I'd never heard of—and a few other minor bits and pieces. Nothing of significance, and I'm struck by how little time I have actually been away. It feels like weeks, but it's only been four days, and the rest of the world has proceeded at its tedious and familiar pace.

I open Google and type in *Manos*. The list of results is unhelpful: a low-budget horror film, a scattering of sites in Greek, some games, some charitable organizations. Nothing obviously significant. I add the term *Rethymno* to the search and then, on impulse, the date of our visit to the cave five years ago. Now, most of the results are in Greek, and I have to run each one through Google Translate. Most are newspaper stories. *Manos*, it seems, is a name. A man's.

Or a boy's.

The picture loads slowly, but I know him immediately. I have his face filed away on my laptop back home.

Waiter boy.

The kid who worked at the Taverna Diogenes. The one who had mooned around Melissa in between waiting on us and leading tourists on snorkeling trips around the bay.

Manos.

I remembered now. But we hadn't seen him that last day. I was almost sure of it. We had gone to the restaurant for our last meal, expecting the sponges he had promised, but he hadn't been there. It was one of the various little disappointments and frustrations of our last hours, and Melissa had sulked through the meal, then complained of a headache and gone to bed.

I read the page quickly. The translation was wooden, clunky, but its core required no subtlety. On the last day of our trip, Manos Veranikis, son of Maria, proprietor of the Taverna Diogenes, had been killed in a freak diving accident.

Chapter Twenty-Nine

I hadn't realized my hand had bled enough to leave a trail, and I can't see to know if that trail will lead to my hiding place. I watch unblinkingly as he sweeps the flashlight beam across the ground from the open cell over the threshold to the tunnel, conscious of the way my right hand is quietly exploring the ground for a rock or hunk of discarded machinery that I might use as a weapon if the worst happens.

He hesitates and then slowly, inexorably, he pans the light toward me, creeping foot by foot along the railway line. If there is a speck of drying crimson there, he will spot it long before my useless eyes find it. The light is fifteen feet away. Ten. Five.

It stops and snaps abruptly back. It finds the drop he saw first, then begins to trace the tunnel in the opposite direction, the way I went first before doubling back when I felt the track descending.

My heart leaps. If my hand bled just enough for a few spatters before stopping, it might lead him the wrong way.

He begins to walk the line, his pace quickening, and I risk another look. In the darkness of the tunnel, with the tank on his back and his slow, careful movement, it's like we're underwater, not on the Daedalus reef but in some deeper, lightless place, like a wreck. He takes another step away from me. *Apparently he has found the trail he was hunting, and I think wildly of Ariadne's thread spooling out behind me. But he's wrong. He's going the wrong way, and I have to bite down a shout of defiance and triumph. He moves off farther, and I hear the wrenching of another heavy door.*

This is not the way he had come in. When he first came down he appeared in the tunnel quite suddenly, not with the long lead-in I would have seen and heard if he had come from all the way down there, and that means that the stairs he used are close to the cell. One of the doors I had taken for another prison. It has to be.

I swallow, fighting my own indecision, knowing he might come back at any moment, knowing that he will soon realize the trail he is following has dried up, knowing that I have to go. Now.

I come up out of my wooden, joint-aching crouch and begin to pad quickly along the track till the curve straightens out, then I set my heels against it and take three long strides toward where I think the wall should be, right hand out in front of me, fingers splayed. When I hit solid stone, I take three strides back to the track, move a few feet farther down, and repeat the process, all the while straining to hear the sound of the man in the mask coming back.

On the third attempt I find the door. Fumblingly, my hand locates the latch and presses it. It gives with barely a sound, and the door pulls open. Beyond it, lit by a soft gray bleed from somewhere above, is a staircase.

It is the closest thing to light I have seen for hours, and it works like a beacon on my mind as I step into the stairwell and start to climb.

I'm getting out. I'm escaping. He'll realize his mistake and come back, but it will be too late. I'll be long gone . . .

But where will I be? I had thought I was under the villa where we had been staying, but this tunnel, the railway line doesn't fit with that. I climb, reaching as I do so in my mind for the last thing I remember before waking up in the cell, and it comes with startling, horrifying clarity.

I see the body on the living room floor, the back of his head bloody, the blood I can still smell on my own ravaged hands.

I can't remember hitting him. Just looking down at him.

And then I'm in a much older memory of darkness and blood, one touched also with gas and oil and with the scent of hot, friction-burned metal.

Mom? Gabby?

And now I know why I've been thinking about my sister so much. After all these years and in this, of all places. It's not just because Gabby was where my lies began. It's because I killed her.

Chapter Thirty

I stared at my phone, processing what I was reading. Manos Veranikis—Mel's waiter boy—had been swimming off the stone outcrop just west of the Minos hotel's private beach, where he sometimes took snorkelers. He was gathering sponges to sell, diving from the rocks. He was by himself, which he shouldn't have been, so there was no one to raise the alarm when he apparently hit his head and lost consciousness. He drowned, and his body washed ashore later that evening.

Sponges. Jesus.

I saw again his mother's face in the restaurant, the recognition of Melissa and the sudden, irrational fury. Maria blamed Melissa for her son's death, and now I understood why. We had gone to the Diogenes on our last night, but he hadn't been there. Mel was disappointed because he had promised us sponges. I saw him in my mind's eye, miming the basketball-size one he had planned to bring her.

Was that how he died, trying to bring a souvenir for a tourist lady he had a crush on? Could it be that simple?

God, I thought. *How awful. How utterly, pointlessly wretched.*

That poor boy. And his mother. No wonder she hated us. No wonder she had been ready to flay Melissa's skin from her face with her nails the moment she realized who we were. I felt suddenly stupid and worthless, a tourist who had gathered up those bits of the place and its people that seemed nice and fun and then left, knowing nothing, unaware that one of the people who actually lived there had died trying to make us happy.

I felt sick to my stomach and sat very still for a long minute, trying to decide if I was going to throw up. I replayed it all as best I could, both the recent visit to the Diogenes and the last one five years ago. The boy had been dead by then, but the restaurant was still doing business and we hadn't noticed anything amiss.

They hadn't known yet. How long after we left had the police arrived? How long before Maria—our comic, boisterous Greek servant and entertainer—had been made to identify the remains of her child?

God.

But then other thoughts came and I, tourist still, moved on. If this was the key to the mystery word *Manos*, as seemed likely, why was Gretchen so convinced we were in danger?

You most of all.

It didn't make sense. Or rather, it made perfect sense up to a point but didn't explain what had happened to Gretchen or why she had made her odd pronouncements. It explained Maria's anger when she recognized Melissa, but it had nothing to do with Gretchen's shredded underwear, and the simplest explanation was that the two things were, therefore, unconnected, that they were separate issues. One was an accident—tragic and perhaps influenced by Melissa's flirtatious manipulations, but an accident nonetheless, though one that perhaps some local had seen fit to underscore by piling the leaves into the shape of the boy's name.

It was a poor revenge, I thought, ashamed of myself. We hadn't even known what the word meant. Maybe that had only been a beginning, and there was more—worse—to come. But if so, if someone blamed us for Manos's death and meant to do something to us as a result, how did Gretchen know, and why would she think I was the one most in danger?

Thinking of Gretchen brought me back to the other matter. She hadn't even been with us last time, so ravaging her clothes was either a mistake or was unrelated to the boy's death. A mistake, though unlikely, wasn't impossible. I thought of those big windows in the villa. If someone had seen her going to her room, they might have mistaken her for Melissa and targeted her by accident. She did look a lot like her.

But tearing up someone's underwear to revenge a child's death? No. It felt petty, wrong. I couldn't believe it. Either that was an unrelated bit of spite from someone else, or Gretchen had done it herself in a melodramatic—and frankly psychotic—bid for attention.

My gut said that was it, and not just because I couldn't think of who would hate her enough to do something so mean-spirited and creepy. I had believed her when she told me she knew it wasn't me who had cut up her clothes. Maybe this was all just willful self-delusion, an extension of the bad dreams she told everyone about in which she had been interrogated by monsters, and that her warning to me about being in danger was just more amateur theatrics. Some people like being at the center of drama, even when it's the drama of malice and intrigue.

Especially then.

There was no doubt the woman had issues, and I of all people should understand that. She was sad, lonely, overwhelmed by her more sophisticated and glamorous friends—myself, obviously, excluded—and she wanted the limelight. If she had grabbed it in a way that was preposterous and inconvenient for everybody, there was still no more point in attacking her for it than there was in indulging her fantasies. Leaving the bathroom and heading back to the car, I resolved to be Gretchen's friend until she felt comfortable enough to tell me the truth. After all, if anyone should understand someone lying to make a shitty situation seem better, it should be me.

So I gave her a welcoming smile when Simon led her to the car. He was using his cell phone, talking, I assumed, to Melissa.

"I have her," he said. "We're on our way back."

Gretchen looked wan, her face pale and un-made-up, her eyes sunken and bloodshot. She gave me a weary *hi* and the kind of shrug that could have been an apology but could also have just been a comment on her lot in life. I offered her the front seat, but she shook her head. She wanted to be as alone as the car would let her. I couldn't blame her for that.

His task complete—or half-complete—Simon's mood improved considerably. And he flicked on the radio. By the time we were back on the coast road and speeding toward Rethymno, he was humming along to Pearl Jam and drumming his fingers on the steering wheel. Gretchen said nothing, just stared blankly out the window as the dusty scenery slid past. She looked numb and exhausted, and she clearly didn't want to talk. Perhaps later, I thought, I could get her on her own.

I wanted to talk about Manos, to tell them what had happened to him, if only to explain his mother's bizarre behavior at the restaurant, but I couldn't. Partly it was the fear that, after a cursory sympathetic remark, Simon would shrug it off as irrelevant to him, to us, that it would make me like him less. But it was partly something else too, a lingering anxiety that Gretchen hadn't been lying, that there was still something I didn't understand that made the situation far worse than I could imagine.

Marcus had reacted to the word *Manos*. The name. Did he know about the dead boy? If so, why had he pretended not to? Why had he lied to me?

I shifted in my seat. I was missing something important, and though I had no good reason to think so, I couldn't shake the sense that it was something bad. Something terrible.

The thought took hold, and for all Simon's chipper observations on the weather and the view, I found myself getting more and more apprehensive with each mile we traveled, as if the villa was a kind of prison where terrible things might still happen. I could have escaped, I thought, I could have left the airport bathroom and tried to book myself on the next flight to anywhere or checked into a local hotel and sat out the trip there. I hadn't because that would have been crazy, a ridiculous and defeatist overreaction to a little strangeness and tension, but I couldn't shake the idea completely.

You could have gotten away, I said to myself. *But you missed your chance. And now? Well, we'll see soon enough, won't we?*

We rounded a bend in the road and a pair of large pink-faced vultures looked up at us from the carcass they were picking over. *A dog,* I thought. They had white furry collars, but their heads were bare. Simon pointed without taking his hands off the wheel.

"Cool," he said.

I just nodded.

Chapter Thirty-One

I freeze in the stairwell, though I know he may be on his way back up, may only be seconds behind me, laboring along the tunnel in his scuba mask, blade at the ready. My legs just won't move.

You killed your sister. All those years ago. You killed her and your mom, and you've been lying about it and everything else ever since.

No.

Yes. It's true. You know it now. You remember.

I do. I see it. I have always remembered waking up in the darkness of the flipped car, Gabby still and silent in the seat next to me, my mother crumpled in the driver's seat. A silence that sucked in the whole world, the darkness of a black hole from which nothing can escape. I remember the hell that was the wait for someone to see, strapped into my seat on my side, my face pressed to the window against the road. The Toyota's frame had crumpled in the roll and my seat belt was jammed, though that was nothing compared with the damage on the left side, which had taken the full force of the impact. I remember the disorientation, not understanding which way was up, and then the slow, dragging horror as I made sense of it all but could do nothing but weep and wait.

Eventually there were lights and sirens and men with tools who cut the car apart and told me I was a very lucky girl. They gave me candy and hot chocolate and sympathy. Lots of that, though it would never be enough. They gave me what they could, and they asked me what I remembered.

And I lied.

That was when it started. I told them my mother was tuning the radio, got distracted, lost control.

Mommy.

I didn't say I poked Gabby one too many times, a hard stick in her ribs with the forefinger of my left hand. I didn't say that she screamed. That my mother turned round to tell us that if we couldn't behave till we got home . . .

And that was all it took. A momentary glance away from the road, and then a curve she hadn't seen properly, misjudged in the darkness, over compensated, and then off the road and down the steep embankment, rolling into trees.

That was the truth, and it began with me.

I stand barefoot on the stairs in the gloom, blinking back tears and then, somewhere in the bowels of whatever structure I am in, I hear the slam of another door, and I'm back in the present and moving, refocusing, trying to find what I need to do and hold it in front of me where I can see it.

Get out. Get out. Get out.

I'm up the stairs and faced with another door.

Don't be locked.

I try it, and it opens, though I have to push through what feels like a heavy swag of carpet to get out. For a moment, I'm disoriented, but I know where I am. I'm in the foyer of the villa. There is a table lamp by the ancient rotary phone, though it's on my left instead of my right, and I reach for it, snatching the receiver from the cradle.

Silence. No dial tone.

I slam it back down, but by the light of the lamp I see the door to the stairwell I have just climbed, and with a surge of triumphal resolution, I pull the carpet hanging aside and shut it quickly, dragging the heavy bolts into place afterward.

My hand is trembling as I do it, but I do it, and it's done, and I'm safe.

I sag to the ground, suddenly light-headed, conscious now that I can feel the slight tremor of the generator running when my hands touch the floor. Everything is as it was. It seems impossible, but the generator means everyone is here, doesn't it? Maybe they don't even know I was gone.

I get woozily to my feet and walk round to the living room. There are lights on here too, but it is deserted. There is no body on the rug.

You imagined it. Or made it up.

No. I walk over to the spot where I remember standing, looking down, then get on my hands and knees and feel the rug. It's wet, but with water, not blood.

Cleaned. Hurriedly and probably ineffectively, but cleaned.

I stand up again, conscious that I'm weaving drunkenly in place now and that my head is starting to throb. This doesn't make sense. The room is beginning to swim. There was something I had to do, but I'm not sure what it was.

I turn back to the foyer.

There is a snake on the tower stairs.

It's long and green and bright as spring leaves.

Wait.

No. It's not a snake. It's a hose. Like you'd use to water the lawn.

I've seen it before, but not here. Not in this room. My brain lurches and fumbles. My stomach turns, but now I remember. I saw it in the basement. It was coiled around some tools. It was next to the generator.

And now I understand.

Chapter Thirty-Two

It was late when we got back to the villa. Roadwork in one of the villages outside Rethymno had added almost an hour to the journey. At one point I pulled out my cell phone to see if we still had a signal. We didn't, but the last thing I had been looking at—the Manos story—was still up on my screen. I whisked it away again as fast as I could, but I couldn't be sure that Simon, unreadable in his sunglasses, had not seen.

There was a funereal mood back at the house. Everyone lined up to welcome Gretchen with hugs and pats and simpering smiles, as if she had just come home from war. All except Brad, who gave her an arch look and tipped his imaginary hat like a character out of *Yankee Doodle Dandy*. Gretchen looked hurriedly away and avoided his eyes for the rest of the afternoon.

But then, so did everyone else. At first I thought I was imagining it, but I kept an eye on him as the rest of us talked and ate and (of course) drank, and it was clear that if the group felt some unease about me and Gretchen, they felt more about Brad, and I found myself wondering what had been said in our absence. For his part, Brad thumbed through magazines, read or played on his tablet, and sat in the corner, moving only to refill his glass—a bottle of red he was not sharing—or go to the bathroom. I don't think he said a word all afternoon, but at one point he started humming deliberately. It took me a moment to realize he was imitating the keyboard riff from Prince's "1999." He caught me looking at him and gave me a bleak, mocking smile.

Are we having fun yet? It seemed to say. *Enjoying the millennial reunion? Who wouldn't want another two thousand days of this?*

In spite of her previous pronouncements about me—or even because of them—Gretchen seemed at pains to keep me close, to make a show of how unified we were, though she never said that she no longer held me responsible for what I still thought of, absurdly, as *the panty incident*. In fact, we didn't talk about it at all, and I suspected some kind of mutual gag order had been decided upon, as if to spare both our blushes. Or because they suspected someone else had been responsible but didn't want to open that particular can of worms.

It was a fitting image: slimy, repulsive, and stinking of decay.

That's maggots.

Same difference, at least in this instance.

When I went into the kitchen to get ice for my drink—I had moved on from wine to vodka and didn't give a shit who knew it— Gretchen came with me. She eyed the basket of crusty bread on the counter, then opened the fridge and lifted out a cucumber, a fat, ripe tomato, a jar of black olives, and a block of feta cheese. The light from the fridge was cold and blue. It hollowed out her fragile beauty and made her waifish.

"Do we have anything less Greek?" she mused, half to herself. "I mean, it's good and all, but I could murder a pizza."

"I don't think so," I said. "Drink?"

"God, no. I think I need a break."

I nodded, sipping mine absently while she assembled a rickety sandwich, and suddenly the weight of my past lies was too much to bear and I wanted to be done with it all.

"My sister died a long time ago," I said without preamble, like I was confessing to a priest in the hope not just of forgiveness but of redemption, the chance to start over.

She looked up, her eyebrows raised, and started to say something puzzled, but I shook my head.

"I know," I said. "I told you she worked in the movie industry doing CGI. I lied. Sorry."

She put the knife down and considered me.

"Why?" she said at last.

"I honestly couldn't tell you. It's something I do. Did. I'm trying to quit."

She gave a snuffling laugh. I had meant my confession, but I saw suddenly how it opened a door to ask something in return.

"Gretchen?" I said.

"Don't ask," she said quickly. "I know I shouldn't have blamed you, and I'm sorry, but I didn't want to talk about it. Still don't."

I nodded, but I wasn't letting her completely off the hook.

"You said we were in danger—"

"I was being stupid," she said quickly. "Forget it."

"O . . . K . . . ," I said.

"Really."

"One more thing."

"Do I have to?" she said, not so much defiant as whiny, like a kid being sent for a bath.

"Yesterday afternoon," I said. "When the rest of us went to the fort and you stayed with Mel."

She was immediately on her guard, pushing her hair behind her ears as I'd seen her do sometimes when she wasn't comfortable.

"What about it?" she said, slicing the tomato with more care than was strictly necessary.

"Did you see Brad?"

She put the knife down again and turned to face me, lips pursed and face red, like she was ready to tell me where to get off, but then she deflated and looked at her hands. For a long moment she said nothing, and when she finally spoke her voice was barely above a whisper.

"He texted me," she said. "Offered to buy me a drink at a hotel in the town center."

"And you went," I said.

She checked that no one could hear from the other room, then nodded quickly.

"It was just a drink, right?" she said. "Except that it wasn't. He had a room. He said he and Kristen were on the outs and maybe I'd like to . . . you know."

I buried my surprise and just said, "And did you?"

She shook her head.

"I went to the room," she confessed. "But it all felt too weird. I'm not . . . I don't know. It's not my style, you know? I like Kristen, and even though he said . . . anyway, no, I didn't." I nodded again, thinking that was the end of it, but then she added, "He was actually quite sweet. And sad. Not like he normally is at all. I actually considered . . . but then . . ."

Her face tightened, all the tenderness that had been there a moment before now turning into something else entirely. Again she checked the doorway and stooped, as if trying to make herself small, before she leaned in and whispered.

"He called me *Melissa*. Not once. Four or five times. He said I looked like her and being with me would be like being with her. Freaked me out. I mean, I was insulted, you know, because he obviously wasn't really interested in me, but it was more than that. It scared me. He's, like, *obsessed* with her. Asked me to sit like her. Talk like her. I couldn't deal, so I took off."

"And he was . . ."

"Not happy," she said with a bleak smile. "But then you'd already figured that out, huh?"

"Yeah," I said, thinking of the butchered underwear strewn about her bedroom floor. "I think I had."

Chapter Thirty-Three

I took a health and environmental science class in college. It was mostly pretty dull stuff, but one of the case studies stuck with me. A Minnesota family in the nineties started getting frequent bouts of what they thought was flu: lethargy, occasional nausea, disorientation, an inability to focus, and memory loss. They were treated and released over and over, with doctors considering chronic fatigue syndrome to be the leading possible cause of their symptoms. This went on for three years. In that time the kids' grades crashed, the father lost his job, and the mother became so depressed with her failure to complete even simple tasks that she became suicidal. The only time they improved was when they went away on vacation, but as soon as they got home, their symptoms would creep back in. Almost five years after the syndrome began, a random home improvement revealed a leak in the exhaust line of their furnace. Prompt blood tests confirmed that the cause of all their sickness was chronic exposure to low levels of carbon monoxide.

Cases where the dosage was much higher—when people stayed with a running car in the garage, say, or when they used a charcoal stove indoors— had more dramatic and alarming results, frequently leading to unconsciousness within ten or fifteen minutes and death in twice that. The gas is light and odorless. Most people don't notice it even as they start to succumb to symptoms.

I stare at the hose on the stairs, and I know why we have been so tired, so woozy, so forgetful. I had thought we were being drugged, but we weren't. We were being poisoned.

Marcus is upstairs. So are Gretchen and Kristen and Brad. I have no idea if they are alive.

I run clumsily to the front door, but it has been locked with a key. I follow the hose down the cellar stairs to the generator, past the scuba gear, not thinking about who might be down here, stumbling and falling on the steps. My skinned knees flare and my shattered left hand shrieks with pain as I land awkwardly on it, but I get up and blunder over to the throbbing yellow generator and shut it off. The exhaust line has been fitted to the hose and fastened in place with pipe grips.

The gas is light. That means it will rise, and the sealed windows of the villa that make it so stuffy will hold it. The second and third stories are now a gas chamber. I look at the scuba gear, but I don't have time to mess with regulators. Instead I snatch up the small tank of pure emergency oxygen, then turn to the tools and garden implements. I pick up a picklike mattock, but it's too heavy to wield one-handed. Among the dust and cobwebs is a ball-peen hammer, the kind with the rounded striking head.

That will have to do.

I hit the wall hard with my left shoulder as I navigate the spiral back to the foyer but keep going, breathing as shallowly as I can while I climb. I can't smell the poison. I can't taste it. But I know it's there and that there's nothing I can do that will keep it out. The air is probably loaded already, which means I have only a few minutes of consciousness. Maybe not even that.

I round the corner onto the landing of the third floor at a ragged trot and make for Marcus's door. I weave as I walk, listing like a rowboat taking on water, and fall heavily against the door. It is locked. They all will be, a precaution against whoever broke into Gretchen's room. I set the oxygen tank *down but waste no time knocking. There is a good chance they are already unconscious or worse.*

I swing the hammer wildly at the door handle, hitting, missing, hitting again, using all the strength I still have. The handle buckles but the latch holds, so I try charging with my right shoulder. The first hit is too close to the hinge, but the second, with a blundering run from the top of the stairs, splinters the wood around the faceplate, and the door judders open.

Marcus is motionless on the bed, wearing the shorts I saw him in the night before, the sheets kicked haphazardly aside, lying on his belly, his face buried in the pillow. He always slept like that. I don't wait to check his pulse or breathing but stride across the room, hammer raised.

The energy of my step drives the swing of the hammer, and the window explodes.

I lean out into the night and suck in the air. It's cold as deep water, and it fills my lungs like life. I use the hammerhead to clear as much of the glass from the frame as I can, but as soon as I try to pull Marcus closer, it's clear that I can't do it with one hand. I should be distraught, emotionally overwhelmed, but all my remaining mental strength has been honed to a fine point, to completing a single set of things I need to do, and I feel nothing. I take another breath of the air outside, then go back into the hall and down one flight.

After the impenetrable darkness of the cellars, the dusk up here barely slows me down. I go to Gretchen's room next, still feeling unsteady, but I crash into the door like a battering ram, turning my shoulder into it at the last second. The latch holds, but the door itself cracks along a seam where I hit it. I use the hammer to clear the wood, then reach in and unlatch the door.

Gretchen is huddled on the bed under a protective mound of blankets. I practically throw the hammer through her window, take another breath past the shattered remains, and turn around, only then seeing that there is another figure curled up on the floor beside the bed. I bend, trying to get my eyes to focus.

It's Kristen.

Dimly, I think another piece of the puzzle has slotted into place.

But I can't abandon Brad, even if Kristen wants nothing more to do with him. I go back out, moving down the hall to the last door. I'm flagging now. I can feel it, and it's not just tiredness. My movement is sloppy, my balance precarious, and my mind is wandering. It's the gas. It's in my lungs, my blood. I hit the door to Brad's room, but I've lost all the punch I had a moment ago, and it holds. I try again to no avail. I'm suddenly impossibly tired. It's like being carried away on a thick black river and wanting nothing more than to float with the current. I try once more, but my shoulder charge is weak and uneven. I hit my face against the jamb and collapse to my knees.

I have no choice. I need air. I crawl back the way I came, back into Gretchen's room, clambering roughly over Kristen's prone body to lay my head on the windowsill and drink in the night. A shard of the windowpane gouges my cheek, but I stay where I am, breathing deep and full until my head clears, and I remember the O2 tank I left in the hall upstairs. I stagger out, flounder my way up the steps, and pick it up. I fiddle with the regulator, taking a quick hit as I make my way back to Marcus, and the oxygen hits my brain like an adrenaline firework.

I roll Marcus onto his back and clamp the regulator to his face.

"Breathe," I say. "Breathe."

And then I'm moving back into the hall and down once more, wondering vaguely if that delay will cost Brad his life or if he's dead already. I am lining up to charge the door when a firm hand grips my shoulder and spins me round.

Chapter Thirty-Four

I don't know what woke me. It wasn't a sound as such, or not one I consciously recognized when I opened my eyes. For a while I lay in bed, straining my ears to focus, and then there was something: a muffled thud, like someone overturning a soft but heavy chair. It came from below.

I had my little stub of candle in its holder and had borrowed a box of safety matches from the kitchen, the waxed kind that smelled of paraffin. I struck one and lit the candle, then swung my legs out of bed and planted them firmly on the floor. I don't recall really deciding to do anything, and I think I might have still been half-asleep, just acting without really thinking.

I could have wrapped a towel around myself and stuck my head out into the hall, but I didn't like the feeling of being naked, or nearly naked, after what had happened to Gretchen. So before I opened the door, I dressed: bra, underwear, a sundress, and sandals. It took me barely longer than the towel would, and I felt somehow secure, like a person ready to face the world. Still, it was a strange decision, and I don't think I was thinking clearly. My head felt thick, fogged by more than sleep, and my feet were unsteady, as if I was drunk.

I stepped out into the hall and along to the spiral staircase, my candle flame fluttering so the shadows leaped. I thought vaguely of what Marcus had said about Plato's cave, about taking the shadows for the thing itself, but my brain was too sleepy to do anything with the image. Instead I tiptoed down into the foyer and looked around. The front door looked solidly locked, but it felt strange to be down there alone in the dark, and I couldn't remember why I had come down.

A sound, I thought. *I had heard a sound.*

Suddenly I wanted to get this over as soon as possible. I might have gone back up the stairs if the candlelight hadn't caught the odd flash of green on the ground.

A garden hose, like one I'd seen in the basement. It seemed to be running from the cellar stairs into the living room.

I wasn't scared, just curious, as if I were still in a dream where things didn't really make sense but everyone behaved as if they did.

I followed the hose into the living room.

I could tell something was off as soon as I went in. Moonlight came through the great high windows, and I could see something out of place in the middle of the living room carpet—a sprawling, mounded something, like a large dog stretched out and fast asleep. If my eyes had been better I wouldn't have needed to stoop to see what it was, wouldn't have had to touch him, to roll him over, feeling the warm wetness on my hands and smelling the sharp, metallic tang of the blood all over him.

"Brad!" I gasped, kneeling beside him.

If I'd had my glasses, I wouldn't have had to kneel, and I might have noticed the figure I had walked past to get to him, might have sensed them moving behind me before the blow fell. The back of my head flared with sudden agony, and the world went first light, and then very, very dark.

Chapter Thirty-Five

The hand on my shoulder belongs to Melissa. She's holding a battery-powered lantern and is standing at the top of the stairs, looking perplexed and angry.

"What the hell is going on?" she says. "Did you break something?"

"The windows," I said. "We have to get this door open."

"What are you talking about?"

"Just help me with this door."

"It's locked."

"Force it!"

She knocks, and I push her aside and charge the door again. This time it shudders in its frame.

"Jan! What the hell!" Melissa exclaims.

I hit the door twice more, my shoulder aching with each lunge, and at last it bursts open. Brad is lying on the bed motionless. It takes me a moment to see the dark stain on the pillow, brownish at the edges but thick and black around his head.

When Melissa sees the hammer she tries to grab it, shouting something, but I shake her off, and the iron head crashes through the window. The room floods with wholesome air, and I stagger out into the hall and slump to the ground while Melissa bellows her disbelief. I know I should get the oxygen tank and share it with the others, but for a moment I don't have the strength. I can feel the temperature dropping as the night air rushes into the stuffy house, and I just sit there, my back against the wall, breathing it in. I doubt it will save Brad.

Time passes. A minute or two, perhaps, but I'm still not thinking clearly and can't be sure. But then I hear movement, and I look up to see a shadow in the stairwell. It shifts and turns into Marcus, looking dazed and unsteady.

"Jan?" he says. "What's going on?"

"The generator," I say, my head still foggy. "The exhaust was connected to a hose. We all have carbon monoxide poisoning. Keep breathing from the tank. And share it with the others."

"What?" says Marcus. He looks even less focused than me, though whether that is the corrupted air he has been breathing or the high from the shot of pure oxygen I gave him, I can't say.

"The tank in your room," I say. "Get it. Use it."

"I don't understand," says Melissa. She's more alert than us, having only just come upstairs. Maybe her side of the house wasn't affected since the hose ran right up the tower stairs.

"Help him," I say. "Help them all."

"I can't tell if they're breathing," she says. "Brad's head is all cut. I can't tell if it's bad, but there's a lot of blood."

"Give them the oxygen anyway. The ventilation is getting rid of the carbon monoxide from the air, but we have to get it out of their bloodstream."

"I don't understand," says Marcus. "Why won't they wake up?"

"It's the gas," I say vaguely.

"Will they be OK?"

"I don't know, Marcus."

"I don't understand," he says again.

I just sit and breathe, suddenly too tired to explain.

"Why would anyone connect a hose to the generator?" says Melissa.

"To kill us, Mel," I reply, exasperation breaking through my weary confusion for a second. "First just to confuse us, disorient us—but now, I

think, to kill us. They've been pumping low amounts in at night, which is why we've been so . . . weird and tired. It makes you unfocused, forgetful. But tonight it's more and—"

"Why do you know all this?" says Marcus.

It's an odd question, but I shrug it off.

"I studied this stuff," I say. "It doesn't matter. Tonight the dose is way higher."

"Why?" says Melissa.

"Because someone wants to murder us all in our beds!"

"You weren't in your bed," she says. Another odd remark. She seems thoughtful rather than alarmed. Cautious.

"No," I say. "I was chained in the basement with the generator."

"What?" says Melissa, incredulous now.

"I don't understand," says Marcus woozily. He's still badly out of it.

"I was chained to a metal ring in the wall of a cell in the basement."

It sounds preposterous, even in my ears, and I see bafflement settle into Marcus's face, like something heavy that makes his whole body droop.

"This is crazy," says Melissa. "You were chained up in a cell? Where?"

"With the generator!" I shout. "I already said."

"Show me," says Melissa.

"What?"

"Show me."

I say nothing.

"It doesn't matter right now," I say. "We need to look after—"

"You are saying someone tried to poison us but it doesn't matter?" says Melissa, aghast. "It does to me. You say you were chained up in the basement. I want to see where."

I give her a weary look and then something rises in my heart, a mixture of anger and righteous indignation.

"You want to see?" I say, getting to my feet. "Fine. You'll see."

I turn and stride erratically for the head of the stairs, leaving Gretchen, Kristen, and Brad in their rooms, steadying myself on the rail and picking my way carefully so that I don't trip on the hose. Melissa is at my shoulder and actually catches hold of my elbow as we walk, like we are on some girls' night out.

She guides me, following the bright line of the hose in the gloom, to the half-open door into the cellar, Marcus stumbling at our heels. The stairwell is dark, and I am struck by a sudden dread of going back down there, even with the others. I think of the thick liquid blackness of the cell speckled with my blood, the creeping bull-headed man-monster I locked down there . . .

My head swims. Something isn't right, but I can't focus to see what, and Melissa is already propelling me down the stairs, the battery lamp held over her head, Marcus behind her. I see the stack of tools from which I took the hammer, the bright-yellow generator, nestled there like something toxic poised to strike: a scorpion, perhaps . . .

"Where?" snaps Melissa.

"What?" I say again. The thick fog of confusion is filling my head once more. Something is wrong.

"You were chained up in a cell."

"Yes. I broke my hand to escape."

"Where?"

"What?" I say, my head thick, my voice faraway.

"Where is the cell, Jan?" says Melissa.

I turn around stupidly, then realize that she is pressing the lantern into my good hand. I take it and hold it up. There is the passage to the stairs we have just come through and the mesh door on the other side of the chamber. I go through it, picking my way between ancient wooden crates and pallets till I come to another heavy door, its timbers barred. I don't want to open it, but I feel Melissa and Marcus watching me, waiting. I hold the lantern in the fingers of my left hand, not touching it with my shattered thumb, and use my right to press the latch until I feel the door shift. I pull it. It sticks. I yank harder, an unfocused anger building inside me, flowing down my arm and into my hand. The door scrapes open.

It is a cupboard. There are shelves, mostly empty, some with moldy boxes and folded hessian sacks spotted with mouse droppings. There is no passageway. No door.

I turn, bewildered. The light from the lamp falls on Marcus's face, and I see not confusion, but disappointment and a swelling horror.

"It was here," I say. "I was chained up down here. I know I was."

"No, Jan," says Melissa. "I'm sorry, but you weren't. You made it up, didn't you?"

And then, as I stare at them both, Marcus speaks.

"God, Jan," he says. "What did you do?"

Chapter Thirty-Six

"Nothing," I say. "I didn't do anything. I escaped from the cell, and I saved your life . . ."

As soon as the words are out, I know they are the wrong thing to say.

"Oh," says Melissa, realization dawning. "That's what this is."

"What?" I say. "No, I mean, I really . . ."

"Fuck," says Marcus, turning away, his eyes wide with shock. "You set this up so you could rescue me? What the fuck, Jan? People could have died! They still might."

"No!" I say. "It's true."

"It's not, Jan, is it?" says Melissa. "You want to be the hero, to make everyone like you, so you arranged this. You are lying to us again, aren't you? I think you even lied to yourself."

"Is that right, Jan?" asks Marcus, appalled. "Is this another fib to make your life feel better?"

No! It isn't. I haven't been lying. I didn't make it up.

"That's pathetic," says Melissa. "I'm sorry, Jan. But it is, and I'm not going to cover for you this time."

"No!" I say. "It's all true. I was chained up. There was a cell . . ."

"Where, Jan?" says Melissa, and her confusion has gone too. So has her compassion. Now her face and voice are hard, simmering with barely contained anger.

"Here!" I say. "Or . . . somewhere. There were railway lines and—"

"Railway lines?" Melissa sneers. "Jan, this time you've gone too far."

"I'm telling the truth!"

I didn't invent it all to make my life feel better, more interesting, to make myself a hero. I didn't. I swear to God. Not this time.

Melissa turns to Marcus, taking charge. "We need to call the police and an ambulance," she says. "I don't know as much as she does about carbon monoxide poisoning, but we need to get help now."

"There were railway lines," I say, stuck in the mud of my own thoughts. "I came up into the foyer and turned, but the phone table wasn't there . . ."

"Be quiet, Jan," says Melissa. "We're trying to figure out what to do."

"It wasn't there," I muse aloud. "I mean, it was there, but it wasn't where it should be, where I thought it would be." I stretch out my right hand, as if reaching into my memory to snatch up the dead phone receiver, then retract it and reach with my wounded left. It is almost there in my head now. I just have to push through the fog a little farther. "It was on the other side, because . . . because . . ."

Push through . . .

There was something like . . . fabric. Like carpet hanging. And I turned to the left because . . .

The house is symmetrical. Simon's voice in my head. It was what he said when we arrived on the first day. The house had been rebuilt over generations, but at its heart, it was balanced, symmetrical. And that meant . . .

"There's another cellar," I say. "There's another door on the east side of the foyer. Behind the tapestry. You can't see it, but there's a door and stairs down to a labyrinth passage. The cells. The railroad tracks."

"It's over, Jan," says Melissa. "Drop it."

"No," I say, the certainty growing in my mind. "It's true. There's another staircase."

"Jan," says Marcus. "There's no railroad in Crete."

"A mine, then," I answer, shoving past him, making for the door.

"Marcus," says Melissa in a low, serious voice, "I don't think she should be allowed to wander around . . ."

"No mines either," says Marcus irritably. He grabs me by my wounded hand so that I cry out, and he looks down. "Jesus, Jan. What the hell?"

"I told you," I say. "I had to break my hand to get out."

He looks at me then, and I see doubt in his face.

"There is no cell, Jan," says Melissa. "No chain, no ring on the wall. You smashed your hand with the hammer on purpose, didn't you? Didn't you?"

"Jan," says Marcus, and some of the old care is back in his eyes now, the old pity, though I think it might still be directed at the lengths I will go to get him back. I snatch my hand away, furious at his disbelief.

"He chained me up, Marcus!" I roar at him. "He asked me questions!"

"Who?" says Melissa, still defiant, disbelieving.

I stare at her. If I was clearer in my mind, I might not say anything yet, but as it is, the hesitation is only momentary.

"Simon," I say.

Her jaw drops slowly open. She tips her head slightly to one side, as if trying to home in on a distant sound, her eyes turning to slits.

"You're insane," she says, and she actually takes a step back, as if she's afraid of me.

"Jan, listen to yourself," says Marcus. "That can't be true."

"It is," I say. "I'll show you."

And I'm moving again, faster now, clearer in my mind and full of a desperate determination to show them once and for all. The cell doesn't matter. The ring in the wall. My hellish captivity. None of it matters. But they will see that I am telling the truth. I will show them that, or I will die in the attempt. It is suddenly and clearly the only thing I want out of what is left of my life.

I'm beyond Marcus before he thinks to come after me, round the corner, and halfway up the stairs into the foyer. I hear them coming after me, but I ignore them, bursting into the open space of the foyer and crossing to the telephone table and the hanging tapestry beyond it. I drag it aside, and there's the door, bolted by my own hands.

I throw one back, but then I'm pulled away. Melissa has hold of my right wrist and she's staring into my face with an animal ferocity.

"That's enough, Jan. We're going to sit here quietly while we wait for the ambulance, and then we're going to talk to the police . . ."

I start to speak, but I see Marcus's face and stop. He's confused again, but now he's staring at the door half-hidden by the tapestry.

"How wide were the railroad tracks?" he says.

Melissa gives him a disbelieving look.

"What the fuck are you talking about?" she says.

"How wide?" he says again, looking directly at me.

I shake my head and motion with my hands. A foot. A foot and a half. I don't remember.

"Too narrow for a train," says Marcus.

"See?" says Melissa.

"But not for a gun carriage," he says. Melissa sputters wordlessly at him but he adds, "There's a gun emplacement in the cliffside. I saw it when I went walking but couldn't find a way up to it. It was probably a German antiaircraft battery. I hadn't thought about it, but I'll bet the house was used as a command post. Officers' HQ, maybe. There'd be a mini garrison quartered here. Bunks. Storage rooms. A place to hold the AA guns out of the weather . . ."

He says it dreamily, putting each idea together like a child lining up dominos.

"But . . . ," he says, turning to Melissa. "What's going on, Mel?" he says. "Where's Simon?"

"Asleep, as we should be," she shoots back, but there's something hunted in her face, like a cornered animal.

"You know Jan," she says. "This is one of her stories. Her lies. Why would Simon lock her up and ask her questions? It's crazy."

"Gretchen said she had a dream," says Marcus, still just thinking aloud. "People asking her questions . . ."

"Coincidence," says Mel. "Come on, Marcus, you can't think—"

"Manos," I say.

That stops her. She turns very slowly to me now and her face is white. "What did you say?"

"Manos," I say again. It sounds soft in my mouth, like a prayer. "The waiter from the Diogenes. The boy who died. That's what Simon was asking me about. I think he asked Gretchen about it too because you told her once, when you first met. In a bar. He wanted to know if she had told anyone else . . ."

"I don't know what you are talking about," Melissa shoots back, but she's on the defensive now and I don't believe her. "Manos? What does that have to do with us?"

"Simon was angry," I say, lining up the remaining pieces till the picture comes together. "That day, our last day, five years ago. He was mad. I didn't know why because I never saw you in the cave with Brad, but he was. He was sick of your flirtations and whatever else they turned into. He was angry, and he took the Jet Ski out. I remember seeing him bouncing along the waves. He was going so fast. And then he went round the cove. Where the boy was diving for sponges."

"That's enough," says Melissa. "Stop talking now, or I swear to God, Jan . . ."

I see it all like the picture in Marcus's slide show, and I remember that last morning, Simon's grimness when he took the Jet Ski out and his fury when he brought it back, running it up through the shallows and onto the rocky shingle.

Fury, and deliberation.

He had wrecked it on purpose, and the only reason to do that was because he was looking to cover up damage the Jet Ski had already sustained . . .

God.

The truth hits me cold and clear as the night air from the shattered window upstairs.

"Simon hit him, didn't he?" I say. "Ran him over. By accident, perhaps, but . . . well, he didn't help him. He left Manos there to drown, and then Simon came back to the hotel and ran the Jet Ski aground so that no one would see the damage he'd done to it when he hit the boy."

"You're insane," she says. "Delusional."

"And you thought I'd seen," I add, realizing. "You thought I knew, that I told someone."

Something happens in her face, a narrowing and tightening, as she stills, listening.

"It wasn't just the name in the leaves, was it?" I say. "It started before the trip. Someone sent you something." As soon as I said it I realized the full horror of that truth. "Oh my God. It's why the trip happened! You probably had no intention of following up on all that 1999 stuff, did you? There wasn't going to be a real reunion. But then someone wrote to you. Yes? A letter maybe. Or an e-mail from some untraceable account. You wanted us back here to find out who it was, so the 1999 party became a real thing. What did they ask for, money?"

"You're making this up," she says, her voice flat, hollow.

"You know I'm not."

Marcus is watching us, like he is out in the darkened house of a theater, gazing up at the stage.

"Maybe Simon didn't tell you right away," I say. "About Manos. You don't have to take the blame for any of this or cover for him. He was the one on the Jet Ski, not you."

"You don't know what you're talking about. If it had happened I would have known. I would have seen it. I was with him the whole time."

"No, you weren't."

It is Marcus. We stare at him in stunned silence, and I think again of the theater, as if he is in the audience but has stood up in the middle of a key scene and joined in.

"What?" says Melissa, thrown, all her righteous fury draining away.

"I was on the headland," he says. "Jan and me . . . we weren't getting along so I went for a walk. Bird watching, if you can believe that. I had binoculars."

"No," says Melissa. "No!"

"Yes," he replies. He speaks quietly, simply, like he is explaining something hard to a slow student. "I didn't see the thing itself, but I saw which way Simon took the Jet Ski. And I thought it was weird later, when he said he'd gone the other way round the bay, and I remembered seeing him fiddling with the nose of the thing before he got in range of the beach, like it was already damaged—before he ran it aground. I didn't know about the dead boy—Manos, I mean—not till recently. You asked me to put together the slide show of the trip, remember?" he said to Melissa. "And I wanted to add the names of places, little maps and stuff, you know? So I looked up the restaurant online. The Diogenes. Found the story about the waiter, realized he died the same day as when Simon took the Jet Ski out . . ."

"No," says Melissa again. "That's not proof of anything."

"And I thought about how he ran the Jet Ski aground and how pissed he had been in the cave, and how that boy waiter had annoyed him, and I wondered . . ."

"Why didn't you say?" I demand, almost as horrified by him as I had been of her.

He sags, and for a second his eyes close, then he shakes his head and shrugs, like he is shifting the weight of the globe itself off his shoulders.

"I didn't know anything," he says. "It just felt . . . weird. Coincidences. But the police had ruled it an accident, and I didn't really know so . . . I just wanted to get a reaction, see if there was more to it . . ."

"It's not true," says Melissa.

I ignore her.

"Why didn't you tell me?" I say.

"We barely talked . . . ," he begins, then shrugs again, a weary, defeated gesture. "Not about anything serious. Not till this week. Sorry. I should have."

"Marcus, did you blackmail him? Marcus, I can't imagine . . . it's almost worse!"

"It wasn't like that," he says. "No demands. The e-mails, the letters, they only said one thing, the same thing I wrote in the leaves on the patio. The boy's name. I wanted to see if they'd react, you know? I had no proof of anything. I didn't really know anything. But I wondered, and the more I thought about it—about them—the more it seemed plausible. An accident, or worse."

"Worse?" I said.

"If Simon ran him over," he said, "the question then is whether he did it by mistake, or if he saw him in the water . . . and then . . . Simon had been so angry . . . it felt right. I could almost see it in my head. And I dreamed about it, the black stuff in the water turning pink . . . it made me furious to think that's how it might have gone down, and they had just walked away from it. I didn't want them to forget. I didn't want them to think that everyone else had forgotten. And I thought that if I pushed it a little, maybe something would come out, some bit of real evidence I could take to the police . . ."

"You should have said."

"I know, Jan. But all I had was a hunch. Swear to God. And then I saw them here and they were just, so them, so perfect, so unburdened by anything, and I couldn't stand it. So I left his name outside, and I made sure we went to the restaurant, and I left the gate open so that they'd feel hunted, exposed—"

"Shut up!" says Melissa. "Shut up."

"And you thought it was me," I say to her. "Lying Jan, playing head games with her friends. Well, you'd show her, wouldn't you? Gas her. Chain her up till she talks, and when you're absolutely sure she hasn't told anyone else, get rid of her and anyone else who might be a threat. Flood the house with carbon monoxide. A tragic accident from which you walk away untouched, still flawless, still—"

"Shut up!" roars Melissa.

And now she's clawing at my face with her nails, and Marcus is on her, trying to hold her back. He's still unsteady, though, and she elbows him hard in the gut, so he shrinks away, doubling up in pain.

"You think you are going to mess up our lives like you messed up your own?" she yells at me, a Fury now, her face hard as steel, her eyes like lances. "You? A pathetic, lying, glorified fucking checkout girl? You? You are nothing! Do you know what we are worth?"

I wince at the truth of her words, and though I try to dodge as she comes for me, I stumble and lose my balance. I brace for the weight of her dropping on me, but by the mad light of the lantern as it rolls away, I see that she is unfastening the bolts to the hidden door. It takes a second for me to realize what is happening, and then the horror of it hits me as the door jolts open, and the Minotaur who has been waiting behind it comes out.

Chapter Thirty-Seven

I know it is Simon under the mask. I knew that the bulk of his body is just the shadow of the air tank on his back in the gloom. I know everything. So I can't explain the scale of the horror that descends upon me as the door kicks open and he bursts through.

Melissa steps back, and—too late—I see the little microphone pack tucked into her waistband and remember the wireless link to the scuba suits. There's no point pretending we don't know what he did five years ago and what he planned to do with us on this trip. He's heard it all.

He has one of the pickaxes from the cellar in his hands, and he comes through swinging, not at me, but at Marcus.

Eliminate the threat first.

Marcus is bigger than me, stronger, but he is also still sluggish from the gas. He is also just beginning to wrap his head around what has been happening in the house, and I think, essentially good and civilized as he is, that he doesn't quite believe that Simon will kill him right there and then.

I know different.

As Simon hefts the pick, I lunge at him, catching him side-on in a clumsy bear hug that throws him off balance. His hammer blow at

Marcus still connects, but it strikes his shoulder instead of his head. Marcus cries out and falls back, clutching the wound and half crumpling in a heap. Maybe part of the pick caught his head, after all. Or maybe he is unsteady and is trying to lower his center of gravity. Either way he slumps against the wall and slides down onto his butt, legs twisted and splayed. His left hand moves between the shoulder wound I had seen and the cut on his head, which I hadn't.

Simon takes a step toward him, trying to shake me loose, but I hang on like a wildcat. I don't know what else to do. I cling to him, stupidly, desperately, trying to tangle my legs in his, but he jabs the shaft of the pick hard into my belly, and I slide off him, breathless and wheezing. For a second I am bent double, fighting for air in mad and terrified panic, and then he turns and lunges at me again, this time with the steel head of the pick.

I have enough presence of mind to leap back, realizing too late that I have fallen through the open door. I tumble hard, missing the foyer threshold and dropping down the steps, hitting my head, shoulder, and knees so that my body becomes a siren, my brain so full of its lights and shrieking that I am aware of the door closing after me only when I hear it latch.

I have landed headfirst against the bend in the stairwell, my feet above me, and as I fight to right myself, my injuries crying out in protest, I think of only one thing.

No. Please. Not Marcus . . .

I claw my way back up the stairs, my hot, swollen left hand tight and useless against my breasts, snatching at the door handle and pulling at it with my right. The door shakes in its frame, but it isn't going to open that way. I slam at it with the heel of my right hand, the echoes drowning out my moaning sobs, drowning out everything but Mel's sudden shout.

"No!" she yells. I stop, though I know instinctively that she isn't talking to me. "Not with that! It has to look like an accident."

"It's too late for that." Simon's voice, still distorted into that slow rolling creep-show Darth Vader sound. Before it had frightened me. Now it just makes me angry, outraged.

"It's not," Mel says, calmer now. "We can fix it. Stick to what we said we were going to do. You deal with her, and I'll get the generator running."

"What about him?"

"Look at him. He's not going anywhere."

So Marcus has been hit harder than I thought. He is unconscious, or close to it, and Melissa is going to finish the job.

While Simon comes for me.

I let go of the door handle like it's hot and turn back down the stairs. It's pitch black again, but I am almost used to that now, and my feet feel the edges of the stone steps, guiding me as I scamper down.

You're leaving Marcus. They are going to kill him, and you are running away.

I have no choice. I will go back for him. I swear I will. But I have to survive the next few minutes first and find a way to get past Simon. I reach the foot of the stairs and turn, arms spread, fingers splayed, toes feeling. I'm back in the labyrinth, in the darkness of the tunnels, and the Minotaur is coming.

I move faster than I should for safety, but there is no time to waste. My feet sweep the stone floor for anything I might use as a weapon, but they find only the rails I had thought were train tracks. They orient me, but I hesitate, hating the idea of moving back toward the dank cell that was my prison and that I worked so hard to escape.

But there is nowhere else to go, and before I have made the decision, I hear the door to the stairwell and know he's coming.

I pace the tracks lightly, silently, my mind working twice as fast, trying to think of something, anything that might work to my advantage. His footsteps echo in the stairwell, and as I half turn toward them I see the shifting pale bleed of light from the bottom. He has a lantern.

Shadows loom and flicker, showing the rough texture of the walls, and then I'm turning away and almost running to the empty cell where I was chained in the dark.

I don't choose it. It chooses me because it is the only place that feels familiar down here in the dark with the monster at my heels, and before I can think through what I am doing, I have ducked inside. Almost immediately I see the arched passageway come to life in the yellow glow of his lantern. Thoughtless, despairing, I move as far away from it as I can, huddling in the far corner, dropping into a childish crouch, left arm hugging my knees, right hand slamming splayed against the floor.

There's something under my right heel. Something small and slender. As if in a dream, I grope for it, remembering the sound it made as it rolled away from my grip when I was still chained.

A nail. Rusty, but solid, long as nails go, maybe five inches, and with a broad striking head. I snatch it up, watching the light brightening through the doorway, listening to Simon's shuffling steps and labored breathing.

"You can't run, little Jannie," says the singsong monster voice. "There's nowhere to go."

He's right, but I don't care. The cell reminds me of what he did, what he's going to do, and I am suddenly full of a bright and glistening rage, hard and sharp as a sword. I stand up and move soundlessly to the door, squeezing into the shadows beside it, back to the wall, arms raised and ready.

The lantern is a mistake. It shows me exactly where he is. The scuba mask is another mistake. It kills his peripheral vision, so he has to lean all the way into the cell and turn before he can see me, and by then it's too late. My left arm goes round the back of his head and locks under his chin. I jerk him back, and my right hand punches the nail through the wet suit over his ear. I push, feeling the tip probe for the space at the center, guiding it with my fingers like a surgeon.

Simon stills with sudden horror, feeling the nail tip entering his ear. His body goes limp and he stops fighting to get out of my grasp. The lantern is fixed to his belt, and his hands are both holding the pickax out in front of him, but they too have gone still with dread at what I am about to do.

"Jan . . . ," he begins.

"Don't speak," I say. My fingers have pressed the nail tip as far as it will go before drawing blood. If I slam the heel of my hand hard against the nailhead, it will go straight through the eardrum and the temporal bone of the skull into the brain. He may not know that, but his body senses it.

Death is two inches away.

His eyes are wide under the diving mask. He does not move. All my fear and horror have become his. His life is in my hands.

I am Theseus, come to purge the labyrinth.

I draw back my hand, then smash it against the side of his head with all the force I can manage.

I don't hit the nail. I go higher. His unresisting head slams back against the doorjamb, and he slumps to the ground, the pick sliding from his hands to the floor. I doubt that I have long, but I don't need much time. Not for him. I've already seen by the lamplight the dull, ancient brown metal of the key. I snatch it from the ring and pull him roughly to the concrete bed stand.

The key fits the manacle and pops it open.

I wrench his right arm around, conscious that he is already coming to, but the cuff fits tight around his wrist, tighter than it did around mine. It snaps closed. He is not going anywhere.

I take up the pick and the lantern and leave the cell without glancing back. In seconds, amazed at how short the passage actually seems when I can see, albeit in my fuzzy, unspecific way, I am back at the stairs and climbing.

The door at the top is not fully closed, and I can feel the thrum of the generator again. I push through it in a single motion.

Marcus is lying on his back on the foyer floor, his right arm flapping vaguely like a wounded bird. He is gurgling horribly. Melissa is squatting on his chest like some malevolent succubus, one hand pinching his nose closed, the other forcing the green hosepipe into his mouth.

I have reversed my grip on the pick, so I hit her with the handle. She turns into it, expecting Simon, so I see her furious incredulity just before the shaft breaks her nose.

She rolls sideways, clutching her bloody face, but then she comes up with a kitchen knife. I don't know where she got it from or when, but she has it now, and she's struggling to her feet, her eyes locked on me, her mouth spitting curses.

She steps over Marcus, but as she slashes at me, his eyes open, and he grabs her ankle. She twists away, stumbling, but as her furious gaze goes to him, I swing. The first blow finds her gut and doubles her up, but then I hit her again, in the back of the head. I hit her hard. Hard enough to do real damage, and she collapses instantly.

She slumps to the floor, and for a moment, after I have tugged the hose from Marcus's mouth and left him rolling and gagging, I consider forcing it on her. I might thread it between her flawless lips and push, holding her nose as she had done to him. It would be that simple, and no one would say I had not been sufficiently provoked. I would not be convicted for her death, and for a wild and terrifying moment, I don't really care either way.

But I don't do it.

Clumsily, I lash her hands behind her unconscious body with the hose and coil the length of the thing around her till she looks like the meal for some great python, and then I go down and shut the generator off.

Marcus is stirring, sitting up, coughing, spitting. It is the sweetest sound I have ever heard, but I don't tell him that.

"Marcus?" I say. "Are you OK to drive?"

After he checks on Gretchen, Kristen, and Brad, after he leaves in the Mercedes in search of a police station or, failing that, a cell phone signal, I sit on the floor in the foyer, staring at Melissa. Her head is bleeding a little, but I don't tend the wound. I don't go near her. I watch her sleep, if that's what it is, and I keep the kitchen knife and the pickax in easy reach.

When Kristen comes down, babbling, crying, telling me she can't wake Brad properly, that he comes to, then drifts away again, that she thinks there's something seriously wrong with him, I speak to her soothingly and tell her help is on its way, but I don't look at her. I keep my eyes on Melissa.

It's dawn before the police arrive, but they make up for the delay with seriousness and professional compassion. It's hours before anyone asks me what happened, and by then it has already started to feel like something I dreamed.

Or made up.

Except that I don't do that anymore. I know how that sounds, but I'm sure of it. I know it in my bones, as I might know that I would never wear a certain coat again having cast it onto a bonfire and watching it burn. I was done with that. I had cast it off and done more to it than chained it in the basement where I might one day return, the key pressed hotly in my hand, just to see if it was still alive.

Chapter Thirty-Eight

The woman was wearing a white bikini. Not especially small, but cut to suggest it was revealing more than it really was. She looked like a Bond girl. She was striding out of the waves and walking toward us. Marcus said nothing, but I could feel him looking, so I put him out of his misery.

"Check out Venus born upon the foam," I said.

"What?" he said.

I nodded toward her. "Like you hadn't seen," I say.

"Oh, her," he said. "I see what you mean. Kind of obvious, though."

He was trying to be loyal. We had quarreled that morning, not for the first time on this trip, and he was trying to avoid another. The thought irritated me.

"You can admit you find another woman attractive, Marcus," I said. "I'm not that fragile. Jesus, she looks like a movie star."

"You hate it when I look at other women," he said.

"When you ogle them, yes. I'm not talking about that. I'm just saying if someone beautiful walks by, you're allowed to say so. If you don't, if you pretend not to notice, then you're lying and that's insulting."

"I don't ogle women."

It was true. He didn't.

"*What about that waitress last night? The one with the waist-high neckline.*"

"*I just . . . God, Jan, it's like you want to fight. I looked up and smiled. That was all. I don't see why you have to go out of your way to find some reason to . . .*"

"*Hey. You're American, right?*"

It was the girl in the white bikini. Talking to us.

"*Sorry,*" *she said.* "*I wasn't spying on you or anything, but I heard you talking before . . .*"

Marcus gaped.

"*Yeah, we're from the States,*" *I said.* "*What's up?*"

"*Hi,*" *said the girl.* "*I'm Melissa. My husband is sitting over there behind the white umbrella, trying to look cool in his new shades. Look, this is gonna sound weird, but we're trying to make a reservation at the restaurant tonight, and they're saying they only have a table for six. It's dumb, but everything is booked up and they don't want to waste seats. There are only four of us. We're with a couple of people we just met. So we were wondering if you'd like to join us. Seven thirty tonight. Totally fine if you can't. But we kind of need to know. Dinner is on us, by the way.*"

"*Oh, I don't know,*" *said Marcus, smiling doubtfully.* "*We were gonna go into town, and we really couldn't accept . . .*"

"*Food from strangers,*" *she finished for him.* "*No worries. Have a good—*"

"*Wait,*" *I said.* "*We can go into town tomorrow. Might be nice to meet some new people.*"

I gave Marcus a look, my eyes shaded against the sun, and he floundered.

"*We're in,*" *I said.* "*I'm Jan. This is Marcus.*"

"*Are you sure that . . . ?*" *Marcus began.*

"*Yes,*" *I said, feeling suddenly sure that this was what we needed.* "*We can go into town tomorrow night.*"

We didn't, of course. We had every meal from that night on with Melissa and Simon, Kristen and Brad, holding on to them so that we spent less time sniping at each other, and they had been a godsend. It struck me as slightly odd that she should invite us like that, that they couldn't have just slid the concierge a few euros and kept the table to four. And as we got ready to join them that night, I even wondered if the spectacular bikini entrance had been deliberate too. In fact we had been so charmed by them—so dazzled—that we didn't look the gift horse in the mouth, but later I found myself wondering if we had always been designated as audience to their greatness, as if they'd needed people to perform their perfection to. They'd recruited us as ordinary people, lesser people who would bask in their reflected glories as a way of making them feel better about themselves. We just happened to be in the right place at the right time. Could it have been that simple?

Maybe.

What the hell did I know? And even if I was right, I couldn't put all the blame on them. We had loved it, Marcus and I, the glamour, the sense of being part of their social circle, like we had been scooped up from our quiet gray lives and raised above the clouds to a place of golden light and the promise of continual happiness. It was the life we had been promised by every magazine I had ever looked through, every TV commercial I'd ever seen. So we embraced it and clung on, even when the cracks started to show, even—God help us—when we secretly knew what they were under the shine.

I think of Melissa rubbing suntan lotion into Simon's back on the beach, kneeling astride him, turning to look at me and smiling, aglow with sex and charm and the easy confidence of wealth. I can almost smell the warm coconut oil, hear the music from the hotel's sound system, feel the glow of my skin under the sun, Marcus lying, eyes closed, beside me. It's idyllic, glorious, and I want it back so much that it tugs at my gut, my heart, like the most exquisite pain. And then, quite suddenly, the light changes, and now we're in the dim lobby of the villa, and Mel is straddling not Simon, but Marcus. He's faceup and she's shoving a hose into his mouth. She snaps her head round to look at me, and her face is full of malice and rage, her eyes black and toxic. It's as if she's trying to eat him, like she's a vulture on the road, protecting the carcass she's found from interlopers. Yes. That's it. She's a gaunt, ravenous thing, starving to gobble up that crumb of the world that someone tried to take from her.

I don't know why I keep coming back to her. It was Simon, after all, who set this all in motion, his crime five years ago that made everything at the villa necessary for them. Maybe women always seem worse when they turn nasty because we expect better of them, though that is clearly stupid. The papers called her Lady Macbeth, a lazy and inaccurate reference, but I sort of understood it, particularly when I learned that the first time I had been visited by the monster in my cell, it hadn't been Simon under the scuba gear, it had been her. They traded off. Like they were sharing chores.

Was that love? The willingness to do absolutely anything for each other? To imprison, torture, kill to keep their perfect and exclusive bubble intact?

The idea bothered me. It didn't seem like love, but I watch the parents in the park with their kids, the obsessive care and attention that feels so proprietary, so consuming, the families so ready to circle the wagons and point their guns and knives at whoever is outside the limits of their love, and I'm not so sure. Strange that love can turn so poisonous, so corrosively selfish. I think of the Goya painting, the wild-eyed Cronus devouring his child, and I see the mad hunger I glimpsed in Melissa as she squatted over Marcus with the hose.

It's hard to remember her now as she was when we first met, when she and Simon seemed so gloriously unblemished, and I can't do it without delving back through old photographs. There, in those first days of the 1999 we promised to celebrate, I see captured not so much who they were, but how we saw them, and each untainted image is full of light and energy and laughter, a joy so unconscious and complete that it brings tears to my eyes. I don't hate Simon and Melissa for what they did to me. I hate them more for what they did to a Greek family they thought beneath them. I hate them for what they showed the world to be.

But that is unhelpful. Whatever the world is, I still have to live in it. We all do. Maybe that's the truth at the heart of the labyrinth myth— that we're wandering, lost, always trying to stay one step ahead of our personal monsters, always ready, sword in hand, spooling out Ariadne's thread in the hope that one day we will make it out in one piece.

Chapter Thirty-Nine

The trial lasted weeks, but we didn't have to be there the whole time. Marcus was grilled for withholding his suspicions, but in light of his cooperation with the police, he wasn't charged. His tip about the Jet Ski turned up other witnesses who had seen Simon in the snorkeling area that day, and though no smoking gun came to light—the Jet Ski itself having been cleaned and repaired too many times to retain any blood or similar evidence so long after the crime—the circumstantial case was very strong. Add to it what Melissa had drunkenly confided to Gretchen the night they met for the first time since their school days, and I was surprised it took as long as it did.

We returned to the house only once, three days after we left it, and I showed them where I was held—the concrete bed, the manacle on the wall. Marcus came with me and looked, shamefaced, but when he tried to apologize for his lack of faith, I just shook my head and kissed him.

Maria, Manos's mother, came to the trial every day, supported by an assortment of relatives and friends all dressed in sober black. I remembered the day we went to the Diogenes, the fury on Maria's face when she recognized Melissa. It was Marcus who had suggested we go to the taverna that day. He had been fishing for a reaction.

Simon, understandably, hadn't wanted to go, but Melissa forced the issue. I wondered about that now. Was she testing the water to see if they were in the clear, or was it something darker, more sinister? Had she gone back merely to see if one of us—nudged by the restaurant where the boy had worked—would give some sign of what we knew, or was she there to rejoice in her secret knowledge? If nothing else, the fact that she never considered how Maria might respond spoke of both her arrogance and her contempt for the woman and her family. That Maria blamed Mel for what was then considered the boy's accidental drowning must have come as a surprise to her; but the brazenness with which Mel had outfaced her, the way she had made herself the victim after the fight, getting us all to rally round to make sure she was OK, sickened me. I remembered wondering if all those restaurant owners and shopkeepers, the hotel staff and the cab drivers, all secretly hated the wealthy tourists on whom they depended, and I felt again a sense of responsibility and shame for all that had happened. Maria said nothing during the trial but our eyes met once across the courtroom. I put my hand on my heart and just looked at her, my eyes streaming, till she nodded once and looked away.

Brad did not recover. Not completely. I mean, he can walk and talk, and he looks the same as he always did, except that he always has a slightly hunted, anxious look, as if things are happening around him that he does not understand.

"He forgets things," says Kristen, when we find a moment alone together. "Little things, like where he put the keys, but also movies we saw the day before. All of it, just gone. He's not sure what happened here, but he knows he's . . . well, different. It's ironic. I don't think he could do the job he used to do now, so his losing it matters less. And he is—God forgive me for saying this—nicer now. Not as mean, you know? He used to be funnier, but there was often a little cruelty in his jokes. Now . . . it's like he got old overnight. But it's not so bad. He's become quite sweet, and most of his humor is directed at himself, at the things he doesn't seem to be able to do . . ."

She wipes away a tear and pulls herself together with a shudder that turns into a smile.

"I thought you guys had been breaking up," I say. "Before that night, I mean. I thought—"

"We were," she says quickly.

"But now you are staying with him, in spite of everything?"

I try to say it kindly, like I am impressed, but I am a bit baffled by it all. It isn't like Brad can't feed himself anymore and needs help going to the bathroom, but he isn't the man he was and will surely be relying on her income, if nothing else.

"He doesn't remember," she says, and the smile is different now, fragile as eggshell, her eyes frank but unfathomable. "We broke up, but he doesn't remember. I just haven't the heart . . ."

"Are you sure?" I say. He had, after all, been obsessed with Melissa, had tried to seduce Gretchen *as* Melissa, and had ravaged her underwear when she turned him down. "You don't owe him, Kristen. He might not be the person he was, and I'm not saying you should punish him for what he did, but that doesn't mean you have to take him under your wing."

"I know," she answers. "But—and I know this doesn't make any sense—it's like what happened to him made him the man he should have been, the man he would have been if it wasn't for all that other crap: the competitiveness, the need to prove himself funnier, smarter, richer, better than anyone else. He sees Melissa and Simon for what they are and seems bewildered that we were even friends with them. It's weird, but without all that stuff in his life, he's . . . different, like all his armor has been taken away, and for the first time in years, I can see the guy I fell in love with."

I don't know what to say to this, so I just nod and smile and eventually say, "OK. If that's what you want."

"I think it is," she says, and that 'I think' makes me feel better, though I am not sure why. "Hey, I never said thank you," she adds. "For what you did. I mean, I think you know, but in all the craziness, the investigation and all, I don't think I ever said it. You saved our lives. I didn't think I'd ever say that when I wasn't working from a script, but it's true. You really did. I can't tell you how grateful I am. If there's ever anything—and I mean anything—that I can do . . ."

"You would have done the same," I say. "Ninety percent of it was self-preservation."

She looks taken aback by the admission, then nods.

"Will you keep working?" I ask. The civil suit against Simon and Melissa's estate would mean that we all received significant lump sums. Not enough to live on forever, but more than I had ever had or imagined I would have. I had two steel pins in my left hand, and though I was assured I would regain full use of it in time, I couldn't do the job at Great Deal I'd been doing. It was something of a relief and had made a decision for me that I should have made years ago.

"Oh yes," she says. "I love what I do. And I know it sounds awful, but all this—the press coverage—has only helped my career. I shouldn't say it, but it's true."

I smile.

"Kristen, you mind if I ask you something?"

"What?"

"Are you actually English?"

Again, I had caught her off guard. She opens her mouth to say something airy and confident, then thinks better of it.

"The studio was looking for a Brit," she says. "I had been in a show over there and working under my stage name. But I was born Sarah Kristen Congrieve. In New Jersey. My agent knows. So does the *End Times* producer. But we kept it from the media to give my character a little . . . what does my agent call it? *Verisimilitudinous mystique.*"

I smile and nod and say nothing.

"You should visit the set," she says. "Everyone would love to meet you."

I have attained a little celebrity of my own.

"Maybe after this semester," I say. I had quit my job at Great Deal as soon as I got back to the States, citing the physical injury rather than the mental strain. I think Camille was relieved, though everyone was nice and supportive. They got me flowers. I am taking classes now at UNC Charlotte, retaking courses and rebuilding my ravaged GPA. Whether I will actually apply for med school when it is all done, I am not sure, but that is the plan, and this time there'll be no fudged info on the applications, no flights of fancy during interviews. I've said things like that before, but this time I don't just mean it. After all, I've meant it before. This time, I *know* it's true. Because nothing puts your life in focus like someone trying to take it from you.

Liars are quick to use the most extreme phrases to underscore the truth of their fictions.

Honest to God.

To tell you the truth.

Swear on my mother's grave.

Well, I really did that last one. I had always known where Gabby and my mother were buried, but I never went. Not once. It was easier that way, both to dodge my responsibility for their deaths and to pretend none of it had happened.

I didn't feel guilt over the accident. Not now. In my first meeting with Chad after the trial in Heraklion, he had told me that I had just been a kid, doing what kids did when their sisters got on their nerves. It had all gone horribly wrong, of course—my mother losing concentration, the car missing the bend—but it might not have. It might just have easily been the kind of near miss that happens to drivers daily and that they have forgotten by the time they go to bed that night. I had certainly not intended any of what happened, and the sense that what I had done had actively killed them both—though it had burrowed into my head and heart, where it had turned rancid, rotting through the rest of me—was clearly just the poison of grief and confusion.

Nothing I couldn't have figured out for myself, of course; nothing, in fact, that I hadn't figured out almost as soon as I realized the truth, back in that lightless cell at the heart of the Cretan labyrinth, but it felt good to hear it from someone else. I went to the grave the following day.

It was cold and wet, a gray December haze hanging over the city so that Charlotte's multiplying towers vanished halfway up in mist thick as smoke. The headstones were not as faded as you might expect, the names still hard and clear. I laid flowers and wept for them both, and for myself who had been left behind without them, and I said that I was sorry. Then I promised never to lie again, and though I knew I was being melodramatic and perhaps unreasonable, I meant it, and have lived accordingly since. If I feel tempted to spin a little elaboration, one of my spiraling falsehoods that usually began small, a bit of fun to add a little glitter to the world, I've found that I can rotate my left hand a quarter turn, then clench my fist. The action sends a shot of pain up my arm like lightening.

It hurts like hell but it clears my head.

I walk back to the car through the wet grass, looking down at my shoes, whose leather is stained dark, and there is Marcus, waiting at a respectful distance. I am not sure what the future holds for us, but it feels like there might be one, and that is a long way from where we were before the reunion—a long way, indeed, from where we had been at the end of the previous trip. Nothing binds people together, I guess, like shared experience, even if that experience is full of fear and sadness. It is too strange, too darkly funny to actually say out loud, but Simon and Melissa may actually have done me a favor—several, in fact—without meaning to, so a part of me almost feels sorry for them.

Almost. They will serve multiple life sentences for what they did to us and, most damningly, what they did to a boy-waiter who had been fascinated by the shine about them, and whose life they had thrown away like leftover food pushed to the side of the plate as they left the table and got on with their lives.

Kristen and I promised to stay in touch, but I don't know if the group of six we had been can function as a foursome. Gretchen remained friendly through the trial, but if I thought her a third wheel before the events of that awful night, she embraced that role even more completely after it. She was, I think, more saddened by Simon and Melissa's betrayal of her than she was outraged, and though I tried to convince her otherwise, she seemed to feel guilty.

"I don't think it was my fault," she said when we had gone for coffee in a Heraklion café-bar during the first week, when all the important information was already out in public. "Not really, but I wonder if I forced their hand, you know? After that stuff with Brad, when I freaked out but couldn't get out of the country. If I'd just not said anything. If I'd just gotten my passport without talking to them, without agreeing to come back and stay one more night, I might have left and there wouldn't have been any point in them going after you."

"But Melissa switched your purses on purpose," I said. "So you couldn't leave."

Gretchen sipped from her cup, leaving a ring of rose-colored lipstick on the ceramic.

"Probably," she said, still looking to give her shiny friends the smallest of outs. "Those purses were exactly—"

"She switched them, Gretchen. She admitted it. You were a target for them before the trip even began. It's why they invited you. And once they figured out it wasn't you sending the messages with Manos's name in them, that it was one of us, they were going to get rid of us all no matter what you did or said."

I thought back to the trial, as I had done constantly since it ended. At first, Simon said virtually nothing under cross-examination, offering mere shrugs, denials, and claims that he couldn't remember. He implied the whole thing had been a mistake, the result of a faulty generator and our—mainly *my*—paranoia and deception. Melissa, by contrast, had been defiant, denying everything but somehow managing to blame everyone else, as if everything that had happened was due to the stupidity and mean-spiritedness of other people and a hostile universe. This impulse toward self-justification was bizarre and, in some ways, more frightening than anything she had said or done the night she set out to kill us all. For someone who had always seemed so composed, so attentive to the way others viewed her, this careless dropping of the veil was shocking and contemptuous, as if no one had the right to judge her so she didn't care what they thought. That included the jury, whom she frequently sneered at in ways that made for newspaper headlines. I was reminded of the look in her eyes when, after she had been yelled at by the dead boy's mother that day at the restaurant, Brad had refused to play along with Melissa's pity party. There had been a feral rage in her face at the thought that someone had the audacity to disrupt what she felt she deserved. It had been the same look she had had that night in the foyer, when she had attacked me for exposing what she and Simon had done.

But she continued to deny everything, even as she scornfully remarked that it was absurd that she might lose her liberty over the death of "some Greek waiter." The court translator hesitated over the statement, barely keeping her fury in check, and the prosecution repeated the statement several times in his closing remarks. Each time, Melissa just rolled her eyes and sighed. I was surprised no one from the public gallery went for her, the tension, the hatred was so thick in the courtroom. I felt ashamed to have been her friend.

Though the evidence remained open to interpretation, the process of laying out who Melissa had become was excruciating, her beauty and charisma peeled back to show a heart so hard and shriveled that it was painful to look at. I felt the eyes of the jury on the rest of us too, all of them silently, fiercely asking the same question: *How did you not know?*

I couldn't answer that. Simon had turned out to be shallow, selfish, and ruthless in a bland, predictable, and petty sort of way, but it didn't shock me—maybe because he was a man. I'm used to the way men, suitably draped with respectability, with money and status, are absolved and dressed with things that, if squinted at without your glasses, look like virtues: strength, confidence, and ambition. Melissa was more of an enigma, her sense of sneering superiority to all around her—including, I would say, Simon—less easy to explain and harder to swallow. A double standard, perhaps.

Even so, the evidence against them was largely circumstantial, and it was still possible that, however much the jury hated them, they might still get away with it. The turning point came when Simon abruptly changed his plea to guilty. It was clear that the trial was going badly, and everyone in court—and, for that matter, in the papers—figured he was cutting his losses, but I felt that there was more to it than that. I think I saw the moment he made his decision. Melissa was on the stand. From time to time she had tried to play the radiant and misunderstood goddess, but her furious contempt kept showing through, and the mood of the room was solidly against her. The prosecutor asked her whose idea it had been to go scuba diving and, when the question had been translated to her satisfaction, she rolled her eyes.

"Si," she said. "Of course."

"Of course?" said the prosecutor.

"Si never misses a chance to show off."

She smiled as she said it, but it was a knowing, disdainful smile, and I happened to glance at Simon. He blinked, as if slapped, and bit down on his lip, his eyes lowered. Five minutes later he started whispering to his lawyer, and the trial was halted for the afternoon. When we returned, the tenor of the proceedings had changed and Simon was on the stand, listlessly but clearly recounting what they had done and why.

It came, to everyone but Melissa, as an immense relief.

There were no huge surprises, but I was still amazed by the calculation behind that last night when they had tried to kill us all. They had already interrogated Gretchen and had no reason to believe she had told anyone what had happened to Manos Veranikis. Their plan, Simon said, had been to probe the rest of us for what we knew or suspected, me in particular, but Brad, already a thorn in their sides after his freak-out with Gretchen's underwear, disturbed their set up of the generator hose. Melissa panicked, hitting him from behind, then I had come downstairs, and that brought everything else forward.

"We knew then that we would have to kill them all that night," he said, almost casually. "That had always been the plan, but we hadn't meant to do it so quickly. We still wanted to know who Jan might have told—we assumed she was the one sending the messages because it was the kind of thing she would get off on—so we chained her up in the basement and tried to get her to tell us what she knew. That was a mistake," he added, giving me a quick, blank look. "We should have killed her first.

"Anyway," he continued. The courtroom had become utterly silent as he spoke, his words echoed by the Greek simultaneous translator, the prosecutor holding back, letting him talk. "We got Brad back up to his room. He was sleeping alone because his wife didn't want anything to do with him. Then, while we took turns to question Jan in the basement, we flooded the west side of the house with carbon monoxide.

"It was a simple plan. Perfect, really. Mel's idea, of course. The east wing, where our room was, is self-contained, so we could stay there. We'd use the scuba gear to make sure we didn't get poisoned, but we figured we'd just pretend to find everyone dead in the morning, discover that the hose had come disconnected from the genny, and no one would be the wiser. Apart from us, everyone who knew or had even the smallest suspicion about what happened to Manos Veranikis would die in that house. A tragic accident. We would walk away and get on with our lives."

The baldness of the admission was staggering, as was his composure when, at the end of it, he looked at his wife and added, "I guess this time, you don't get what you want."

I never heard Melissa speak again.

I thought back on some of this as Gretchen nodded vaguely.

"I don't know," she said. "They just seemed like such *nice* people—Mel, anyway. So welcoming and . . . I don't know. Maybe it's our fault, you know? That we somehow messed everything up. I mean, I know they did terrible things, but if we had never met them . . . who knows?"

"Gretchen, practically the first thing Mel told you when you met her in that bar was that Simon had killed Manos Veranikis a few years earlier."

"Well, that wasn't the first time we spoke. Remember, we were old school friends."

I brushed past this embroidery.

"Even so, she told you her husband had killed someone!"

"Well, yes, but it sounded like it was an accident."

"Which they didn't report."

"No, but now they're saying he did it on purpose. That doesn't seem right."

"Simon was angry at Mel for the way she played with men. When he saw the boy—one of the people she had led on quite deliberately—he lost it and ran him over. It wasn't a coincidence or an accident."

"You don't know that, though. Not for sure. You can't know what was in his mind. Not really. And even so, that wasn't Mel's fault, was it?"

I tell Marcus all this when we are back in Charlotte, the day I went to the graveyard, and he just shakes his head.

"She wants to hold on to her impression of who they were because they made her feel better about herself. Like she was singled out by rock stars or royalty to be their friend. Of course she wants to think the best of them."

"They tried to kill her!"

"Yeah," says Marcus, giving me a sideways grin. "There is that."

"I don't think I'm going to be close friends with Gretchen."

"Despite the bond of imprisonment and attempted murder? Hard to believe."

We walk a few paces in silence, leaving the cemetery and moving to Marcus's rain-misted Camry.

"What about us?" I say. "You think we're going to be close friends?"

He gives me that little side look again, and his smile this time is smaller, more watchful.

"I think it's possible," he says, turning away so I can't read his face. "What do you think?"

"Definitely possible," I say. "One condition, though."

"What's that?"

"We never buy a generator."

"Deal," says Marcus. "When the lights go out, we'll light a candle."

"And hold hands."

He turns to me at that.

"You OK?" he says.

I look past him across the car roof, back to the wet, indistinct gravestones beyond the cemetery railings, and I nod, turning away from them and facing the future.

"Yeah," I say. "I'm good."

Acknowledgments

Thanks to Gray Reinhart, John Hartness, Sean Higgins, and Scott Abell Johnston for their help on carbon monoxide and breathing apparatus; Cannon Cory on commercial real estate; Gregory Wilson on store operations; and Chris Bruney on diving. Special thanks to my first readers, Finie Osako, Kerra Bolton, Sarah Werner, David B. Coe, and wonder agent, Stacey Glick. Lastly, thanks to my editor, Kelli Martin; Danielle Marshall; and all at Lake Union who helped to make the book a reality.

About the Author

Andrew Hart is one of the pseudonyms of *New York Times* bestselling and award-winning author A. J. Hartley. His sixteen novels straddle multiple genres for adults and younger readers and have been translated into dozens of languages worldwide. As Andrew James Hartley, he is also the Robinson Professor of Shakespeare Studies at the University of North Carolina, Charlotte. His website is www.ajhartley.net.